I'm not like most other vamps. I don't do black. I don't prowl the streets, biting unsuspecting victims (unless he's really, *really* cute). I don't sleep in a cramped coffin. I don't go all orgasmic at the mention of Marilyn Manson. (He-llo? The guy is so totally un-hot, even if he does have the whole night-creature look going on.)

My favorite color is pink. Biting is *so* over. I'd rather drink my dinner out of a martini glass and follow it up with a Cosmopolitan chaser. I sleep in a king-size bed on a pillow-top mattress (yum). I score a ten on the O-meter when it comes to Matt Damon, Brad Pitt, and Toby Keith (I know, I know, he's so *not* my type, but there's just something about the cowboy hat). I've also been known to cry during the MasterCard commercials. And—this is the eighth deadly sin as far as my kind are concerned—I'm a closet romantic.

I absolutely, positively *love* love.

Dead End Dating

A Novel of Vampire Love

KIMBERLY RAYE

BALLANTINE BOOKS • NEW YORK

An Ivy Books Mass Market Original

Copyright © 2006 by Kimberly Raye Groff
Excerpt from *Dead and Dateless* by Kimberly Raye copyright © 2006 by Kimberly Raye Groff

Published in the United States by Ivy Books, an imprint of The Random House Publishing Group, a division of Random House, Inc., New York.

IVY BOOKS and colophon are trademarks of Random House, Inc.

This book contains an excerpt from the forthcoming book *Dead and Dateless* by Kimberly Raye. This excerpt has been set for this edition only and may not reflect the final content of the forthcoming edition.

ISBN 0-345-49216-1

Cover illustration by Marcin Baranski

Printed in the United States of America

www.ballantinebooks.com

OPM   9 8 7 6 5 4 3 2 1

For James H. Adams,
the best father in the world.
I miss you so much!

Acknowledgments

I would like to say thank you to my agent, Natasha Kern, for her expertise, guidance, and genuine faith in me. This book would not have been possible without her.

Thanks also to Nina Bangs and Gerry Bartlett for reading on the spur of the moment and encouraging me during so many discouraging times in my life. You guys are the best!

Thanks also to Charlotte Herscher for being such a kind and patient editor. You kept me going in more ways than you can possibly imagine.

And a special thanks to my husband for being so wonderful when I'm *not*. I don't know what I would do without you.

One
❤ ❤ ❤

For those of you who don't already know me, my name is the Countess Lilliana Arabella Guinevere du Marchette (yeah, I know), but my friends call me Lil.

I mean, really, what were my folks *thinking*? It's hard enough being a single, jobless, five-hundred-year-old female vampire in this day and age without the whole pretentious French royalty thing *and* an ancient lame-ass name that doesn't even fit in the box on a Visa application. Talk about another cross to bear. (Oops, poor word choice. My bad.)

Let's just say life is tough for any woman, and death isn't much better. We're still expected to live up to this whole Night-Feeding Barbie image—perfect figure, perfect hair, perfect clothes, perfect incisors—and procreate, hunt for the family, *and* make sure little Morticia doesn't color on the walls and baby Vlad doesn't eat the eyes off his Count Dracula doll. Talk about stress.

For the typical committed female vampire, that is.

I, on the other hand, haven't had a decent date in the past one hundred years, much less found Count Right, so my life is a bit simpler. Notice I say "simpler" rather than lonelier. Because I am not, repeat *not*, lonely.

I'm a single, hot, happening vampire with a flair for accessorizing, a handful of super-sweet friends—literally—and a very expensive therapist. 'Nuff said.

Now where was I? Oh, yeah—me making my own way in the world. First on my list is finding an apartment. A girl can live with her parents for only so many centuries without having a nervous breakdown. Second is getting a job. Neither of which should pose a problem for someone like me. Pure vampires (those born rather than made) are an ambitious, take-charge-and-make-things-happen race, and so most of us are filthy rich. If I were so inclined, I could easily use my family's green to find a suitable apartment in Manhattan (complete with a live-in maid, which is almost worth being eternally indebted to my folks considering the fact that I *hate* to clean) and go to work for my father managing his New York University location of Midnight Moe's.

What is Midnight Moe's, you say?

Think copy machines. Think printing services. Think two hundred locations nationwide (near a university near you).

Think *bor-ing*.

While I have nothing against copying or printing, I

simply can't see myself standing behind the counter from dusk 'til dawn, wearing a lime green polo shirt with "Midnight Moe's" embroidered across the pocket, and matching Dockers. Lime green is *so* not my color (I'm a winter, and anything out of my range makes me look, well, dead.) As for the Dockers . . . they're *Dockers.* (Shudder.) So you can see why the thought of spending eternity gainfully employed in the family business is enough to make me want to stake myself.

You've probably guessed by now that I'm not like most other vamps. Except maybe one, that is. My father says I'm the spitting image of my great aunt Sophie, who nuked herself, just last year, in a tanning bed she purchased off the QVC channel. She was a total nonconformist when it came to the whole vamp image, with her blond highlights, pale peach nail polish, and addiction to Hawaiian-print sarongs.

Personally, I wouldn't be caught dead in a Hawaiian-print *anything*. Likewise, why would I crawl into a Sun-sation 5000 when Clinique makes the most rockin' sunless tanning spray in the perfect shade of medium gold? *Not!* I don't care for pale peach, either, but I do have highlights and I'm definitely a nonconformist (aka the daughter that was switched at birth or so my mother tells the women in her Happy Hunting Club).

You see, I don't do black. I don't prowl the streets, biting unsuspecting victims (unless he's really, *really* cute). I don't sleep in a cramped coffin. I don't go all orgasmic at the mention of Marilyn Manson. (Hel-lo? The guy is so totally unhot, even if he does have the whole night-creature look going on.) Nor am I a cold,

ruthless, unfeeling bitch, unless you're the Princess Co-
lette du Guilliam, the blond-haired, blue-eyed *slut* who
stole my very first boyfriend.

My favorite color is pink. Biting is *so* over. I'd
rather drink my dinner out of a martini glass and follow it up with a cosmopolitan chaser. I sleep in a
king-size bed on a pillow-top mattress (yum). I score
a ten on the O-meter when it comes to Matt Damon,
Brad Pitt, and Toby Keith (I know, I know, he's so *not*
my type, but there's just something about the cowboy
hat). I've also been known to cry during the Master-
Card commercials. And—this is the eighth deadly sin
as far as my kind are concerned—I'm a closet romantic.

I absolutely, positively *love* love.

I love everything about it, from that first initial
glance between two strangers, to the earth-shattering
moment when both realize that they are meant to be
together forever (deep sigh). My favorite movie is
Pretty Woman, followed by *An Officer and a Gentle-
man* and *The Terminator* (the movie itself isn't all
that touching, but the one love scene really rocks).
My favorite holiday is Valentine's Day, and I have a
heart-shaped tattoo at the left side of my bikini line.
And I actually jumped up and down when Carrie
ended up with Big in the final episode of *Sex and the
City.*

So it only stands to reason that I should forgo Moe's
and opt for something a little more romantic to pay the
bills.

Vampires need love, too.

Okay, most of my brethren would argue this with me

because they (a) don't believe in the concept and are, for the most part, vicious bloodsuckers, and (b) aren't nearly as enlightened as I am. But while the average Joe Vamp doesn't buy into the "L" concept, he's still hard-pressed to find an eternity mate for all those practical reasons mentioned above (see little Morticia and baby Vlad). Who better to hook him up than yours truly?

For a fee, of course. After all, a girl's gotta eat (okay, so this girl's gotta keep up her supply of MAC bronzing powder, but you get the idea). Which is why I'm not limiting my services to vamps. Hence my fantabulous entrepreneurial brainstorm: *Dead End Dating*. A Manhattan-based, equal-opportunity matchmaking service for the smart, savvy, sophisticated single sick and tired of dead-end dating, and the smart, savvy, sophisticated single *vampire* looking for just that.

I know, I know. It's brilliant. What can I say? Genius runs in my family (ever heard of Marie Curie?). Anyhow, it's a great plan, one that I've already put into motion. Last week, I leased the perfect office space just around the corner from my favorite Starbucks (ah, the smell of mocha latte and maple scones), and I hired my first employee: Evie Dalton. Evie is as human as they come, but I'm a sucker (no pun intended) for an impressive interview ensemble—DKNY miniature jacket, boot-cut Gucci corduroys, Kenneth Cole boots, and the pièce de résistance—a rhinestone belt to *die* for.

So here I sit on a clear, moonlit October evening in Manhattan, my laptop open in front of me, ready and willing to change someone's destiny. To pluck them from the pit of loneliness and lift them into the blessed light of companionship. To save them from the jaws of isolation and deliver them into the warm, comforting embrace of . . . Well, you get the picture.

Who knows? Maybe I'll find my own eternity mate while I'm dishing out happily ever afters.

Of course, I'm not getting my hopes up, mind you—I'm even pickier when it comes to men than I am with accessories. For now, I'm willing to settle for paying the bills, particularly the whopper of a Visa bill that's headed my way after funding this latest venture.

Not that I'm worried. Once my ad runs in all of the local papers, the masses will be climbing over one another to get to my office (I'm picturing a half-off sale at Barney's). The funds will roll in and I won't have to crawl back to my folks in Connecticut and endure yet another Sunday night dinner with a prospective Count Right. Did I mention that my mother has a habit of fixing me up? She doesn't buy into the whole non-lonely spiel.

Anyhow, I just know Dead End Dating is going to be *it*. The next big thing. My ticket to complete financial independence and personal fulfillment. Or, at the very least, a really cool way to pay next month's rent.

The matchmaking biz *totally* rocks.

TWO
♥ ♥ ♥

The matchmaking biz *totally* bites.

Not the matchmaking part, mind you. It's been all of two weeks since I opened Dead End Dating and I've yet to actually make a match. It's the *biz* part that's started to chew me a new one.

I stared at the stack of bills that Evie (black capris, white mini T-shirt, and a set of pink rhinestone bangles) sat on my desk next to my only two client folders.

Yep, ya heard me. What with 95.7 million singles (75 percent human, 10 percent vampire, and 15 percent Other), I've managed to attract a whopping *deux*.

I swallowed and tried to ignore the sudden hollowness in the pit of my stomach. Ignorance was good in a situation like this. Bliss. Especially to a card-carrying optimist like myself. There's simply no way to handle being alive for a gazillion years if you panic at life's

every twist and turn. You have to keep your cool and
withhold all hysterics until you've got a bona fide problem on your hands.

"I really wasn't expecting monthly bills until we'd
been open a full month," I told Evie.

"These are hook-up charges for new service. You've
got your electric, telephone, Internet—the usual." She
handed over another stack. "*These* are the monthly
bills."

Okay, so this was a bona fide problem, but I tried
for a smile anyway. "Any phone calls today?" When
facing a negative, it's best to put it in proper perspec-
tive by focusing on the positives.

"Only two. The first was Mrs. Wilhelm." Louisa
Wilhelm made up client folder number one. She was
a widow—about ten years ago her eternity mate went
parachuting and landed a little too close to the sharp
end of an oak tree branch. She was also my mother's
best friend. "She wants to know if you've found her
an escort yet."

"But she just signed with us last night."

"That's what I told her, but she said that the soiree
is in three weeks." "The soiree" referred to the annual midnight ball and charity auction sponsored by
the Connecticut Huntress Club, in which my mother
served as vice president. Mom also handled the re-
freshments every third meeting and, along with passing out glasses of chilled AB negative, handed out
tidbits about *moi*. Namely, that I'm smart. And beautiful. And successful. And desperately in need of an

eternity mate to complete my desperately incomplete life.

But I digress. Back to the soiree.

We're talking *the* event of upper-crust vamps.

"She said we should hurry up," Evie went on, "because if she wanted last minute, she could just wait for Marvin Terribone to ask her the day of, like he did last year. She wants to teach him a lesson and make him jealous." Evie leveled a stare at me. "She wants results by tomorrow."

I was pretty sure the news qualified as a negative, so I turned to my laptop to find a positive. I brought up my new website—www.deadanddating.com. (Yeah, it says dead *and* dating, but dead *end* was already taken as a domain name, and so I'd had to settle for the next best thing.) The site offered three free matches to anyone who took the time to fill out the carefully worded questionnaire and join the Dead End Dating family database. I'd had ten hits in the past twenty-four hours and all of three applicants.

Three.

And they were all women.

Definitely a negative.

"Maybe Mrs. Wilhelm swings both ways," Evie offered as she came around to peer over my shoulder. The luscious aroma of mocha latte clung to her and teased my nostrils.

"And maybe I'm the next Miss Hawaiian Tropic." While vamps were like humans in that their sexual preferences tended to go in various directions, Mrs. Wilhelm was like a trillion years old. As in really *old*.

As in really old-fashioned. And snotty. And pretentious. Even if she did butter her bread on both sides, she wasn't likely to admit it.

Add a capital B to the bona fide.

"I told you we should have advertised in Times Square," Evie said.

"I'm on a tight budget."

"How tight?"

"Nonexistent. I've maxed out my credit cards, so short of hocking my great, great, great, great, great grandmother's engraved goblet, the only sign I'm likely to have in Times Square is one I paint and wear myself."

"If it's any consolation, you're having a really good hair night."

Did Evie actually believe I was so shallow that I could be distracted from a major crisis with a compliment?

I smiled. "I used a new shampoo."

"And that blush is incredible."

My smile widened. Hey, we're talking blush as in MAC. "It's a new combination blush/bronzer called Sunlight Sparkle. It's pretty hot, huh?"

"Totally hot."

"Smoking hot," I added.

"*Blazing* hot."

"*Hellaciously* hot." Now that I'd exhausted my "hot" adjectives, it was back to reality. I sighed, stiffened, and prepared myself. "What about the second call?"

"Your father. He said he has your new uniforms

and that you should pick them up this week on account of the fact that you start training in the store at Midnight Moe's next week."

Okay, so maybe I didn't prepare myself quite enough because this news made my stomach do a cartwheel *and* a double back flip. "But I've already told him I'm not starting anything next week." I shook my head. "I'm not working for him."

"I don't think he's clear on that. He also said that he got you your very own name tag. Beige with lime green lettering. To match the shirt." Evie must have read the look of horror on my face. "Then again, maybe I misunderstood him. It has been a long day."

If only.

My father had selective hearing when it came to his four offspring—me and my three older brothers. Namely, he tuned out any and everything that didn't pertain to one of three things: (1) making money, (2) the Knicks, and (3) making money. Since he didn't consider my new venture anything more than a temporary, and not very well-thought-out endeavor—like the time I told everyone I wanted to be an artist; I did all of three pictures before deciding I would rather sit for a portrait than paint one—making money wasn't a likely possibility. Unless I managed to lure one of the Knicks into my clutches for a little matchmaking— I should be so lucky—I wasn't going to hit pay dirt for number two, either. Which meant when I'd turned down the offer to manage the second NYU location of Midnight Moe's, he hadn't been paying attention.

He expected me to don the lime green shirt and the

Dockers and report for duty just like my three brothers. But the thing was, I wasn't like them.

I had dreams of something bigger.

I had aspirations.

I had *goals*.

Even more, I had good taste.

"I'll just have to pull out the big guns," I told Evie.

"Are we talking a Beretta or an Uzi?"

"You've been watching too much *CSI*."

She smiled. "There's no such thing." Her expression grew serious. "So are you going to sell the goblet and get us into Times Square?"

It was my turn to smile. "Who needs Times Square when we've got two hundred and twenty locations nationwide?"

"I thought the whole point of going into business for yourself was to make your own way."

"I am making my own way," I told my oldest brother, Max. Short for Maximillian Gautier Bastien. What can I say? My parents are *so* fourteenth century.

"You're using our copy machine."

"True, but I'm running the copies myself." Did I have to explain everything?

I stood behind the counter at the first NYU location of Midnight Moe's on West Fourth Street, near Washington Square Park. Long fluorescent bulbs crisscrossed the ceiling and showered the inside in bright white light. Signs dangled here and there, advertising various services, from BINDING to CUSTOMIZED BUSINESS CARDS.

Printers whirred and copy machines *ka-chunk*ed. The sharp smell of paper and ink mingled with the various scents of humans, vamps—both made and born—and Others who filled the store.

"It's not like I'm borrowing money," I pointed out.

"You're using our paper. And our ink. Both cost money."

"That's one way of looking at it," I said to Max.

He was tall, with short, dark hair, rich brown eyes, and the typical vamp aura that oozed sex appeal. He'd been twenty-three when he'd lost his virginity and stopped aging. Fairly young for a born vamp since most couldn't physically have sex (the motor started and the engine revved, but there was no shifting gears into drive) before the age of twenty-five (the dormant period usually required for a certain gene that controlled both the aging process and the ability to orgasm). When the gene reached maturity, the flood gates opened. It was hello Mr. Orgasm and bye-bye aging.

Thankfully, it didn't take regular orgasms to keep the process at bay; otherwise I'd be dust by now.

My brother was one of the few vamps whose first orgasm had come sooner. He'd been a ladies' man ever since, his appeal multiplied by the fact that he had an extraordinarily high fertility rating—a little number that reflected how likely he was to hit a bull's-eye when it came to procreation. While a vamp's fertility rating meant squat to a human, it made him all the more sought after by his own kind.

Likewise, we female born vamps had our own measure for success—the orgasm quotient, or OQ. Not to be confused with the ever-popular OC, which I'd never actually gotten into on account of the fact that I watched very little television. The OQ was the number of times a female vamp could orgasm during a single sexual encounter. The higher the number, the more likely she was to conceive.

I know, I know. Are we a bunch of rabbits, or what?

"Let me get this straight," Max told me as he watched me punch in an obscene number of copies. "There's another way to look at this situation that doesn't involve you mooching off of Moe's?"

"I'm not mooching off of Moe's. I'm extracting payment from you."

"For what?"

"Keeping my mouth shut."

"You never keep your mouth shut."

"What about when you moved in with that stripper for six months? And pretended to be human? I still can't believe she bought it. Then again, I don't think she was dealing with a full deck."

"Diane was very smart."

"If you consider her bust measurement in lieu of an IQ score."

"Okay, so she wasn't that smart. She had stamina and endurance."

"I hate to break it to you, but humping a pole isn't an Olympic sport."

A small smile touched his lips. "Not yet." He turned

his attention to a pudgy blond guy who dumped an armload of office supplies onto the counter.

While Max rang up the customer and bagged his purchases, I gathered my stack of pink flyers. The moment he handed over the man's change and turned back to me, I shoved the advertisements at him. "All you have to do is put one in every customer's bag."

He shook his head. "Dad will blow a major gasket if he finds out I'm helping you."

"He'll blow one anyway when he finds out his oldest, most reliable son isn't so reliable, after all."

"How's that?"

"Before the stripper, there was that nun from the church over on Forty-sixth Street."

"She wasn't a nun, and it wasn't a church. It was a Catholic girl's school. She worked in the office."

"What about that custom jewelry designer? What was her specialty again? Jeweled crucifixes?"

"She admired the shape, not the religious connotation."

"What about the cop who worked in special investigations? The woman had a sixth sense that could have spelled major trouble for us if she'd started asking questions."

"She never asked questions. She just begged for sex."

"The vegetarian."

"America's all about freedom of choice."

"The IRS agent."

"Okay, okay. I'll hand them out." He took the flyers and set them next to the cash register. "You really think this whole matchmaking thing will work?"

I recited the statistics. "You've got a mega amount of single people and not nearly enough places to meet and greet. If you do manage to meet someone, you have no way of knowing what they're *really* like."

Max gave me a pointed look.

"I'm not talking about vamps. Obviously, we're hypersensitive and a little more in tune when it comes to the opposite sex. But humans aren't. And neither are werewolves or the dozens of Others out there."

"Maybe."

"There's no maybe about it. I'm right on this. Say this girl goes out with a guy she happens to meet at the local coffee shop. She's desperate to stop wasting her time, settle down, and find the right person, but he's nothing more than a serial dater in an Armani shirt." I shook my head. "It's too hit and miss. On top of hooking yourself up, you've got blind dating, which is the most unproductive activity *ever.*"

"Since when did you become an expert?"

"Since I've been on way too many blind dates." His eyebrow kicked up a notch. "Okay, so I've been recording *Dr. Phil.* It's strictly for research purposes. He's a really smart guy."

"He's a human."

"Nobody's perfect."

He grinned. "Speak for yourself."

"Let's face it," I went on. "The world is full of lonely people in desperate need of intervention." To make my point, I swept a gaze around the store, pausing on a girl who sat at a nearby computer. "Alone," I told my brother before shifting my attention to a twenty-something man fighting with a copy machine at the front of the store. "Alone." Another girl dawdled in front of the Liquid Paper display. "Alone."

I glanced at a born male vamp who leaned over a nearby color copy machine. I knew he was born because I could smell him. Born vamps had a wildness about them that gave off a sweet, rich, intoxicating aroma. From decadent fudge brownie to carrot cake with cream cheese icing. While the scents varied from vamp to vamp, they were always sugary, potent, and unmistakable. My nostrils flared. This guy smelled like a Twinkie. "Alone," I gave the verdict.

"How do you know he doesn't have an eternity mate waiting in the car?"

"Duh, he's not wearing a commitment charm." The charm was a small crystal vial that all committed vamps wore suspended on a chain around their neck. It held a drop of their significant other's blood. While it looked like a hip piece of jewelry to the average human, it symbolized the sacred union between born vamps.

Not that my brother had noticed. Men. Sheesh.

I continued my prospective client search. A man stood near the computer terminals available for rent. "Alone," I said again. A woman picked up a roll of packaging tape to go with the box she'd just retrieved. "Alone." My gaze lit on the customer Max had just rung up. The man had paused in the Hi-Lighter aisle. "Painfully alone."

"Why do you say that?"

"Because he already spent twenty minutes trying to decide between the neon green and the fuschia pink, and now he's second-guessing his final choice." I eyed my brother. "If he had a significant other, do you think he would be wasting time *here*?"

Max (FYI—chocolate cake drenched in caramel sauce) shrugged. "So maybe you're on to something."

"I am." I plucked a flyer from the top of the stack and turned to follow Mr. Hi-Lighter, who'd finally given up the debate and headed for the door. "Later, bro."

Three

❤ ❤ ❤

"Hey," I called out when I reached the door. Obviously, Mr. Hi-Lighter wasn't used to having majorly hot babes call after him. He didn't so much as miss a step as he walked down Fourth Street toward the subway station.

I usually avoided the subway the way most people avoided Porta Pottis (a girl just didn't know what she'd find crawling around in there during the middle of the night). But my instincts were prodding me on. I had a feeling about this guy.

He looked so sad.

So lonely.

So geeky.

He needed me.

I started after him. I'd made it all of three steps before a strange sensation washed over me. My ears perked up and the hair on the back of my neck prickled, and I had the strangest sensation that I was the one being followed. I glanced around and saw . . . nothing. Just the empty sidewalk and the neon green MIDNIGHT MOE'S sign glowing in the distance.

Shrugging off the feeling, I turned my attention back to Mr. Hi-Lighter, who'd managed to get a pretty good lead on me. I picked up my pace, which should have been enough to run this guy down in no time (just one of my many vamp talents). I gained on him as he neared the subway station and descended the steps, but I couldn't seem to close the distance between us. He was moving too fast.

Faster than me?

That could only mean . . . Nah. He couldn't be. I would have made him right away. That was the thing about vamps. We had heightened senses. We could see things that other people couldn't. Hear sounds that weren't audible to the average ear. Smell scents sharper and more intense than the average nose— another reason I avoided the subway.

I followed as he pushed through the entry gate. My nostrils flared and I drank in a deep breath of . . . graham crackers? Way too bland for a born vamp. As for a made vampire . . . the few I'd actually met had smelled like old mothballs and greed.

Obviously the past five hundred years were finally catching up to me. I just wasn't as fast as I used to be. That, or Nike had finally hit pay dirt with their running shoes.

Pushing through the gate, I bypassed a group of college girls, backpacks slung over their shoulders, and a gay couple walking hand in hand. I started down the platform just as Mr. Hi-Lighter came to a stop at the far end near a group of young guys.

They wore classic gangbanger with slouchy jeans that barely clung to their hips, muscle shirts, and enough gold jewelry to reduce the national deficit by a good quarter.

"What do you think you're doing?" one of the guys asked Mr. Hi-Lighter.

"Waiting for my train."

"It ain't your train, dumbass." The guy—tall with buzzed dark hair, an olive complexion, and a tattoo on his bicep that read BORN TO DIE—walked up until he was nose to nose. "It's *our* train."

"That's right," another one said. He had deep red hair, freckles, and a Stone Cold Steve Austin attitude. "And this is our platform."

"So get lost," Born to Die said before giving the geek a quick shove.

Mr. Hi-Lighter stumbled back a few steps, right into another one of the guys who'd come up behind him.

"I guess this asshole's hard of hearing." The guy behind shoved the geek back toward his friend. "Otherwise, he'd be gone by now."

"I don't want any trouble."

"Then you shouldn't have stopped on our platform uninvited." Born to Die pulled out a knife. "It's gonna cost you."

I picked up my steps, but I was still too far away to stop what happened next. The knife pressed against

Mr. Hi-Lighter's throat. His breath caught, his nostrils flared, and his eyes turned a telltale midnight black.

I stopped in my tracks and waited for the transformation that would come next. A wolf or a jackal or something equally vicious. Something that would rip these clowns to pieces.

The air shimmered and blurred, and a split second later, an old woman's voice crackled across the distance.

"Antonio Dante Moreno! You should be ashamed of yourself."

The guy with the knife stumbled backward, his eyes wide as he stared at the tiny old woman. Tight, meticulous snow white curls covered her head. She wore a flower-print dress, orthopedic shoes, and a spaghetti-stained apron. One twisted, arthritic hand gripped a large stainless steel ladle. The smell of Dippity-do and garlic clung to her.

"Grandma Maria?"

She shook a gnarled finger at the gangbanger. "You ought to be ashamed of yourself, Antonio. Why, your papa, bless him"—she crossed herself with her free hand—"would turn over in his grave if he could see you now."

"I . . ." He swallowed, his gaze stunned and frightened at the same time. "Y-you can't be here. You're d-dead."

Her gaze narrowed and drilled into the young man. "You'll be the one dead when I tell your uncle Gino that you were out getting into trouble when you should have been home studying for your algebra test. You're this close to failing. *Failing*," she wailed. "Why, no one in our family has ever flunked out of school."

"I—I didn't mean . . ." He shook his head. "I—I'm sorry."

"This is too weird, man," one of the other guys said. "Too fuckin' weird."

"Watch your language, young man." She bopped him with her ladle before turning to smack each one of the group soundly on the head. "All." *Bop*. "Of." *Bop*. "You." *Bop-bop*.

"I—I'm getting the hell out of here," one of the guys blurted.

"Me too."

"Wait for me."

The young men scrambled for the steps. A few moments later, the old woman's figure blurred and shimmered. Just like that, the pudgy man from Moe's stood on the platform in her place.

I blinked and tried to come to grips with what I'd just witnessed.

It wasn't the transformation itself that had me so freaked out. I'd seen more than my share. Heck, I'd done my fair share. My particular favorite was a white Alaskan husky with vibrant blue eyes and a vicious bark.

But I'd never morphed into an Italian grandmother, for Pete's sake.

No wonder this guy was alone.

Being a geek was bad enough. But a geeky *vam-*

pire? Talk about a sucky existence—and I don't mean that in a good way.

This guy needed my help, all right.

And I needed his.

I tightened my grip on the flyer and stepped forward.

Four
❤ ❤ ❤

"I don't need a date." The geeky vampire stared at the flyer I'd just handed him and shook his head.

"Not a date. A *mate*." Did I have to spell out *everything*? "An eternity mate."

"I'm afraid I don't really understand."

"My name is Lil Marchette, and I've just opened up an exclusive service that helps unattached vamps, like yourself, find that special someone. For a small fee, of course."

He stared at me as if I'd just confessed to being a vamp hunter. One with really good taste in accessories, of course. His voice vibrated with shock. "You're a *vampire*?"

"Duh."

His gaze roamed from my expensive honey-colored hair with platinum highlights to the tips of my favorite

Anne Klein slides, and back up again. "You don't look like a vampire."

"Neither do you. Especially wearing the apron and the Dippity-do."

"I haven't nailed the whole metamorphosis thing yet. Most vampires just pick something ruthless and go for it, but my special talent is mind linking. Whenever I'm stressed, I get my wires crossed. Instead of digging into my own mind for something frightening, I end up pulling something out of whoever's in front of me."

"Frightening, as in a little old grandma?"

"A little old Italian grandma."

Okay, he had a point.

"Thanks," he went on, "but I, um, really don't think this is for me." He handed back the flyer.

His hand brushed mine and he actually blushed, and I started to think that maybe I was trying to bite off more than I could chew.

Hel-*lo*?

Vamps mesmerized and intrigued and intimidated and, in my case, looked really hot and happening carrying the latest beaded Donna Karan handbag in cream mocha. They did not *blush*.

My gaze swept the length of Grandma Fang, from his battered brown penny loafers (can we say *over*?), up the length of his blah-blah beige khakis, his yellow button-down shirt with the white undershirt peeking over the top button, to his round face and pale, watery blue eyes.

He'd obviously been in his mid-to-late thirties when

he'd lost his virginity and stopped aging. Judging from the way he avoided my gaze and kept blushing, that couldn't have been more than a few years ago.

"How old are you?"

"One thousand thirty-six."

"I know most young vampires aren't really thinking about the future and continuing the bloodline, but—what did you just say?"

"I'm one thousand thirty-six."

"*Years?*"

He nodded and I just stood there dumbfounded for a few moments. The subway roared by us and groaned to a stop. The doors slid open, and a few people filed out onto the platform. An older woman, arms overflowing with grocery bags, clicked by me. The smell of cheap hairspray slid into my nostrils like a heavy-duty dose of smelling salts.

The shock beating at my temples subsided and gave way to a totally fantabulous idea. (Did I mention that I do my best thinking when I'm totally stressed? There's just something about the added pressure of impending disaster, be it war, famine, or pinning on the Moe's name tag, that makes my creativity positively hum.)

I was definitely hitting a ten on the in-over-my-head-o-meter. At the same time, I couldn't shake the excitement zipping up and down my spine.

This was *it*.

The mother lode.

The oldest, most clueless, most dweebish vamp in existence (make that the *only* dweebish vamp in existence because the very nature of our species contradicted the whole geekoid persona).

If ever anyone needed to get an afterlife and find a mate, it was this guy.

And I was just the girl to help him.

I'm a sucker for happy endings, after all. An advocate for l-o-v-e. A firm believer in relationships, even though I haven't actually had a decent one in the past one hundred years.

As a die-hard, card-carrying romantic, I *had* to help him.

The fact that he would be good PR for my business and prove to the entire bloodsucking community that I knew my stuff when it came to matchmaking was just a great big cherry floating in my already delish green apple martini.

I smiled. "One thousand years old, huh?"

"And thirty-six."

"Well, then." My smile widened. "It's your lucky day. We're running a half-price special for anyone over one thousand thirty-five."

The brown wooly mammoths that doubled for his eyebrows climbed a notch. "Really?"

He was obviously as cheap as he was dweebish.

"Half price for a full consultation and four prospective mates *and* we'll pick up the tab for your first official date." My smile widened so much I thought my face would crack. "All you have to do is fill out the Dead End Dating profile and wish list, and we'll get started."

I gave him my most impressive *you want to do this*

look, which had been known to influence not only humans but the majority of unattached heterosexual male vamps. I even narrowed my eyes just a hint and threw in a dose of sexy, sultry, *you want to do this because you want to do me*.

Not that I would ever allow him to lay one finger on me. I don't do dweebs. Okay, *okay,* so at the moment I wasn't doing anyone. But he didn't know this, and, frankly, there are times when a woman has to use everything in her power to make things happen. Be it ancient *vampere* magic or a full-blown tease.

I expected a dutiful nod. At the very least, a little drooling. I *am* pretty hot.

He merely blinked his pale, watery eyes and stared at the flyer again.

Okay, so I really hadn't done the sultry, sexy *do me* look in a long time. (Try one hundred and sixty-some odd years . . . He'd been fighting the Mexicans for truth, justice, and the Texas way, and I'd been a sucker— literally—for a man in boots and spurs.) I was obviously out of practice. That, or this guy wasn't just a dweeb.

I eyed him. "You do like females, don't you?"

He actually looked offended and relief swept through me. "You bet I do."

"So what's the holdup then? You should have dozens of little . . . What did you say your name was, again?"

"It's Francoise. My friends call me Francis."

It figured. "Look, Frank, a guy like you owes it to the entire community to continue the grand tradition of vampires everywhere. Procreation of our kind is a privilege. It's a duty." I clamped a hand over his puny shoulder and stared at him as if he were the last drop of AB negative at an all-you-can-eat vamp fest. "The survival of our race depends on you, Frank."

He stood silent for a long moment. "I, um, never really thought about it that way," he finally said.

"It's about time you did. Every day, more and more humans are born. The world is overrun with them. Throw in several hundred thousand werewolves, a few thousand werevamps, and a hodgepodge of Others, and we're talking a major population explosion. Meanwhile, strong, virile, fertile male vampires like yourself sit idly by and do nothing."

Obviously, there were no strong, virile, fertile male vampires sitting idly by, but he didn't seem to realize this, and I was definitely on a roll.

"Before you know it, we'll be extinct," I went on. "Fortune hunters the world over will be digging up vamps and selling their fossilized fangs on eBay."

I was definitely making him think. I considered humming a few bars of Queen's "We Are the Champions," but I didn't want to overkill. So I just tightened my grip on his shoulder as if the fate of the world rested with him and waited for his answer.

"It really would be nice not to be alone so much of the time. I mean, I'm not exactly alone alone. I do have Britney and the twins, but they—"

"I thought you didn't have any little vampires running around?" I cut in. No way did this guy have baby vamps, much less twins. A male vampire had to have a fertility rating that went off the charts to dish out a set of twins. Which would have made him something of a legend. Which would mean I would have heard of Francis long before now.

"The twins are a pair of kittens and Britney's my cockerdoodle."

That made sense. Sort of. "Your *what*?"

"A cockerdoodle. You know, part cocker spaniel, part poodle. A cockerdoodle."

"Please stop saying that word."

"What word? Cockerdoodle? That's what she is. A—"

"I know, I know. I just don't want to hear it."

He gave me an odd look. "She's a real looker. I've had her for ten years now, and she's won ten dog shows. Not that I care about the competitions themselves. I just enter her to have something to do in my free time."

"That's a great hobby. My mother has at least a half-dozen friends who live and breathe dog shows." Of course, most of them had large-breed dogs. Dobermans, great Danes, huskies—the kind that ate cockerdoodles for breakfast. But that was beside the point. "Showing dogs is great common ground. You've got the whole primal animal appeal. On top of that, it's competitive. I'm sure there are oodles of female vamps who are really into it."

"What about scrapbooking? See, I save all the pictures and ribbons and things from Britney's shows and keep them in several books. It's sort of a hobby of mine, too." He held up the bag with his Moe's purchases. "That's what this stuff is for." Excitement lit his gaze. "I even bought pinking shears to bevel the edges on the pictures."

I clapped him on the shoulder. "I won't tell if you don't."

"I guess scrapbooking's not very macho."

"Not even close. So what do you do for a living?"

He shrugged. "Nothing much now. I used to be in real estate and I made a few good investments, but I haven't done anything lately."

"Real estate, huh?"

"My family owns a lot of land in the old country."

"You own land in France?" He nodded. "What part?"

"Most parts." He must have noticed my stunned look. "I go all the way back to Napoleon. The first one. We used to play chess together."

"What did you say your name was?"

"Deville. Francoise Deville."

The name set off an alarm in my head, and my hands started to tremble. I hadn't just stumbled upon a really old geek. I'd stumbled upon *the* really old geek. From the oldest family in France. And the richest. And that was saying a lot when you considered that we vamps had some major bucks.

"Where are your parents? Brothers? Sisters?"

"Most of my family is still in Paris. My parents live in the country."

"Do you ever see them?"

He shook his head. "They don't really like to have me around. I'm sort of the black sheep."

"I hear ya on that one." Boy, did I ever.

"You really think you can find me an eternity mate?" he asked after a long, silent moment, his voice quiet.

Hopeful.

Scrapbooking and cockerdoodles aside, the guy was sort of sweet.

In a pathetic, desperate, dysfunctional sort of way.

My chest hitched a little, and I suddenly felt even more determined. "You bet I can. Of course, I might have to GQ you up a bit first." I pushed a strand of hair off his forehead and tried to envision him as Brad Pitt à la *Troy*.

Okay, so forget Brad Pitt.

Maybe a young George Clooney.

All right, all right. George was out. But there was always Matt Damon.

I squinted my eyes and let Frank's image blur. There. Definitely more Matt Damon.

Sort of.

"We'll definitely need to do a mini-makeover. It's part of our VIP Service Package."

"A makeover?" He touched his hair. "You mean I'll have to get it cut?"

"Shaped," I corrected. "And colored."

"You want to *color* my hair?"

From the look on his face you would have thought I'd suggested a torture fest with garlic and the first *American Idol* CD. "You'll definitely need a facial, too. Maybe some contacts."

He shook his head. "I don't know about this."

"Obviously. Otherwise, you would have been snatched up long ago."

"You really think so?"

"Sure, I do." I patted his arm. "Just leave everything to me. You're in capable hands."

While my *do me* look was definitely rusty, I still had it when it came to touching. Another pat on his shoulder—coupled with a little stroking persuasion from my fingertips, of course—and his expression went from worried to slightly confused. (Okay, so I'd lost a little in the touch department, too. I'd been going for relaxed.)

"What's the name of your business again?" he asked me.

"Dead End Dating, and we're the best." Or we soon would be, once we took Francis from humdrum to hunky. Until then . . . "Did I mention that the half price is payable up front?"

Five
♥ ♥ ♥

I left my new friend Francis at the subway station, his phone number and address already entered into my BlackBerry and a check for half of my fee stashed in my purse, and walked to the corner to catch a cab home. I was so pleased with my night's work that I decided to head home on a high note rather than going back to the office to face the dismal number of profiles on the Dead End Dating website.

I stepped down off the curb and signaled for a cab. I know, I know. I should do something vampy like change into a bat and fly back to my place. But black is *so* not my color, and a pink bat doesn't actually fit with the whole low-profile thing my kind have preached for the last trillion years. I could run, too, but my feet hurt. It's tough being a fashion vixen.

I put my fingers on either side of my mouth and let

loose a shrill whistle that would no doubt have every dog within a ten-block radius whimpering. A yellow cab squealed to a stop in front of me, and I pulled open the door.

The creepy feeling hit me again when I climbed into the cab. I chanced a glance behind me. Of course, no one was there. Just the empty sidewalk and the darkened building that housed a bakery and a small convenience store. The musty smell of garbage drifted from a nearby doorway, mingling with the sharp scent of the cab's exhaust and . . . something else. Not necessarily something unpleasant, just . . . different. It was stronger, slightly more musky, and definitely out of place on a New York street.

Like the scent of an exclusive men's cologne in the middle of a cheap flea market.

I couldn't help the sudden goose bumps that chased up and down my arms. As if someone were watching me.

Someone or something.

"Awful late for a pretty gal like you to be out and about."

The voice drew my attention to the rearview mirror to find the cabdriver's gaze boring into me.

"I'm a night owl."

"Me too." He was an old man with steel gray hair and a mass of wrinkles. He wore a button-down plaid shirt, the cuffs rolled up to reveal beefy forearms sprinkled with white hair. He glanced over his shoulder and smiled, giving me a glimpse of straight white dentures. His brown eyes crinkled and more wrinkles cut into his weathered cheeks. "Most of the other cabbies can't stomach the late shift 'cause of all the crazies, but me, I like it. It keeps things interesting."

He looked nice enough. Like someone's grandfather. But there was just something about the strength in his hands as he gripped the steering wheel that made me uncomfortable. I glanced up and caught his stare in the rearview mirror, and goose bumps chased up and down my arms again. I could picture his hands wrapped around something soft and slender, his forearms flexed with force as he tightened his hold . . .

Okay, so he had some pent-up rage, but he'd never acted on it. Not yet.

I quickly closed the window in my head that let me see into his character, a trait that all born vampires shared. We could look into any human's baby blues, and see the real person. The one most people tried to hide from one another. While I could see how such character insight could be beneficial—it meant no going into business with a human crook or hiring a receptionist that might be a mass murderer or climbing into a car with an SOB—short for Snipers of Otherworldly Beings, an organization of the enlightened few who actually believed in vampires and other supernatural creatures, and made a living trying to rid the world of us. At the same time, I knew more than I wanted to about most humans.

Namely, that they could be more evil than any vamp. And much more ruthless.

I shook away the deep, disturbing thought and

pulled my cell phone from my purse. I didn't do *deep* very well.

"So where are you headed, little lady?"

"Manhattan." I gave him my street address and settled back into the seat. Before he could initiate any more conversation, I flipped open my phone and punched the button to check my messages. I had ten.

The first played and a familiar female voice filled my ear.

"You're not going to believe what happened to me tonight. I was walking down Fifth Avenue and I looked to my left, and there it was in the window. *The* most kick-ass Louis Vuitton handbag. It has a blue jean print and a snakeskin handle and I just *had* to have it. I can't wait for you to see it. Where are you? Oh, yeah, you're doing the work thing. I hope you're having as much luck as me! I'll call back later." *Click*.

Nina Lancaster was the blond half of The Ninas— my two best friends in the entire world.

The three of us had been hanging out for more than three hundred years. We'd played hide-and-go-seek as children, nursed dozens of broken hearts, and sampled our very first full-blooded Italian together—his name had been Giovanni and he'd tasted even better than he'd looked. Nina Lancaster was the daughter of Victor Lancaster, an ancient vampire and hotelier who, unlike someone who shall remain nameless, didn't force his daughter to wear a name tag or tacky clothing. Rather, Nina played hostess at the Waldorf Astoria to feed her designer handbag addiction.

Nina Number Two, aka Nina Wellburton, was the brunette half of the duo. Her father had made his fortune in female sanitary products—made Moe's sound good, didn't it? Nina Two supervised the accounting department in New Jersey where her father's production facility was located and wouldn't dream of dropping an obscene amount of money on a handbag. "You can't eat a handbag," she always said. "You can't eat those shoes." Nina Two was a closet penny pincher.

Ouch.

But what can I say? We grew up together. We're best buds. Not to mention, she was one of the few vamps I knew who wasn't self-indulgent, which made her different from the pack, which made her like me.

But with less attractive hair, of course.

I deleted the message and waited for the second.

"You won't believe what Nina did." Pause. "All right, so you'll believe it. She threw away a month's salary on a *purse*. I mean, I know it's a Louis Vuitton, but there is such a thing as self-control." Worried sigh. "She has no control. She's floundering in a sea of addiction, and I think we need to plan some sort of intervention. I mean, we *are* her best friends. It's our duty to pull her back from the brink of destruction." Thoughtful pause. "I'll call back when I come up with a plan. Oh, and I hope work is going well." *Click*.

I deleted the message and waited for number three.

"It's Nina again. Where *are* you? You have to see this purse. I stopped off at Nina's and showed it to her and she flipped, as usual. She's been staring at spreadsheets too long. She obviously can't appreciate a work of art when she sees one. I think she's repressed. She's practically locked up in that office of hers all night. I think we need to save her from herself before it's too late. Maybe we can sneak into her office, fire up her computer, and do a screen saver with the latest Dolce and Gabbana ad. It features this silver lamé top and a pair of studded hip-hugger jeans and . . ."

The cab pulled up in front of my building just as I deleted message ten—a detailed plot from Nina Two to kidnap Nina One from the Waldorf and take her to a Shoppers Anonymous meeting.

My apartment was located in a renovated duplex on the east side of Manhattan. The building itself was dark and quiet. There was no doorman to pull me from the car and pay the cabdriver for me. No front-desk man ready to carry my bags and punch the button on the elevator. There wasn't an elevator, period. Just several flights of stairs that led to the fifth floor and a long hallway with only two doors, one on either side.

I hadn't met the woman across from me, but I'd heard she was an accountant. Single. No children. No pets. She smelled like cheap perfume and ate a lot of Thai food.

I paused at my door and my ears prickled.

". . . on the national front, the number of missing women continues to mount. Just three days ago, Candace Flowers disappeared from her Chicago area home. That makes a total of nine women to vanish in the Windy City in the past two months alone. A whopping number that surpasses the recent string of kidnappings in Los Angeles . . ."

She also slept with the television tuned to CNN, the volume turned low so as not to disturb the neighbors. But I wasn't the average girl next door, and I heard everything loud and clear.

Zzzzzz . . .

Okay, so she snored, too.

Sliding my key into the opening, I twisted the lock, turned the doorknob, and flipped the switch just inside. Warm yellow light pushed back the shadows.

The place was about the size of my closet in my parents' penthouse over on Park Avenue—they still kept digs in the city even though they now spent most of their time at their estate in Connecticut. Rather than small, I liked to think of it as quaint. Cozy.

All right, all right. It was *small,* but it was all mine—at least for the rest of the month—and it was just a few blocks from Dead End Dating.

Of course, all mine also meant *all mine.* As in no eternity mate. No boyfriend. No platonic roommate. Not even a cat.

Not that I wanted any of the above. I was happy with my life. Extremely happy. Wildly, fantastically happy.

Yeah, yeah. So I'm not *that* happy. But I'm working on it. First my career, then my own love life (an eternity mate who adores me and a half-dozen little vamps with my sense of style).

I set my purse on a small antique phone table I'd

talked my mother out of when I'd moved a few weeks ago. Along with a sofa and two chairs. Unfortunately, the sofa took up half my living room, and I'd had to return the chairs for lack of space. My parents had bought heavy-duty blinds for every window as a house-warming present. I'd splurged on some Egyptian cotton sheets that were now calling my name from the king-size bed that took up my entire bedroom.

I was halfway undressed by the time I walked across the room to the blinking answering machine that sat on the floor next to the spot where a chrome and glass Huervo dining room table would eventually sit *if* my work with Francis panned out and I started raking in the dough. (Hey, a girl could dream.)

I punched the blinking button with my toe and my mother's voice filled the room.

"Your father has called you three times and you haven't called him back."

"Because I know what he wants," I said out loud.

"Midnight Moe's has been good to us," the message went on. "I know it's not exactly a glamorous business, but it's lucrative."

Guilt—oh, wait, that was my mother's voice—followed me the few steps into the kitchen where I opened my itty-bitty refrigerator and surveyed the contents. I reached past a styrofoam Starbucks container, four juice boxes, and a six-pack of Diet Coke and pulled out what looked like a bottle of red wine.

The label read BOTTLED ESPECIALLY FOR GARNIER'S GOURMET, an upscale deli and bakery located in the

Village. Garnier's offered their human customers the widest selection of French cheeses in New York, and their vamp clientele a civilized, and discreet, alternative to dinner.

". . . trying your father's patience," my mother went on. "He's been so upset that he actually forgot to trim the bushes on the east side yesterday, and you know he *always* trims the east side . . ."

My father always trimmed the bushes on the east side because they bordered the neighboring estate owned by one Viola Hamilton, president of the Connecticut chapter of the Naked and Unashamed Nudist Sisterhood, aka the NUNS. The NUNS were a group of female werewolves and, therefore, the plague of the great state of Connecticut as far as my father was concerned.

Viola hosted the sisterhood's weekend meetings, and so she liked the bushes high and full to maintain her privacy.

And my father liked to piss her off.

". . . he's terribly upset about this whole plan of yours. And so am I . . ." my mother went on.

I uncorked the bottle, poured a glass, and nuked it in the microwave. Settling on the sofa, I took a sip. My tongue quivered at the first drop. The liquid teased my taste buds, slid down my throat, and worked its way through my body. Warmth rushed along my nerve endings. While it wasn't the same rush that came from drinking from a flesh-and-blood human, it was just as satisfying.

Sort of.

". . . know how embarrassing this is for us? What with you living in that hole in the wall? And finding eternity mates for a living? My word, you can't find your own. How are you supposed to find one for someone else?"

Forget the sipping. I downed the glass before my mom could point out the fact that I hadn't had a real date since my great-uncle Gio took the plunge with mate number four—his three previous mates had all met with untimely deaths, and so eternity equaled about a hundred years in Uncle Gio's world.

My parents were convinced my uncle had just had a rotten string of luck, but I knew the truth. While Uncle Gio was rich, cultured, and good-looking, he was also one of the few vampires with a bad sense of humor. I'd heard my uncle tell enough knock-knock jokes to suspect that my aunt Jean hadn't just fallen three stories onto a flagpole by accident. Ditto for Aunt Gwen, who'd mistaken a bottle of holy water for her favorite Chardonnay, and Aunt Monique, who'd mistaken a bulb of garlic for soap and dropped about two dozen into her nightly bath.

". . . let me introduce you to Stella Burbank's oldest son. His name is Paul, and he's got a very impressive fertility rating. He's absolutely perfect for you. Or he will be if you forget this crazy idea and let your father give you a real job—" *Click.*

I'd crossed the room and hit the off button with my toe. I punched delete and turned toward my bedroom.

I already had a real job and it felt . . . good.

I was tired, my mind in a mental scramble from thinking so much, and I was exhausted. A smile played at the corner of my mouth. While I'd been ready to drop more times than I could count—from dancing all night at one of my favorite haunts, or having a midnight gabfest with my girlfriends—this was different. I felt as if I'd actually *done* something tonight.

I checked the blinds to make sure they were secure; while I wasn't going to go up in smoke from a little indirect sunlight, it was murder on the complexion. I crawled into bed, pulled the covers up to my neck, closed my eyes, and conjured my most favorite fantasy—me, the beach, a few margaritas, and Orlando Bloom.

Oh, and a pink Donna Karan hand-stitched bikini with conch shells dangling from the straps.

Now, *that* was a fantasy.

Six

❤ ❤ ❤

" . . . It's your destiny to work at Moe's . . ."

My mother's voice peeled back the blanket of happy I was currently buried under and slid into my ears.

". . . not to mention, it's your duty. You're a Marchette. We *are* Moe's . . ."

Sleep tried to suck me back under, unwilling to give me up before sunset. I could still feel the exhaustion in my body. A feeling that only eased when night fell.

". . . even your cousin Victor is stepping up to do his share. He called your father just last night. He's the last person I expected to hear from since he's still mixed up with whatshername . . ."

"Whatshername" referred to Victor's wife, Leeanne. Leeanne came from a long line of werevamps. And what, pray tell, is a werevamp? Think Dracula meets the wolf from Little Red Riding Hood. See, a long time ago one of my ancestors jumped ship and got jiggy with a werewolf. Then, before anyone could say boo, said vampire ended up pregnant. Who woulda thunk it? Anyhow, the rest is history, and now there's an entire race of vampires/werewolves running around the planet. Or corrupting it, as my father would say. The only thing he hated more than werevamps were made vampires. My family is *so* totally into the we're-better-than-you-are-because-we're-the-elite-race mentality.

Not that the fuss everyone had made had stopped Victor. He'd fallen hard and fast for Leeanne—proof beyond a doubt of the big L. That's love, not lust. Then again, I suppose it could be lust as well. Or just lust all by its lonesome. Those werevamps *were* majorly irresistible (boy, did I know that one firsthand). To make a long story short, Victor hooked up with Leeanne five years ago, and the family disowned him. Until now. My father had such a soft spot for anyone wearing lime green.

". . . he's had divided loyalties in the past, but he obviously knows what he should be doing. He's family and family sticks together. They don't pack up and move out on some crazy matchmaking whim . . ."

A dream, I told myself. I was still sleeping the sleep of the dead, and the voice echoing through my head was just my imagination. No decent, respectable, sane vampire would be up before sunset—

Just as the thought struck, my eyes snapped open.

Hey, we're talking my mother here.

". . . but it's your life and you have to live it as you see fit. Though I can't begin to fathom how you could possibly be happy in that cramped hovel you call an apartment day in and day out. But if you want to break your father's heart, that's your business. The least you can do is meet your father's financial advisor. He's perfect for you, dear. Call me and I'll tell you more." *Click*.

I squinted at the clock sitting on the floor near my bedroom door. I still had fifteen blessed minutes and my eyelids knew it. They fluttered, trying to creep shut on me.

I fought back the urge to bury my head beneath the pillow and forced myself from between the sheets. The decent, respectable, sane vampire comment pushed into my head, but I quickly dismissed it. This was totally different because I wasn't bugging the hell out of anyone.

I stumbled toward the small window that flanked the left side of my bed. Careful to stay off to the side, I pulled the cord and lifted the heavy blinds. Fading sunlight spilled into the room. I turned and hopped back beneath the pile of blankets. Settling my back against the headboard, I hugged my knees to my chest, pulled up the covers, and stared past the foot of my bed to the mirror that hung on the wall opposite me.

Here's the deal . . . While I can't waltz outside in the direct light of day, staring at its reflection is a totally different thing.

A quick note about born vamps and mirrors—yes, we can see our reflections. Now whether or not we want to, that's a different story altogether. Personally,

I don't glance into mine until I've had at least a full glass of O positive and a little lipstick.

An orange glow topped the building next to mine, and I watched for the next several minutes as it sank lower and lower. I'd seen the sun set like this many times (I *am* five hundred years old and mirrors have been around forever), and every time, I felt a strange sense of loss when the sunlight disappeared completely.

Not that I thought it was any big deal. Or felt slighted in any way. I was one of the special ones— *crème de la crème* breeding, eternal youth, and all that jazz—and daylight was nothing more than a pain in the ass as far as I was concerned.

No way did I actually wonder what it would be like to stand outside and feel the sun warm my face.

Okay, so maybe I've wondered. But I've also wondered what it would be like to play a duet with Mozart, pose for Botticelli, marry the president of the United States (before the whole Lewinsky thing), and sing the national anthem at a Super Bowl game. We're talking brief, fleeting, it-ain't-gonna-happen thoughts that are nice to have, but in no way do they reflect the real me.

I am totally happy and content.

The phone rang before I could give the subject any more thought—thankfully—and I snatched it up.

"Hey."

"Lil?"

My mother's voice carried over the line, and I mentally slapped myself for not glancing at the caller ID.

But I'd been in a sort of serious moment, and I don't really do serious all that well.

"It's about time you answered the phone."

"Just kidding," I blurted. "I'm not really home right now, but leave a message and I'll call you back. Beeeeep!"

"Lil?"

I held my breath.

"This is your mother," she finally said. "I forgot to remind you about Sunday. Don't be late. Your father hates it when you're late. Speaking of which, I've got to go now and wake him up. He tees off at sundown." *Click*.

Whew, that was close.

I let myself take a deep breath and punched the off button on my phone.

Ugh.

In my whole new apartment/new business euphoria, I'd totally forgotten about Sunday. While humans had the traditional dinner where they gathered once a week to drive each other crazy, we Marchettes had the *hunt*.

Back in the old days—pre-Versace—families had hunted together in packs. But since we born vamps had come into a new enlightened era and now did dinner in a much more civilized way—bottled gourmet—we no longer risked discovery by going out and scouring the countryside for sustenance.

Even so, that didn't mean we should let our survival instincts get soft. At least, as far as my dad was concerned. He felt it his duty to make sure that his children were fully capable of hunting should bottling factories fall off the face of the earth and chaos reign supreme. And so he kept up the Sunday hunt tradition.

Only now we hunted each other—the *it* person. The prize? Extra vacation days from Moe's, which suited my brothers just fine. They hadn't missed a hunt in ages. Since I wasn't now nor had I ever been (at least not that I would admit) employed by Moe's, I wasn't nearly as revved about the weekly gathering. I'd rather wear a pair of jeans from Wal-Mart.

On top of making us hunt, my dad insisted on showing us his latest golf swing.

Forget Wal-Mart. Bring on the Goodwill.

I crawled from beneath the covers and walked over to the window. I was about to close the blinds when I felt the strange prickling sensation that I'd felt last night.

I stared at the alley below, my extraordinary eyesight pushing back the shadows to sweep up and down the narrow walkway. Empty except for a few garbage cans, a stray cat, and something soft and furry that I would rather not name.

Denizen of the darkness aside, I had sort of a phobia when it came to rodents.

I searched the area a few more seconds before shaking away the strange sensation. Punching the button on my CD player, I forwarded through the selections until Kanye West started warning the male population about gold-digging women. I hit the repeat button and set the remote control aside. The steady beat filled my small apartment and drowned out the evening news blaring from the TV next door. I danced into the kitchen, downed a full glass of blood, and then did a little ass-shaking toward the shower. Creepiness and nagging mothers aside, I was in a pretty good mood.

A half hour later, I was dressed and ready to start my evening. The sky was a rich velvet black studded with twinkling stars, and I opted to walk rather than catch a cab.

Along the way, I stopped off at a nearby newsstand for the latest issue of *Cosmo* and ducked into Starbucks. My hands were full by the time I rounded the corner and approached my office.

Thankfully.

Because the hunky guy who was waiting just outside the glass doorway made me want to reach out and think later.

Much, *much* later.

Seven

❤ ❤ ❤

He was a vampire.

That was the first thought I had when I saw the man standing in the doorway of Dead End Dating.

Okay, so that wasn't actually my *first* thought.

Numero uno? My lace Victoria's Secret thong had crawled into a really high place, and I was thinking I should have used my preternatural reflexes and gone after it a block back instead of opting to wait until I reached the office.

Thought number two?

He was a really hot vampire.

In a wild, primitive way. He had dark, shoulder-length hair, a strong, stubble-covered jaw, and blue eyes. Not just any old blue either. We're talking neon blue, so bright and vivid that I could have sworn I heard them humming when they collided with mine.

Then again, the hum could have been my deprived

vampiric hormones, which have been known to kick into overdrive in the face of so much testosterone.

This guy definitely had the whole badass cowboy thing working, from the black Stetson that sat low on his forehead and his long black leather duster, to his black jeans and faded black boots.

Unfortunately, he wasn't just a drop-dead gorgeous bloodsucker. He was also a made one.

I knew that the minute my nostrils flared and the only thing I smelled was the faint hint of leather from his jacket. Nothing sweet or rich or edible, though he certainly looked all three.

I forced myself to swallow and focused on the thong. Ugh. Talk about uncomfortable. I should feel totally out of sync right now and not the least bit turned on. My heart shouldn't pound and my hands shouldn't tremble, and no friggin' way should I feel like planting a big one on this guy's firm, sensuous lips.

Think thong.

Think irritating thong.

Think totally irritating thong chafing the hell out of my ass beneath last season's DKNY jeans which I'd pulled on for lack of anything else (did I mention I hate to do laundry?) with a pink vintage Metallica T-shirt that did absolutely nothing for my complexion.

I couldn't have done a thing about the jeans. But I would have been much better off if I'd worn the cream-colored pullover mini tee with the rhinestones and cap sleeves that I'd bought last weekend. At least that played up what was left of my airbrushed tan and made me look marginally sexy . . .

Wait a sec.

At the moment, sexy wasn't my top priority. Mr. Hot *Made* Vampire was out of the realm of prospective vamps. Which meant no feeling his vibe. No wondering what his lips felt like or fantasizing about the rough feel of his hands on my . . . *No.*

It's not like he was all that and a Bloody Mary chaser. Vintage, at least when it came to an entire outfit, was so *not* in. The trick was to pair key pieces with trendy styles. This guy obviously had zero fashion sense on top of the whole being made issue. A double whammy as far as I was concerned.

Even so, I still wished I'd worn the other shirt. Just because he was clueless didn't mean I had to join the party. Not to mention—vampire classifications aside—he was totally, massively H-O-T. While I had no intention of hooking up with him, I still wanted him to want to hook up with me.

It was the principle of the thing, after all.

I reached him in three strides. "Hi."

"Hey there, sugar."

Sugar? There you go. Talk about superior, condescending macho bullshit. He might as well have snatched my voter registration card and my free will along with it. I absolutely *detested* guys who did that.

My heart kicked up a notch, and my nerves tingled. "Can I, um, help you with something?"

"Maybe." He didn't budge. He simply stood there

blocking my doorway, his gaze fixed on me. A funny feeling wiggled up my spine. A familiar feeling.

Realization slammed into me like a bus with bad brakes. "You're the one who's been following me," I blurted. "It was you."

He didn't so much as flinch at the accusation. No sheepish look of apology to soften the badass image. Instead, he grinned, which lifted the corners of his mouth and revealed a row of straight white teeth. My heart pitter-pattered shamelessly.

"Guilty." His voice went from deep and seductive to cold and businesslike. "My name is Ty Bonner. I'm an independent fugitive apprehension agent. I'd like to talk to you about a string of kidnappings."

My mind rushed back to the news spiel I'd heard coming from my neighbor's apartment about the missing Chicago woman.

Before I could speculate, Ty said, "Why don't we have this discussion inside? Your coffee's getting cold." He motioned to the Starbucks container in my hand.

"What? Oh, this isn't for me. It's for my receptionist." He stepped back and I walked past him.

I meant to saunter, but I was too busy wondering why he would want to talk to me about a bunch of kidnappings and, okay, so I was also wondering why I had such rotten luck when it came to men. The first really good-looking guy I meet and he's *made,* for Damien's sake.

What was I? Cursed or something?

"Well, well. You have been busy," Evie said the

moment we walked into the office. "Way to go, boss. If you keep pulling them in like this, we'll be up and running in no time."

"He's not a client. He's a fugitive administrative agent."

"That's fugitive apprehension agent," Ty corrected.

"A bounty hunter." Evie gleamed at Ty as I set the coffee on her desk. "Sounds terribly dangerous."

"Sometimes."

"Do you carry a gun?" Her gaze traveled the length of him, pausing at several spots in between. "A Beretta? Glock? Ruger? Magnum revolver?"

"Evie's a huge *CSI* fan," I chimed in when Ty raised an eyebrow.

"Actually, I carry a forty-caliber Sig," he told her. "*When* I carry. Which isn't too often. I don't really need a gun." Not with the forces of darkness on his side.

"Stupid me. You're probably a black belt. Highly trained in hand-to-hand combat," Evie said. I could practically see her shiver with excitement. "I bet you kick ass royally with your bare hands."

"I can hold my own."

"You can go ahead and take off," I told Evie, who simply sat there, staring at Ty as if he were a Tootsie Pop and she had a sudden hankering for the chocolate center. "I bet you're tired."

"Not at all." She took a huge gulp of her mocha latte. "This is my sixth one of these today." She set the cup down. "I'd be glad to hang around to take calls while you guys have your, er, talk."

"That's okay. I'll answer the phone. I'm sure this won't take long."

"Really, I wouldn't mind."

"I don't want to impose."

"You're not. It would be my pleasure."

"Go." I directed my *mucho* psychic vamp abilities and willed her to her feet, but she didn't so much as budge. It wasn't until Ty gave her the Look that she pushed back from her desk and stood. She handed me a small stack of messages before reaching for her purse.

"Don't forget your coffee," Ty said, and she smiled.

"Thanks," she said as if he'd been the one to stand in line for twenty minutes for it.

"You're welcome," I said, willing her to leave again with my eyes. I felt a niggle of guilt. After all, Evie was my friend, and I made it a rule never to use any vamp mojo on my friends. Then again, most of my friends were fellow vamps and the mojo didn't work on them.

Besides, this was an emergency. And in her best interest. I didn't know Ty Bonner. He could be sizing her up for dinner for all I knew. From the way Evie was gushing, she'd be a more than willing entree.

"Take off," I said, and she made a beeline for the door as fast as her leather Jimmy Choo wedges could carry her.

Oooh, I hadn't really noticed those before. Nice.

". . . do it?"

"What?" My head swiveled back to Ty. "I'm sorry. I didn't catch that."

"Where do you want to do it?"

A dozen yummy possibilities raced through my mind, and my tongue was suddenly too thick to talk. I pointed to a doorway and motioned him in.

"Impressive," he said once we walked inside. His gaze scanned the interior of my office while I flipped on a few extra lamps on the way to my desk. "You must be doing pretty well for yourself."

I swallowed and forced aside each and every lewd, lustful thought wreaking havoc in my brain (or at least most of them). "Actually, it's my credit card that's doing all the work right now, but I intend to take over just as soon as business picks up." Rounding my desk, I sank into my chair, set my purse on the floor, and eyed him. "So why all the James Bond stuff? Why didn't you just call and make an appointment like everyone else instead of following me around?"

"You're a vampire."

"And?"

"You're a matchmaker."

"And?"

"The two don't go together." He eyed the plaque on my wall that read LOVE MAKES THE WORLD GO 'ROUND. "Vampires don't believe in love."

"True, but they do believe in procreation. Born vampires, I mean. Nowadays, a lot of vamps are too busy making the big bucks to have much time for a social life. They need a screening process. Someone to point them in the right direction. That's where I come in. I match humans as well." At least, I would once I managed to land a few human clients. "But born vamps are my specialty."

"You've definitely got your work cut out for you."

His comment reminded me of Francis and I realized that since Ty had been following me, he'd undoubtedly witnessed the whole subway episode. "For your information, Francis has tons of potential. It's just a matter of packaging it a little better, that's all."

"You'll have to work on more than his package. The guy isn't much of a chick magnet. At least not when it comes to luring female vampires. He isn't the least bit ruthless."

"He is, too." Or he could be. With a little roughing up.

"Maybe as the Italian grandmother. But as himself?" He shook his head and nailed me with his fierce blue gaze.

My breath caught, and my vampire heart went into stutter mode.

Maybe *nailed* wasn't the right word to be thinking of when it came to Ty Bonner. Nix *pierced*. Or *speared*. Or *shish-kabobbed*. Or any other verb that made me think sex.

"I still don't get why you've been following me."

"I had to make sure you were legitimate and that you weren't using this hook-up service as a front for fresh meat."

"Fresh meat" referred to humans, and I knew he was alluding to the black market that offered humans to vampires who still hadn't come into the twenty-first century and learned to drink their dinner out of a bottle like the rest of us. There were a few—very few—who didn't just feed off their victim's blood.

They fed off their fear, as well, and so popping the cork on a bottle of gourmet or calling up the nearest takeout service wasn't nearly enough to sate their hunger.

Every race had its bad apples, and ours was no different. But knowing it and having it pointed out were two very different things.

"I provide a service, plain and simple."

"I know that now after watching you for the past few days." He gave me a strange look before shaking his head. "You're definitely not a flesh peddler. Not vicious enough."

A tiny thrill went through me when he picked up my paperweight and trailed a finger over the engraved LIL, the *i* dotted with a tiny heart. I stiffened.

"Maybe I knew you were watching me and I'm just a really good actress." Okay, so I'm not vicious. I am a bitch at times, but that's as close as I get to the dark side. Still, I felt hard-pressed to defend myself. As much as I moan and groan about certain aspects of my existence, I'm proud of my heritage.

My sudden call to arms certainly had nothing to do with the fact that Ty Bonner seemed almost disappointed.

"I can be as ruthless and as bloodthirsty as any vamp. That's why I keep this dagger on my desk." I fingered the silver weapon.

He didn't seem the least bit impressed.

"Bloodthirsty, I'll buy. You *are* a vampire. Ruthless?" He shook his head. "Hardly."

"I am so ruthless." I pointed the silver blade at him

to prove my point. "I could send you to bounty hunter heaven with just the flick of my wrist."

"Heaven is the last place I'm headed, sugar." He grinned. "Besides, that's not a dagger. It's a letter opener."

"It could be a dagger. If used with enough force."

He shrugged and nodded. "But you wouldn't use it. You couldn't." He shook his head as if he still couldn't quite believe it. "You're *nice*."

My heart did the flip thing again. Dammit. "I am *not* nice."

"You're cotton-candy nice." He sniffed. "You even smell cotton-candy nice."

"That doesn't mean I *am*."

"You brought coffee to your assistant. Your *human* assistant. That's like giving your horse a glass of Merlot."

"Maybe I spiked it with arsenic."

He didn't look the least bit convinced. "You're offering free dating profiles."

"That has nothing to do with being nice. It's completely self-motivated. I'm trying to build my business."

"You gave five bucks to the homeless man on the corner."

He had a point.

I set down the dagger/letter opener and folded my hands to keep them from trembling.

Okay, so I folded them to keep from reaching out and tracing the scar on his cheek. What can I say? I'm fascinated with scars. Born vamps don't have them. If we are injured in any way, a full day of sleep rejuvenates us and makes us whole again. Talk about beauty sleep. Anyhow, a few zzz's worked the same for made vamps as well. Once they were turned, that is. But before then, they were as vulnerable as any human.

The phone chose that moment to ring, and I snatched it up, eager for a distraction. "Dead End Dating. Where true happiness is just a profile away." I know, I know. It was a lame motto. But the Golden Arches weren't built in a day.

"Lilliana Marchette," my mother snapped. "I've been trying to reach you for *ages*. Don't you remember your own mother's phone number?"

"I'm sorry." I raised my voice a few octaves and did my best Evie imitation. "I'm afraid Lil's, um, not in right now. This is her receptionist/personal assistant."

"Excuse me?"

"Evie. My name's Evie Dalton."

"This is Jacqueline Marchette, Lilliana's mother."

"You don't say? It's such an honor to finally speak with you. Lil has said some wonderful things about you."

My mother hesitated as if she wasn't buying it. "She has?"

"Of course! I'm so sorry that you missed her, but I'm sure she'll be happy to call you back as soon as she gets in."

That did it. No way would *I* use the word happy when referring to calling my mother back.

"Tell her to call me as soon as possible. It's imperative that I speak with her right away."

"Will do. And let me just say what a gorgeous daughter you have."

"Why, um, thank you."

"I mean it. She's positively stunning."

"She's always been a beauty."

"And brilliant."

"Well, she *does* take after my side of the family."

"Obviously. Take care now and it was wonderful talking with you." I ignored a rush of guilt, slid the phone into its cradle, and glanced up to see Ty eyeing me. "I couldn't tell her I was too busy to talk to her. That would just hurt her feelings."

"I would have been glad to step out while you took the call."

"Now you tell me." I tried to look annoyed as I leaned back in my desk chair and motioned him into the seat opposite me. "So what do a bunch of kidnappings have to do with me?"

"Nothing." He leaned forward and braced his elbows on his knees. "Yet."

Eight
❤ ❤ ❤

"So you work for a bail bond company?" I eyed Ty.

While I didn't watch much television, I did find time—in between pedicures—to read. I *lived* for Janet Evanovich's Stephanie Plum novels.

"Once in a while." He shrugged. "For the most part, I work for myself. The feds pay big bucks when you bring in one of their Most Wanted."

I noted the stainless steel TAG Heuer that circled his wrist. The closest I'd ever come to a real bounty hunter was a dog catcher I'd met via my youngest brother Jack (he'd dated her and she'd worshipped him—duh). She'd worn a white jumpsuit and smelled like flea powder. She'd also worn a slobber-proof Timex. "You must be good at what you do."

He shrugged. "I get by."

I had the brief thought that I should reconsider my

chosen profession and seriously think about tracking down a few bad guys myself. Not that I would know where to start. But I could learn from, say, Ty. He'd be the lead badass bounty hunter, and I could be his sidekick. Together we could mete out justice to bad guys the world over. He could teach me the ropes. And then maybe use a few on me.

"Handcuffs."

"Excuse me?"

"He doesn't tie up his victims with a rope. He handcuffs them. The kidnappings started in Los Angeles," he went on before I could point out the fact that he'd just read my thoughts.

Because no friggin' way could he read my thoughts.

Vamps couldn't read other vamp thoughts. They could project thoughts and if the recipient vamp had an open mind, then they could do a little silent communicating. But to read another's thoughts . . .

They just couldn't. Could they?

Yes. No.

Or maybe this was an isolated incident. Maybe for some insane reason, he could read *my* thoughts. Just me.

And this would be because?

I don't know. Maybe we were cosmically linked. Maybe we were completely and totally in sync with each other. Maybe we were soul mates.

And maybe I was just a major drama queen, a sappy romantic, and desperately horny. The three obviously didn't mix.

I clung to the last thought and focused on the words flowing from his mouth.

"The local authorities didn't think much about it when the first victim turned up missing."

"So you're from Los Angeles?" You try focusing with so much man candy just an arm's length away.

"Texas. She was a single twenty-something who'd answered an ad from a local singles paper," he went on. "She went out to meet her date on a Friday night and never came home. She wasn't reported missing until the following Wednesday when her landlord went by to collect the rent. He thought she'd skipped out on him, but when he opened the apartment and found all of her stuff inside, he started to wonder."

"I've got family in Louisiana. Whenever I visit my cousin Charlene, we usually pop on over to Texas—Austin specifically—and see what's up on Sixth Street."

"Good for you." He nodded. "Then he called a nearby restaurant where she waited tables. When they said she hadn't shown up for work or called in, he phoned the cops and—"

"Where exactly in Texas are you from?"

He stared at me long and hard. "Skull Creek. It's a little hole in the wall north of San Antonio."

"Skull Creek. I can't say as I've heard of it."

"You and most everyone else. Look, can we talk about the kidnappings?"

"Isn't that what we're doing?"

"I'm talking about them. You're talking about me."

"No, I'm not. I was asking, not talking. Big difference. Besides, I don't like talking to strangers. You've been following me, which means you already know quite a bit about me. I know nothing about you except that you're a bounty hunter vampire from Texas."

"Okay, fine. What do you want to know?"

Everything. The minute the thought struck, I dropkicked it back out. The more I knew, the more I wanted to know. Which was crazy, because I already knew enough.

Made vampire.

And the fat lady sings . . .

I fought back my curiosity and concentrated on the matter at hand. "So what did the cops say when the landlord called them?"

"People go missing all the time in a city that size, and so no one thought too much about it. But by the time the third woman turned up missing, the cops started to see a pattern. The second woman was around the same age, single, no immediate family. She worked as a gofer at an investment company. Number three was early thirties, single, no immediate family. She answered phones for an ad agency. All three fit the same profile: young, attractive, single, and lonely. They'd all answered ads in local singles magazines. And all three disappeared the night they were supposed to meet the men from the ads."

"Did they answer different ads or was it the same ad? In the same newspaper?"

"Different ads. Different papers. But the feds think it was the same guy who placed all three ads, even though they can't prove it."

"What do you think?"

"I don't think. I know. The same man placed the various ads. The same man who met with each of the women handcuffed them and killed them."

"Wait a second. You said the women were missing, not dead."

"As of right now, the feds are after a serial kidnapper. No bodies have been found, and so the authorities have to assume there's a small chance that the victims are still alive."

"But you think they're dead?"

"A traditional kidnapper isn't really interested in his victim. He's after something else. Money. Power. Both. The victim is merely a tool. Used to bargain for what the kidnapper really wants. But this guy's made no attempt to contact the authorities. He just keeps snatching more women and covering his trail."

I swallowed the sudden lump in my throat. "You really think he's *killing* them?"

He nodded. "I can feel it." Because he was a vampire and his senses were heightened. "After he gets what he wants."

"Which is?"

"I don't know. I just know I have to find him."

"How do you know he's here in Manhattan?" I did a mental search for any snippet of news I'd heard regarding a missing person. I made it my business to avoid news, snippets or otherwise, and so the search lasted all of two seconds. "Has there been a kidnapping here?"

"Not yet. They started in Los Angeles. Then they moved to Houston. Then Chicago. It only makes

sense that New York would be next on his list."
When I didn't look all that enlightened, he added,
"New York is one of the top four most heavily popu-
lated cities."

"The other three being Houston, L.A., and Chicago."

He nodded. "Exactly."

"I still don't understand why you're here. If he's
placing ads in singles' magazines, shouldn't you be
down the street at *The Village Voice*?"

"His victim total is growing, which means he's
drawing more attention. He might try to change his
MO a little, to throw off the authorities. But he can't
change it too much. He uses the ads as a screening process, to pinpoint the exact type of woman he wants.
He'll still need the screening process."

"So he might try a dating service?"

"It's a possibility."

"What do you want me to do?"

"Just keep your eyes open. He'll likely be looking
for someone who fits the profile I mentioned. The
kidnapper himself is very precise and methodical. The
feds are looking for someone employed in some sort
of tech field. I agree with them on that, but rather
than a job, I think he's independently wealthy and the
tech stuff is just a hobby."

"Why?"

"Not many people can pick up and relocate after a
few months. Plus, he pays with cash because there's
no paperwork trail anywhere."

"Rich and smart." Sounded like the wish list of every female in Manhattan.

"And psychotic. I don't know how he's subduing them—probably drugging them—but I do know he uses handcuffs. The police would argue that with me. There's no hard evidence. But he's using them, all right."

"How do you know?"

"I can smell them."

"I've smelled a lot of things over the centuries, but I can honestly say I've never smelled handcuffs."

He winked. "A virgin. I like that."

My heart gave a loud *ka-thunk.*

Made, I reminded myself.

He pulled a business card from his pocket and slid it across the desktop. "I'm contacting all the dating services in the area, as well as the singles magazines. Call me if anyone suspicious comes in."

"Shouldn't I just call the police?" Preferably an ugly, pimply-faced rookie who wouldn't wear a Stetson and smile at me as if he wanted nothing more than to lay me down and peel off my designer clothes.

He shook his head. "He hasn't made a move here. Hell, he might not, and I could be way off base."

"But you don't think so."

"I think it's just a matter of time until someone else turns up missing." He pushed to his feet. "Until then, the police aren't going to chase shadows. That's my job."

The view as Ty walked out of my office was one of

the best I'd had in a long time. Tight tush. Strong thighs. Broad back. *Come to mama!*

Not that I was seriously interested. He*llo*? I *was* a realist. I knew he was off limits. Boy, did I ever. Still, there was nothing wrong with watching.

The door closed, and disappointment washed over me. His card burned into my palm as I filed it away in my purse and gathered up my things. I had my first meeting with Francis in less than an hour, and I didn't want to be late. I needed to know what I was really up against. Mount Everest or the Great Plains?

I was about to find out.

There were moments in every vamp's life—even an optimistic, outgoing, fashionista like *moi*—when you asked yourself, "What's the friggin' point?" The world seems totally clueless, humans even more so, and for-ever is a *really* long time.

I found myself having one of these as I stood in a modest brownstone in the heart of Brooklyn and stared at Francis.

A very naked Francis.

Forget getting a life. My newfound protégé needed to get a pair of boxer briefs with built-in crotch sup-port. Pronto.

"Um, Francis. Don't take this the wrong way, but WHAT THE HELL ARE YOU DOING?"

He glanced behind him at the bathroom he'd just exited, and back to me. "You, uh, told me to undress."

"Yes, and I handed you a pair of underwear to change into."

"I thought that was one of those girdle thingies that women wear."

"Why would I give you a girdle?"

"I don't know." He shrugged, and his Mr. Happy bobbed. "I've never had a makeover before. Maybe you're going to use it to tone down my thighs."

"They have Thighmasters for that."

"What about tummy control? Maybe I need tummy control."

"The only control you need is about five inches lower. Do you mind?"

"What?" He glanced down. "Oh." Heat fired his cheeks, and he cupped both hands over his privates before turning and making a run back to the bathroom.

I punched in several notes on my BlackBerry until Francis appeared, package tastefully tucked into the pair of Calvins I'd picked up on my way over.

"Okay, so why is it I have to stand here in my skivvies?" he asked.

"First off, they're not called skivvies. No one calls them that anymore. Second, I need to know what we're up against." I circled him, noting his arms and chest. A semi-broad chest, as a matter of fact, with nice pecs. "Not bad."

"What?" His gaze swiveled to mine as if he couldn't quite believe his ears any more than I could believe my eyes.

"I said, your physique isn't too bad. You actually have muscle definition." *Thank you, thank you, thank you.*

"I do?"

"Of course, it's all sort of pasty white, except when you blush, but the pastiness can be overcome by your powerful aura, which will make you intriguing and magnetic even if you do look like an extra from *Night of the Living Dead*."

"I have an aura?"

"Actually, no. Not yet. That's something that we will have to work on. Along with the blushing. Look, Francis, I know all of this is blowing your mind. I mean, standing here with a really hot girl in nothing but your undies, but you're a vamp, for heaven's sake."

"What did you just say?"

"Hell," I blurted. "I meant for hell's sake. Now, a vamp should act like a vamp." I came this close to touching his arm, and his cheeks fired a vivid red. "That means plenty of eye contact without getting embarrassed."

"But I'm not good at eye contact."

"Then get good. Just take the bull by the horns and stare directly into my eyes." I moved in closer, caught his stare, and refused to let go.

"Don't do that."

"I'm just looking at you."

"It makes me uncomfortable."

"But it shouldn't." I stopped when we were nose to nose. "You should *like* this."

"It's making me dizzy."

"Tough it out. Use your mind. Most of being a hottie is mental."

"I don't know—"

"Lose the uncertainty."

"I'm really not sure—"

"And the doubt."

"Maybe I'm not really cut out for this." Francis voiced the one thought that had been niggling away in my own head since I'd handed him my card in the subway. "Maybe I'm a lost cause."

If I hadn't known better—namely that vampires didn't cry—I would have sworn I saw tears swimming in the depths of his light blue eyes.

Then again, this was *Francis*.

I handed him a tissue and patted his shoulder. "There, there. You can do it." *I* could do it. Sure, it was Mount Everest. But what the hey? I had hiking boots. Gucci, as a matter of fact. I could go the distance.

"You really think so?"

"Sure, I do." Sort of. "We'll just take one thing at a time. First off, appearance. You're in pretty decent shape physically; you just hide it behind slouchy clothes. Which means, we pull out the credit cards and hit the stores." I smiled, despite my doubt, because I *am* the expert, therefore it's my job to be calm and reassuring.

Besides, if there was one thing I liked even more than hooking up lost causes, it was shopping.

With a capital *S*.

Nine
❤ ❤ ❤

While most people would have seen the Friday meeting with Ty Bonner (hot *and* off-limits—talk about a double disaster whammy) as reason enough to spend the rest of the weekend in bed, moaning about my pathetic life, I wasn't getting down in the dumps. The hour I'd spent with Francis had lifted my spirits and given me hope, and so I'd been anxious to crawl out of bed Saturday evening.

Since DED was closed (it was the weekend), I left my apartment and headed over to Fifth Avenue for my six-thirty tan-brushing appointment with Dirkst. An appointment, I might add, that I'd had to make a month in advance because, hey, we're talking *Dirkst*. A veritable genius with a spray gun.

"What do you mean I don't have any sessions left? I stared at the blonde who stood behind the counter wearing a mini white tank top, white capri pants, and a golden tan to *die* for.

"I mean, you don't have any sessions left." She held up the gold gift card The Ninas had given me for my birthday last year. "As in zero. Zip. *Nada*."

"The gift card is for a full year. Twelve months. My birthday was in February. It's only been eight months. That means I should have at least four months left."

"The gift card was for twelve months or twelve sessions. Whichever comes first." Her irritated expression faded into a huge smile, and I knew she was shifting into sales-pitch mode. As if I'd be remotely interested now.

"We're offering a special package," Miss Sales Pitch went on. "Twelve visits for eight hundred dollars."

My preternatural brain multiplied at the speed of light. "That's a two-hundred-and-fifty-dollar savings." I smiled. What can I say? I *love* a sale.

"Will you be putting that on your credit card?"

"I . . ." My Visa had exactly five dollars and twenty-eight cents open, which I was still holding on to in case of an emergency. "I, um, don't think so."

"Check?"

"I'm not really a check person."

"Cash?" Delight glittered in her eyes, and I shook my head.

"IOU," I told her. "I was hoping you could float me today and I'll pay for the special at my next appointment." *You will float me. You'll be glad to float me. And you'll even throw in a free massage because I'm such a great customer.*

I focused every ounce of vamp energy into the silent command. I felt my hands tremble ever so slightly (which indicated *mucho* concentration). My body hummed with otherworldly vamp energy. While my persuasive talents hadn't done much with Francis and one might be inclined to think I'm not all that, I really am.

The clerk merely blinked. Annoyance creased her forehead. She looked as if she had a fly buzzing around her and she was *this close* to whacking it.

"I'm afraid we don't run tabs." *Whack.* "It's pay as you go or purchase a package." *Whack. Whack.*

"I intend to. As soon as possible. Which just so happens isn't this exact moment. That's why I need you to make an exception. Just this once."

You will make an exception, I silently commanded. *You want to. It would be your ultimate pleasure to give me anything I ask.*

She leveled a stare at me. "That'll be eighty-five dollars for today's session, plus a thirty percent tip."

So much for the whole vamp-mind-control thing.

In this specific instance, that is.

While I don't exactly have my own personal stash of mortal minions, I could if I wanted. It's just that there are certain criteria to successfully bend the masses to my will. See, here's the deal: We vamps can transfix with our stares and mesmerize with our charisma, as long as the human we're trying to seduce is a member of the opposite sex. Meaning, I can totally wow a guy with a few powerful thoughts and a little batting of my baby blues. And, of course, flashing a little cleavage (or even a lot) never hurts. But my effort is totally wasted on a woman.

We born vamps are, at our very essence, extremely sexual creatures. We're conceived via sex. We stop aging when we lose our virginity. Women vamps feed on males while male vamps feed on females (or we used to before civilized society provided an alternative bottled means to the whole dining experience). We even procreate. Our very nature centers around our appeal to the opposite sex.

I reminded myself of this as I stood in front of the marble counter.

But desperate times called for desperate measures, as the saying went. I'd waited three weeks for this session with Dirkst, and I couldn't let a few archaic vamp rules stand in the way of airbrushed perfection. I had to at least try.

"So how *will* you be paying for today's visit?" the clerk persisted.

I'll be using my gift card. The one you're about to slide into your register to program for another year's worth of visits.

My face grew warm, and I could see the intense gleam of my eyes mirrored in the clerk's gaze. Normally, my eyes would be a vivid shade of red when I channeled my vamp energy so intensely. But thanks to a new pair of contacts, they just glowed a brighter, purplish shade of blue.

Okay, it's not that I'm ashamed of my vamp heritage. But red? Talk about asking for trouble. Sure, I know the vamp wannabes pay big bucks for a pair of crimson contacts, but real vamps haven't existed for centuries by flaunting their vampness.

Okay, so a few have. With our mind-control abilities, we can impress a plausible explanation for whatever a human might witness. But that itself is exhausting, and with so many people in the world, I'd be controlling left and right. Much better to keep a low profile. As it was, I was ready to slide to the floor and take a little cat nap.

"You obviously can't pay." The clerk shook her head and punched several buttons on her computer screen. "I'm afraid Dirkst won't be able to see you today."

"But I'm his best client."

She gave me a "yeah, right" look. "He has many clients, miss. And a waiting list of over six weeks. Speaking of which, you'll have to prepay your next appointment—if you make one—via credit card; otherwise we won't be able to reserve your time. Dirkst is much too busy for clients who schedule and then can't pay."

"But I—"

"Ask for Janice."

The strange female voice echoed in my head, and I turned. My gaze scanned the pale beige sofas that lined the walls, and I drank in the familiar faces of the women I'd passed on my way to the counter. Human. Human. Not so human (but that's another story all by itself). Human. Human. Snotty, pretentious human. Human. Vamp—

She looked about thirty or thirty-five (human years, of course), with brown hair pulled back into a ponytail that should have looked chic. If she'd had good bone structure. Instead, her face was soft and round. She wore an expensive bronzer and glitter eye shadow à la Nicole Richie. But she didn't look as trendy as Nicole. Or as malnourished.

I knew then, even before I caught a whiff of Chanel, that she was a made vamp. You'll never see a born vamp with a weight problem. Thanks to our lean, mean diet, we simply don't ingest a lot of fat calories. Made vamps, however, are different. They're human. Or at least they once were. And if they happened to be fat or thin or tall or short or if they'd had their hair dyed a ridiculous red or cut in a pixie bob when they were turned, that's the way they stayed. For all eternity.

Ouch.

The woman was definitely plump by today's standards.

Then again, most everyone was plump by today's standards.

Her gaze met mine, and I heard the words again in my head.

"Ask for Janice."

I turned back to the counter and gave the clerk another mesmerizing smile. "Could I, um, speak to Janice, please?"

"You can speak to whomever you'd like, but she won't be able to do anything for you. We have strict policies here."

"Obviously, but I'd like to speak with her anyway. Just to say hi. She's an old friend of a friend, and I wouldn't want her to think I had stopped by without so much as a hello."

She gave me a suspicious look before finally shrugging. She disappeared. A few seconds later, another woman wearing the same mini white tank top and capri pants appeared. She had delicate bone structure, short blond hair, and a certain awareness that glittered in her hazel eyes.

Her stare collided with mine, and I saw a spurt of hunger. "Yes? Can I help you?" Her voice was breathy and inviting and I knew then that Janice was either (a) lesbian or (b) bisexual. Because she wanted me. Bad.

While I don't swing both ways myself, I've never been one to let opportunity pass me by.

I projected my thoughts again and went through the *program the gift card* spiel.

Instead of giving me a PMS look, she smiled, took a fresh, shiny gold card from the top drawer, slid it into the register, and keyed in several numbers. A few seconds later, she held up the card, now good for another twelve visits.

I felt a small niggle of guilt. It wasn't like I was stealing or anything. I fully intended to pay for the visits—in full—with my first big Dead End Dating windfall. Until then . . .

Hey, what was the point of being a vamp if you couldn't be a little vampy once in a while?

I took the gold card, gave Janice my most dazzling smile, and slid the treasure into my purse.

"I'll let Dirkst know you're here," she said.

"I'd appreciate that." I started to turn, but Janice's voice stopped me.

"I'm sure he'll be right with you."

"That's fine." I started to turn again.

"He's always on time, but I'll hurry him up just in case." She winked. "Just for you."

"Thanks."

"No problem."

"Very good."

"I'll be right back." She gave me a little wave.

"I'll be here." I waved back and hurried toward the waiting area before she found something else to say.

"Thanks," I said as I slid into the seat next to the made vampire. "I think."

She smiled. "She can be a pain, but if you're female and you're low on cash, she's the person to see."

I settled into my chair. "I don't know what I would have done if I'd missed my spray session with Dirkst."

"Is he that good?"

"He has the biggest gun in New York, and, unlike most men, he knows how to use it."

She smiled. "Glad I could help."

"My name is Lil. Lil Marchette."

"I'm Esther. Esther Crutch."

Yow. And I had issues with *my* name?

"So what are you in for, Es? Massage? Steam bath? Oatmeal facial?"

"I'm having my thighs wrapped."

There weren't too many things that caught me off

guard. But this did the trick. "But you're a vampire," I pointed out.

"I know."

"A *made* vampire."

"I know."

"Don't, um, take this the wrong way, Es, but the way you are is the way you're going to be. Now and forever."

"I know that, too." She sighed. "But I keep hoping. I mean, they have so many new, innovative treatments these days. One of them is bound to stick, right?"

Wrong.

"I can't be doomed to fat thighs and cellulite for the rest of eternity, can I?"

Yes was there on the tip of my tongue, but she looked so hopeful that I found myself swallowing instead of shattering her hopes and dreams and turning her into a cold, hard cynic like most other made vampires the world over.

I remembered Ty Bonner (whoa, baby), and I couldn't help but think of the glimmer I'd seen in the dark depths of his eyes when I mentioned dating and love and vampires all in the same sentence. Hope? Maybe. Probably.

Okay, so there'd been a hell of a lot of disbelief, too. But somewhere in the mix, I'd definitely seen hope.

After all, made vampires were entitled to the emotion, too, even if their situation was pretty dismal.

While born vamps were, for the most part, attractive, charismatic creatures, made vamps were an entirely different animal.

As I mentioned, they'd once been human. With human flaws. And whatever imperfections they'd possessed when they were turned—everything from acne to jock itch—were with them for the rest of eternity. Ty still had his scars and Esther still had her cellulite.

"A thigh wrap, huh?" I nodded. "Maybe I should try that myself."

Esther eyed me as if I'd sprouted a halo. "You don't need your thighs wrapped. You're just an itty-bitty thing. What are you? A size seven?"

"A five."

She sighed. "I can't remember if I ever fit into a size five. Back when I was turned the clothes weren't divided up into sizes. You couldn't even buy off the rack. You just made your own."

"How long ago was that?"

"About a hundred years ago. I was thirty-three at the time."

Am I good or what? "Where are you from?"

"Texas. Barron's Bluff. A small settlement just south of San Antonio. There's not much left of it now. Just a few run-down houses. But at one time it was a nice place to live." She smiled. "And date. Boy, I had 'em coming out of the woodwork when I was in my prime. But my mama got sick and I had to stay home to tend to her, so marriage was out of the question. I turned into an old maid. Then this crazy miner—at least I thought he was a miner—rode into town and stole me away from my farm in the middle of the night. Me and two other women from nearby spreads. He sold us to the man who drained our blood and turned us. The other two women were the appetizer and dessert. I was the main course on account of I was so healthy looking."

"And you haven't had a date since before you were turned?"

She nodded. "Way before on account of my mama. And now . . ." She shook her head. "It's a different world. Men aren't looking for a soft body to curl up against. They want long, slim legs." She grimaced as she adjusted the purse sitting on her lap. "And tight tummies. And perky boobs." She glanced down. "While I've got the boobs, they haven't been perky since I was eighteen years old."

"Not all men are interested in perky boobs."

"True, but I don't want a human man. I've buried a whole mess of relatives—I wouldn't turn them and doom them to the same fate." She shook her head, and a sadness filled her eyes. "When I get close to someone—*if* I ever do—it'll be somebody like me. The trouble is, why would a made vampire want a not-so-perfect vampire when he can have any human woman he wants?"

She had a point. Born male vamps had to choose a born female vamp in order to continue the race. But made vamps weren't genetically equipped with any such loyalty. Their survival instincts were purely self-sufficient. As in feeding. Since all men—human and vamp alike—were visual creatures, it only made sense that they would opt to suck on a pretty woman rather than an ugly one.

"I know it seems sort of hopeless, but I'm sure there's *someone* out there." What was I saying? "You'll never know if you don't at least try. Wow. An entire century without a date." I sounded shocked, but truthfully, I wasn't nearly as surprised considering I myself hadn't had an official one in just as long. And I was just an itty-bitty thing.

"We called it courting back then. While I never married, it wasn't for lack of prospects. I had three proposals. *Three*." She shook her head. "I just couldn't up and leave my mama. She had Alzheimer's. I didn't know it then, mind you. We had no clue way back when, but I understand now. It was a blessing in her particular case because I was able to go home after I'd turned and still take care of her without her knowing anything was wrong. She never even batted an eye when I started serving her breakfast at night." If I hadn't known better, I would have sworn I saw a brightness in her eyes.

But made vamps didn't cry. Did they?

Honestly, while I am pretty worldly when it comes to born vamps, I've led sort of a sheltered life. My parents, like their parents before them, never had much use for made vamps. They considered them a threat to our race.

Actually, they considered them the plague of the entire vamp civilization, but that, I was starting to realize, was a tad harsh. I mean, Ty hadn't waltzed in and started pillaging my office. He hadn't even posed a threat to my very human, and thus vulnerable, receptionist. The only threat he'd posed had been to my hormones.

As for Esther . . . She could probably give an exercise machine hell, but otherwise she seemed harmless.

"I buried my last relative, a fourth cousin, just three weeks ago. I don't have anyone left now. I'm all that's left." She shrugged. "And what good am I? It's not like I can continue the Crutch name even if I did manage to meet a decent made vampire who wasn't turned off by a robust figure."

Thank the Powers That Be for small favors.

"So what do you do when you're not getting your thighs wrapped?"

"I watch *Bonanza*. And the *Lone Ranger*. And *The Cattleman*. I have a huge DVD collection. The one good thing about today's world—the technology. Otherwise, I'd have a ton of spare time on my hands."

I smiled. "This might be your lucky day, Esther."

Her eyes lit. "Do you know something about the thigh wrap that I don't?"

"I'm afraid not." I reached into my purse and pulled out one of my business cards. "But if you're sick and tired of watching westerns all alone, then I just might be able to help you."

She stared at the card I handed her. "A dating service for vampires? There is no such thing."

"There is now. Call me and we'll set up an interview."

"Really?"

"Sure thing. My receptionist's name is Evie. If I'm out, you can set up a time with her. She's totally sweet." When a hungry light glimmered in Esther's eyes, I rushed on, "Not like that. Sweet, as in nice and understanding. We have a platonic relationship. She doesn't moonlight for any dating services, and I don't use her as a midnight snack." I patted Esther's hand. "So call me, okay?"

"Okay."

A shrill cry punctuated her reply, and I glanced toward the doorway to see Dirkst eyeing me, a look of outrage on his face.

Dirkst stood well over six feet. He had a hard, toned body and a face that would have done a Greek statue proud. He wore white pants and a tight white T-shirt, and he smelled like a mixture of coconut, pineapple, and Obsession for Men.

"You're a mess," he declared for everyone to hear.

"Thanks." I smiled and pushed to my feet. "It's good to see you, too."

"Worse than a mess." His frown deepened as I reached him. "A pale mess."

I directed my most intense gaze at him and focused my thoughts.

I'm a veritable vision of loveliness and you feel out-rageously privileged for the opportunity to gaze upon my beauty.

Dirkst frowned and shook his head. "I'm an artiste," he declared, "not a miracle worker. They don't pay me enough to deal with such a mess."

Okay, so I know Dirkst and I also know his live-in

lover, Ben. I gave them a housewarming present when they bought a flat in SoHo. But as I've said before, you can't blame a girl for trying.

"Hurry it up." He motioned me forward as if I were on fire and he had the only extinguisher in town. "You're fading as we speak!"

Ten

❤ ❤ ❤

I intended to spend the rest of Saturday evening at the office outlining a shopping itinerary for Francis. But after my visit with Dirkst, I decided to do a little club-hopping instead. I was gold and gleaming, and I owed it to the male population to flaunt my hotness. Besides, I still hadn't given up the notion of finding my own eternity mate.

That, and I needed to drum up some business to tide me over through the whole Project Francis. I was counting on Esther's phone call, and I wanted to have plenty of choice prospects for her to choose from.

"I've missed you soooo much!"

The shriek sounded above the music drifting from the well-known New York night spot, and I turned to see The Ninas rushing toward me.

"I'm soooo glad you called." Nina One reached me first. She wore a slinky red dress and smelled sweet and filthy rich, like crème brulée. Her blond hair hung loose around her shoulders, and red sparkly earrings dangled from her ears.

"Me too." Nina Two had gone for her signature no-nonsense look with a basic black cardigan, jeans, and simple black boots. The rich scent of mango sorbet clung to her like a second skin.

"It's been forever since we've done anything like this," Nina One declared, her earrings bobbing around her face.

Forever was a bit of an exaggeration, but it had been several years. Forget trendy bars and appletinis and the Pussycat Dolls. The last time the three of us drank in a little night life, we'd done Jell-O shots at Studio 54 and shaken our rumps to "Disco Inferno."

"We're going *here*?" Nina One glanced at the neon sign above the brownstone door. She said it with the same distaste she reserved for something brown and gunky stuck to her designer shoe.

I couldn't say I blamed her. Back in the day, clubbing meant hitting the trendiest spots, not the most notorious for made vamps.

"We're not here to have fun," Nina Two said. "We're here to help Lil with her business. Though I can't say how this place is going to help with that."

"I'm an equal-opportunity service. Meaning I need to advertise my services to all vamps, as well as humans."

"That makes sense." Nina One glanced at the sign again and wrinkled her nose. "Sort of." She smiled. "And who says we can't work *and* have fun? Why, I haven't had a really good fling since last week." She glanced at a trio of men who walked by her. The minute they felt her intense gaze, they turned and their stares snagged on her. They stumbled into one another, a mesmerized look in their eyes.

"Stop that," I told her. I rummaged in my purse and pulled out a set of business cards. I divided them up between the three of us. "At least until we get inside. Then I want you to sense out the really lonely ones, get up close and personal, and slip them a card."

"What about the cute ones?" she asked as we walked into the club's dim interior. The smell of sweaty bodies and stale beer swallowed us whole. The Black-Eyed Peas blared from the speakers, and the building seemed to vibrate around us.

"If they're lonely, too," I told Nina One, "then be my guest and give them a card. But if they're just cute, forget it. They have to be lonely, too, or at least a little disheartened with the whole singles scene, otherwise they're not viable client material."

"I only do cute ones."

"I'm a matchmaker, not a modeling scout for Elite."

"But wouldn't that be so much more fun? Why, look at that one." She pointed a red-tipped finger toward a man who stood near the bar. "He's wearing Armani."

I concentrated my gaze on him. He turned and his gaze collided with mine and a rush of images came at me. "He's also married. And a player."

Nina One wasn't easily discouraged. "But it's Armani." She plucked a card from my hand. "He deserves one of these just for having good taste."

"She's hopeless." Nina Two shook her head as her blond counterpart rushed off.

"She's just easily impressed." I couldn't blame her. We're talking *Armani*.

"Well, I'm not. I'm here to help and that's exactly what I'm going to do . . ." Nina Two's words faded as a man caught her attention. She turned and stared at the modestly dressed guy who wore glasses and a serious expression. He was Asian, with deep black eyes and dark, wavy hair. "Do you suppose junior-level stockbrokers need help hooking up?" She eyed him a few more minutes. "Make that genius-level brokers who just made a windfall with BEA Incorporated, which he plans to turn around and invest in an eight percent CD?"

"He doesn't really have much of a social life, does he?"

"That's because he takes his job so seriously. Men like him are hard to come by." Her nostrils flared. "And they taste really good, too. Not that I'm considering a taste, mind you. It's just that they do, and that's always good to know in our business."

"When did my business turn into *our* business?"

She ignored the question, her attention fully fixed on the man. "I'm sure every little bit of positive info helps when you're trying to find a date for someone," she went on. "I think I'll just hand him one of these and see if he has any stock tips. I've been meaning to invest some of my savings . . ." Cards in hand, she headed for the stockbroker.

I glanced at Nina One, who now had the Armani suit fixated on her rather than the business card that lay forgotten on the bar next to him.

Okay, if you want something done right, you have to do it yourself.

I ignored several invitations to dance and honed my psychic vamp abilities. A half hour later, I'd singled out every lonely, desperate person in the place and distributed a stack of cards. I'd also attracted a zillion compliments on my new tan and turned down at least two dozen offers of servitude. What can I say? When you're a hot, charismatic vampire, it's only natural that men fall all over themselves to be at your beck and call.

Normally, this would have fed my ego and made me feel utterly invincible and complete. But I couldn't stop thinking about Esther. While I usually ran the other way when it came to made vampires—we're talking *made*—I found myself in a veritable den of them.

Or I should have been. About a zillion years ago (weeks in New Yorker time), the haunt had been notorious for attracting made vampires. Times had obviously changed.

I spotted three. All male. Marginally attractive if you like the type—or if you'd met one Ty Bonner earlier that day and couldn't help but compare them to him, which wasn't really any comparison at all be-

cause Ty had been *totally* hot with his rugged looks
and piercing eyes and (big sigh) . . .

Not going there again, I reminded myself.

Back to business.

Three was good. Great, considering that I rarely, if
ever, ran into made vampires because they tended to
move in a different social set. An antisocial set. So
finding a trio under the same roof (even one notorious for the type) was like a dream come true.

If they'd been lonely, or at least open to the whole
dating concept. But they were younger vampires—
twenty, maybe thirty years—and they were still adjusting to the hunger that had awakened inside of
them with their transformation. Which meant they'd
come to the club with a single purpose in mind: to
scope out potential entrées.

Esther needed a made vampire who could understand the whole getting older and facing eternity all
alone. He didn't have to be the most handsome, but
he had to be worldly and tough to balance out her
more sensitive nature. And he had to be mature.
Someone made a long, long time ago. A guy who'd
seen death and destruction. A guy who could appreciate her fondness for westerns.

A vampire like Ty Bonner.

Ty?

The thought stuck in my head, and I could practically feel his business card vibrate from the Fernanda
Niven metallic handbag currently hooked over my
shoulder.

Ty and Esther?

Okay, so it didn't have as cool a ring to it as, say, Ty and Lil. But it could work. Ty and Es. Ty and Essie. Ty and Estha.

Before I could stop myself, I pulled out my phone and Ty's card. I punched in the number and got his voice mail.

"This is Ty. You know what to do." *Beeep*.

"This is Lil. Lil Marchette. I was hoping you could drop by my office next week. I'd like to talk to you about something. Say seven o'clock? Tuesday?" I hit the off button and slid my phone back into my purse. I'd been about to say Monday, but I hadn't wanted to appear too eager.

Then again, what did it matter? It wasn't as if I was the one interested in him.

I *wasn't*.

"If you want me to behave myself, then we'd better leave now." It was Nina Two. Her eyes were brighter than I'd ever seen them, and her voice deeper than usual. I recognized the hunger immediately, and my own heart gave an excited thump.

"I thought you ate before you came."

"I did, but we're talking BEA windfall and a savings portfolio to die for. I *really* need a drink."

"This whole financial hoarding obsession isn't healthy," Nina One said as she walked up, red dangle earrings swinging with each movement. "Save, save, save. Why, it totally undermines our entire culture."

"What's not healthy is your obsession with spending any and every penny regardless of the consequences."

"There are no consequences."

"What about tomorrow? What about a nest egg?"

"I've got a trust fund. I don't need a nest egg."

"But it's your father's money. Not yours."

"You really do need a drink. You're light-headed."

"Hey, hey. Could you two call a truce? I'm trying to work here." I handed out my last card, along with a silent suggestion that the recipient might want to hurry and call before my business grew so huge that I stopped accepting new clients.

Hey, a girl could dream.

"We'll go back to my place for drinks," I told the girls.

Fifteen minutes later, I was giving The Ninas their first look at my new space.

"It's really small," observed Nina One.

"It's very efficient," said Nina Two.

"Thanks, I like it, too." I ignored the blinking answering machine and walked over to the fridge. My fingers had just closed around a bottle of O positive when I heard the knock at the door.

"Jimmy's Diner," a voice called out before I'd done so much as glance at the door. "You ladies order take-out?"

"Thank God you sprang for takeout," Nina One said.

"I didn't order takeout."

"I did." When Nina One turned a shocked look on

Nina Two, she shrugged. "I told you I was thirsty and I just couldn't do the whole bottle thing after tonight."

"You mean, after Mr. Savings and Loan."

Nina Two glared. "Is someone going to answer the door or are we just going to stand here and talk about it?"

"By all means." Nina One moved so quickly and silently toward the door that it looked as if she glided on her three-inch Pradas. She pulled open the door and stared at the young, attractive Asian man holding a white bag full of take-out cartons. He had dark black hair, black iridescent eyes, and a build that suggested he lifted more than eggrolls in his spare time.

"What can I say?" Nina Two shrugged as all eyes turned toward her. "I'm in the mood for Chinese."

"Imagine that," I said as I reached for a wineglass.

Nina One curved her finger in a "come here" gesture, and the young man's dark eyes grew bright and intense.

"I think I'll just stick to the bottled stuff," I said, but neither vamp seemed to hear me. I busied myself pouring a glass while The Ninas backed the delivery guy up against the nearest wall and leaned into him, one on either side.

I sipped the O positive and did my best to concentrate on the early morning news coming from my neighbor's television.

". . . the Yankees came so close to nailing this last championship, but . . ."

I'm not any more into sports than I am news in

general and so my attention kept straying to the scene in front of me.

Fifteen minutes later, after a lot of moaning and panting (some of it my own on account of the fact that I haven't actually *fed* fed in forever and the experience is nearly as orgasmic as actual sex, which I haven't experienced in forever either—at least not with an actual partner), I watched my two best friends lean away from the handsome man.

Blood trickled from the bite marks on his neck. He looked dazed and delighted for a few seconds (in man terms, that meant he was ready to roll over and fall asleep), before he seemed to snap out of the blissful haze. He retrieved the take-out cartons, sat on my floor, and helped himself to a container of spring rolls to replenish his strength. The delivery guys from Jimmy's Diner didn't just carry food as an effective cover-up. They were the food, so to speak, so whatever dish they carried was to feed them after they'd fed the customer.

Meanwhile, my two best friends collapsed on the sofa and kicked off their shoes.

"You really should let your hair down once in a while," Nina One said as she eyed me. "Since when do you pass up Chinese?"

"Since I decided to open my own business."

"You still have to eat."

"True, but I'm keeping things simple and frugal for right now. I have to stay focused." And feeding—the real thing—was a definite distraction. Not to mention, I really hadn't been in the mood for Chinese.

Now, if the delivery guy had shown up in a cowboy hat and boots, that would have been a different matter altogether.

I was focused, not dead.

Not technically, that is.

Eleven
♥ ♥ ♥

"You're just in time," my mother declared when she opened the door Sunday evening. "Your father just pulled out his golf clubs. Oh, and don't say anything about your father's hand. He and that woman next door got into it earlier this evening when your father went to trim the hedges. He has a bit of a cut. Nothing a little sleep won't cure, but of course he's stuck with it until morning."

Okay, so it wasn't like I could *not* show up. My parents would disown me if I didn't put in an appearance. Worse, they would tell all of their friends what an ungrateful excuse for a daughter I was—which meant I could kiss good-bye the small trickle of clients my mother had sent my way.

This was strictly business.

"Don't you have a gardener who clips all the hedges?"

"Your father knows how riled up Viola can get, and he doesn't want to put Mr. Wellsprings in any sort of danger. Good gardeners are so hard to find."

"Dad just likes to make Viola mad," I pointed out.

"He simply likes to stand his ground, dear. Viola Hamilton is a beast, and your father isn't about to be bested by a werewolf, of all things. Those hedges are on *our* side of the property line, and the sooner she realizes that, the better."

My parents had lived next door to Viola for eighty years. If she hadn't realized it by now, she wasn't going to. I pointed this out to my mother, who merely gave me a "keep quiet and get inside" look.

Strictly business.

I tried to remember that over the next hour as my brothers slowly trickled in and I watched my dad demonstrate his latest twist and putt technique with a bandaged right hand.

But we're talking an *hour*. For one three-second technique. Which meant my eyes were crossing and I was *this close* to throwing myself off the nearest balcony and sprinting back to Manhattan—my favorite Manolo Blahnik stilettos be damned—when my last and youngest brother finally showed up.

Like my other brothers, Jack had the typical Marchette good looks, with dark hair and deep brown eyes and a sexy aura that had women worshipping at his feet.

Or carrying his duffel bag.

"Where should I put this, Jack?" She was a redhead and she was human and she looked at Jack as if he were the biggest, most decadent chocolate brownie on the menu.

Note—Jack was the only brother who always showed up with a little someone extra.

My mother frowned disapprovingly. My father shook his head and grinned. Obviously the "boys will be boys" mentality crossed all race and culture barriers.

"Mom's ready to kill you and so am I." I hugged Jack and barely ignored the urge to tighten my arms and crush a few ribs in the process. But then he would have been inclined to crush me. We would end up wrestling around like when we were kids and the traditional hunt would be ruined due to fractured bones and pierced organs and the desperate need for rejuvenating sleep.

Then again, what was a little excruciating pain and a few extra hours of sleep if it got me out of the hunt?

"What?" he asked me. "You don't like Tammy?" He eyed the woman who stood across the room shedding her coat, her gaze fixed on him. He smiled, and she all but orgasmed right on the spot.

"I couldn't care less about Tammy," I said under my breath. "You're late."

"It's eight-thirty."

"We meet at seven-thirty," I informed him.

"I could have sworn it was eight-thirty."

"We always meet at seven-thirty."

"Since when?"

"Since about five hundred years ago."

"Are you sure?"

Jack may be a mega-hot vampire, but he wasn't the

sharpest thorn on the family tree. He was the youngest next to me, and he was still stuck in the I-can't-see-beyond-my-dick phase that all males go through. For humans, this usually occurs in puberty and lasts through the twenties. For vamps, it's the first six hundred or so years, also known as the Sexed-Up Six Hundred.

I know. It sounds like a NASCAR race. In a way it is. Male vamps spend this entire period honing their sexual techniques and are, for the most part, in a constant race to see how often they can get off.

I smiled. "Jack's here. We can get started now."

My dad poised for yet another demonstration of his swing. "Not yet. We're still missing someone."

I made a quick visual count. My brothers had gathered around Jack to check out his latest minion. My mother stood across the room and poured herself a glass of wine—the real stuff because my father didn't allow anyone to *drink* drink before a hunt. He said it dulled the instincts and killed the driving hunger that made us natural-born predators. "One set of parents. Five kids. And a Tammy. Who could we be missing?"

"Your father invited someone to join us." My mother downed half her glass in one gulp and cast another disapproving glance at Tammy.

A hollowness settled in the pit of my stomach. "Please tell me the someone is female."

"You like females?" My father poised in his putt and shot my mother an alarmed look.

"No, but they do." I motioned toward my three brothers. "The extra someone is for one of them, right?"

"Now, why would we try to fix up your brothers?" Meaning, my parents felt my siblings were doing just fine on their own.

I raised my eyebrows and glanced at Tammy, who'd picked up a wineglass and was now holding it to Jack's lips so he could take a drink without busying his hands.

"He'll grow out of it." My mother leveled a stare at me. "It's you we're worried about, dear."

"Tell me you didn't invite someone for me?"

"His name is Wilson Harvey."

"Once Wilson Harveaux," my father chimed in. "Before his family simplified things for their auditing business."

"An auditor? You fixed me up with an *auditor*?"

"A CPA," my mother clarified. As if it made a difference. "A very successful one, I might add."

"And he's just franchised his firm." My dad was big on franchises (see Moe's). "He's got a good head on his shoulders."

"And he's eager to settle down." My mother smiled. "He was just about to a while back—about ninety years ago—when his intended was involved in a car accident and the steering column pierced her you-know-what." She held a hand to her own chest. "Anyhow, he just hasn't gotten out much since then. Since you aren't getting out either, we thought the two of you could join forces and get out together."

"A date."

My mother frowned. "Our kind don't *date*, dear. We discuss. One good solid conversation is all that's necessary to know if he'll make a decent eternity mate. You ask him the important questions, such as how much money he makes and his fertility rating, he'll ask you the pertinent stuff, and that's that."

No kissing. No holding hands. No flirting or teasing or enjoying each other's company. Just two people discussing fertility ratings and "pertinent stuff."

Okay, so this is, like, my heritage and all. But sometimes I think being a born vampire bites the big one.

Now was definitely one of those times.

"I'm not ready to settle down, Mom."

"Because you haven't met someone who's viable material. Tonight that's all going to change."

"No, it's not. I don't need you to fix me up."

"Of course you do, dear. Otherwise, I'd have a grandchild by now. Why, Loralee Hoffmeyer has twenty-nine grandchildren. And sixty-eight great-grand-children. And one hundred and three great, great-grandchildren. And one hundred and sixty-two great, great, great-grandchildren. And . . ."

My mother went on, her normal pale complexion pinking around the cheeks and nose. ". . . want is one. *One* grandchild to carry on the Marchette name and continue the bloodline. Is that too much to ask?"

"Couldn't you ask it of them?" I pointed to my brothers, who were busy discussing the hindrance of big boobs (Tammy had them) when trying to pierce the lower jugular during a sex/eating fest.

"Your brothers will settle down when the time is right." My mother said this with such faith that I couldn't help but wish I'd been born with a penis.

"It's you we're worried about, dear. At least they're trying out different women and looking." She motioned toward the handsome trio. "But you"—she shook her head—"*you* haven't found one decent prospect for yourself."

I wanted to point out that Tammy was *human,* and the only thing decent about her was the Antonio Mellani handbag she carried, but I knew my mother would just make another excuse. *Jack's young. Jack's in his prime. Jack's perfecting his carnal skills.*

Jack Schmack.

"You have to start thinking about the future. *Our* future. Our kind would have died out ages ago if all females were as picky as you, dear."

"I'm not picky. I just have high standards."

"Then you'll love Wilson." The sound of a doorbell punctuated her sentence. "That's him." She nailed me with a stare. "You'll meet Wilson and talk fertility ratings, and I'll be that much closer to little Annabella Jacqueline Marchette." My grandmother was Annabella and my mother was Jacqueline, and I was shit out of luck.

"Wouldn't that be Annabella Jacqueline Marchette Harvey?"

"Argueing semantics will not get you out of this, Lilliana." She said my name with a stern look that had me closing my mouth before anything else came out.

Wilson Harvey was tall, dark, and handsome with vibrant green eyes and a statuesque nose that hinted at good breeding (is there any other kind among us born vamps?). He wore his dark hair short and neat. He had high cheekbones and a *GQ* face. A three-piece suit molded to his perfect physique. He smelled like decadent rum sauce. Rich and sweet with a potent edge.

Rum sauce and cotton candy?

Not.

I smiled as my mother made the introductions and went to pour Wilson a glass of wine.

"So." I smiled and resisted the urge to turn and bolt. "My mother tells me you're an auditor."

"Yes. I have a two-forty fertility rating."

O-kay. So much for small talk. "That's, um, impressive, Wil."

"It's Wilson. How many times can you orgasm in one encounter?"

This was the "pertinent stuff" my mother had mentioned. Fertility ratings were the cinch factor for male eternity mates, while the OQ told the tale for the females. See, female born vamps couldn't just fake it. They had to actually orgasm, which released an egg, which gave them a shot at conception. So the more, the better.

"I can hold my own," I told him.

He gave me a serious look. "I need a number."

"Maybe two." He frowned. "Or three, or four." I wasn't trying to encourage him. At the same time, I had my pride, and the scream and release capability obviously factored in. "Say, do you play golf? My dad's got this great new move . . ." I effectively turned

Wilson's attention and spent another fifteen minutes watching my father and his golf clubs.

But hey, it was better than talking multiple Os with Wil—*son*.

"I guess we should get started," my dad finally declared as he shoved his driver into a red leather golf bag.

Agreement echoed around the group, and I chimed in, ready to get the whole evening over with as quickly as possible. I would lay low as I always did during the hunt, and my brothers would pursue it with the same zealousness they always did, and I'd be back on my way to the city in no time.

"I thought we'd mix things up a little tonight," my dad said as he wheeled his clubs into a nearby corner. "The past few months, Jack's been *it* eight times."

My youngest brother shrugged and turned his head so that Tammy could dab a drop of wine from the corner of his mouth. "That's right. Why do I always have to be it?"

"Because you can't draw for shit," Max told him.

"Drawing straws doesn't involve skill. It's all about luck."

"And you've got the worst in the family."

"Boys." My father glared at his sons, and they quieted. "I don't think it's fair that Jack hasn't been able to hunt and have any fun, so I thought we would just start rotating. That way everyone will get to hunt on a regular basis." My stomach bottomed out even before my dad turned his attention to me. "Since it's been forever since Lil's had a turn, I thought we would start with her." My dad smiled as I prayed for lightning, or even a thunderbolt, to strike me smack dab in the middle of my suddenly tight chest. "You're *it*, dear."

Twelve

❤ ❤ ❤

I hated being *it*.

Okay, so *hated* was a mild word. I hated Fendi knock-offs and guys who catcalled when a woman walked past construction sites, and I really hated Angelina Jolie. Okay, so maybe *envy* would be a better word when it came to Angie. (Did I mention that I've seen *Troy* eight times and I'm actually a card-carrying member of Brad's fan club?) Anyhow, the point was, the H word didn't come close to what I felt. Next to working at Moe's, being *it* was my ultimate nightmare. The last time I drew short, I ended up with three broken nails, a concussion, and a ruined Christian Dior blouse.

See, the *it* vamp is the one who gets to wear the whistle around his or her neck. Aka the one who gets hunted. Aka the one who gets tackled at the speed of light by desperate, bloodthirsty brothers greedy for more vacation days from Moe's House of Boredom.

Granted, the concussion had healed during sleep. But the blouse didn't fare so well. We're talking permanent death and destruction and a huge dent in my available credit because, of course, I'd had to replace it.

I picked up my steps and rounded the front of the house, the starting point where everyone was currently killing time to give me a sufficient head start. I eyed the thick trees that stretched behind the house and willed myself forward. I crossed the massive lawn, complete with a few hideous lawn jockeys my mother had brought from the "old" country, and approached the forest.

Entering the dense growth, I wandered around a good thirty seconds, making sure that I touched every branch I could reach to give my brothers something to lure them into the trees. I'd just stopped to check the status of my heels (no mud yet) when I heard the faint ring of a bell that indicated the hunt had begun.

Taking a deep breath, I leapt straight up toward a very high branch that overlooked the stretch of grass that surrounded the house, perched on the edge, and held my breath. I didn't see them so much as I sensed them as they rushed toward me, plunged into the forest, and headed straight past.

Smell first and think later. That was my family.

They expected me to try to outdistance them and probably figured I'd be running for my life. But I was smarter than that.

And much more of a chicken.

I counted at least six sets of footsteps before I dropped to my feet and started toward the rear of the main house. I was just about to barricade myself in the pool house and play a few games of solitaire on my Black-Berry when I smelled the faint scent of rum sauce.

I headed around the pool toward the patio and came to a staggering halt when I saw the vamp sitting in one of my mother's wrought-iron lawn chairs.

Okay, so I'd never been that good in math. Obviously, Wilson hadn't followed the others and my count had been off. Rather, he was staring up at the sky as if mentally tabulating the number of stars.

"Gotcha!" I came up behind him and tapped him on the shoulder.

He bolted to his feet and whirled on me, lips drawn back, fangs bared.

I leapt back.

"Lilliana?" The fangs retracted. "What are you doing here?"

"What are *you* doing here?" I eyed him. "I know what you're not doing. I've been standing in the trees over there waiting for you to pick up my scent." I'm such a good actress. "You haven't budged an inch."

He shrugged and shoved his hands into his pockets. "I didn't come here to hunt."

"You came here for a multiorgasmic vamp."

He nodded. "Both my brothers have been committed for over one hundred years. My first sister-in-law scores an eleven on the Orgasm Quotient. Number two ranks a ten. I'm the only one in my family who doesn't even have a decent prospect."

I started to realize that Wilson wasn't alone because he didn't get out much. And my mother thinks *I'm* picky?

"I'm not exactly what you were looking for, am I?" I asked him.

"I need at least a ten when it comes to orgasms, otherwise I'll be the disgrace of the Harvey clan."

He looked so disappointed that I had the sudden urge to tell him that I'd lied and I could do an easy dozen (see the good actress comment above). A baker's dozen if I was really turned on and the sex involved whipped cream and serious toe-licking.

Yeah, a voice whispered. *Like a gazillion years ago.*

I ignored the voice. Time had not, in any way, shape, or form, diminished my orgasmic level.

At least that's what I was telling myself.

"Listen, if you're dead set on ten," I told Wilson, "I think I can help you out. I don't know if my mother mentioned it, but I run a matchmaking service." I pulled a card out of my pocket and handed it to him. "I could help you find a suitable eternity mate."

He eyed the card. "Your mother said you managed the second NYU location of Midnight Moe's."

"That's in my next lifetime." The trees trembled around me, and in the far-off distance I could hear footsteps heading back through the trees toward the house. "Now I'm all about hook-ups," I rushed on. "And I would be happy to help you find that special someone. For a fee, of course." The footsteps grew louder, my heart pounded faster, and the safety of the pool house seemed miles away. I could practically feel my beaded net cardigan tremble in fear. "But I'd be willing to give you a nice discount in return for a favor."

"How nice?" His gaze shot to the trees, and I knew he sensed the others as well.

"Ten percent," I told him.

"Forty percent?"

"Are you crazy? I've got bronzers to buy."

"Thirty, and you'd better hurry and make up your mind because they're getting closer."

Too close, but we're talking *bronzers*. "Twenty-five," I said firmly, all the while shaking in my favorite shoes. "That's my final offer."

He smiled and slid the card into his pocket. "What do you want me to do?"

"Tell me again what happened?" My father's gaze drilled into me as I sat on the sofa next to Wilson. My three brothers perched in various chairs about the room. Tammy knelt next to Jack's chair and massaged his feet—can you say barf? My mother stood by the fireplace with a drink in her hand—the real thing this time since the hunt was now over and dinner was officially served. Every eye fixed on me.

"Well." I licked my lips. Great actress aside, I didn't make it a habit of lying. At least not outright. "I was racing through the woods for my blouse's life when all of a sudden Wilson came at me from out of nowhere. Before I could blink, he pounced, grabbed the whistle, and let loose, and that was that. End of the hunt. Congratulations," I told him, turning to shake his hand. "Well done."

"Thank you."

"Racing, huh?" My father cast a suspicious gaze at my spotless heels.

"Actually, I was going so fast that my feet weren't even touching the ground. Just sort of skimming it. The way you do when you're moving from tee to tee. Or running from Viola."

"I do not run from that woman." My father's expression went from suspicious to annoyed, and I gave myself a great big high five. "I outrun her. There's a big difference. Namely, I am the superior creature. Faster. More cunning. More intelligent. I could crush her like a fly if I wanted."

"She does get pretty vicious when there's a full moon," my mother pointed out. "What with those teeth and those claws and that unnatural strength, I think *crush* might be a tiny bit of an exaggeration."

My father turned on my mother. "Are you saying my teeth aren't vicious, Jacqueline?"

"Well, no, dear."

"Or that my claws aren't as sharp as razors?"

"Of course not."

"Or that my strength—that of an ancient, all-powerful warrior *vampere*—isn't by far more precious and magical than that of a werewolf?"

"I just meant that she can be quite a nuisance when she chooses to be. A pest. Like a mosquito. Or an overzealous human." She spared a look at Jack and his latest overzealous human. "Don't get yourself all worked up, dear. She isn't worth it."

"That's true." His gaze swiveled back to me, and I knew my temporary reprieve was now over. "So he came at you out of nowhere? You didn't hear a thing?"

"I was breathing so hard from all the racing, not to mention Wilson is really light on his feet."

"We're all light on our feet. We also have cunning hearing."

"Yes, well, Wilson exceeds the already high standards. He pounced and I was powerless to resist."

"Powerless? The last time I tried to tackle you during a hunt, you kicked me in the nuts," Rob chimed in. "I couldn't walk for the rest of the night."

I glared at my middle brother. "Yeah, well, you're not half as fast or as determined as Wilson."

"Maybe you're just getting slow," Rob challenged.

"And maybe you're just jealous because Wilson beat you tonight."

"Am not."

"Are too."

"Children," my mother said as she came to stand next to my father. She rested a hand on his shoulder, obviously still intent on soothing him after the Viola comment. "Enough of this bickering. Wilson won fair and square, and that's that."

"But I just don't get it," my father started, and my mother's hand tightened on his shoulder.

"Of course you do, dear. You were young once, and just as fast and determined. That was about the time that we first met. We were at my family's castle. Remember that?"

"Yes." He still looked puzzled.

"You took one look at me standing on the balcony and, just like that, you leapt the five stories to stand next to me. You moved so fast, I didn't have time to take a breath, much less back into the room. Not that I would have. I wanted to meet you."

My father puffed up. "I *was* fast, wasn't I?"

"The fastest. Then again, so am I. I could have retreated inside and slammed the door in your face if I'd wanted to."

"But you didn't want to."

"Exactly." She tilted her head in my direction. "Which is why we're going to leave this topic alone."

"We are?" My father looked puzzled for a few more seconds, before understanding finally hit him. "*We are.* So"—he rubbed his hands together and smiled big enough to show his fangs—"anybody hungry?"

"Hold up. Who gets the vacation days?" Max asked. "I was really counting on them next month. I'm planning a trip to Venice with a few friends."

"I can't very well give Wilson vacation days when he's not in my employ."

"We could give them to Lilliana instead," my mother suggested.

"But she was *it*," Max argued. "The reward goes to the best *hunter,* not the prey. I say we give it to whoever was closest when Wilson blew the whistle."

"That would be me," Rob said.

"Like hell. I was closer than you," Jack said.

"You wish." It was Max's turn. "I was closer than both of you losers."

"There's no reason to fight. I can't take the days. I don't work for Moe's," I pointed out.

"It's settled," my father went on as if I hadn't said a word. "Lil gets the days to use whenever and however she chooses." He glanced at Wilson and smiled. "With whomever she chooses."

"Now that that's settled," my mother declared, a pleased look on her face, "why don't we all head to the dining room for a real drink?"

Thirteen
❤ ❤ ❤

"**H**ow many times can you orgasm in one sexual encounter?" Evie's voice drifted from the open office doorway.

It was six-thirty on Monday evening, and I'd just stopped by to retrieve more business cards before meeting The Ninas at another singles hot spot.

"I don't know." I shrugged and stuffed the cards into my purse. "A few, maybe." I'd managed to keep Evie in the dark about the whole vamp thing, and I wasn't going to stir her suspicion by admitting the truth.

"I'm not asking *you*. We're asking the client in room A, and she wants to know why we need to know."

My hand stalled reaching for another handful of cards. "We have a client in room A?"

She smiled. "Our fourth one today. The flyers that you handed out through Moe's really did the trick."

"*Four?*" She nodded and I smiled. Okay, so it wasn't the line I'd envisioned extending all the way around the corner, but it was a start. Pretty soon, room A would be busier than Grand Central Station.

Wait a second . . . "We have a room A?"

"I figured we needed a space for clients to relax and fill out their profiles in private, so I cleaned out the storage closet and brought a few things from home to dress it up."

Okay, so I knew Evie had it going on the moment I saw her, but I didn't realize that she was as conscientious as she was stylish. "Very impressive."

"Impressive enough to warrant a raise?" She gave me a hopeful look. "I've been dying since I had to give up TiVo, and all accessories, too, on account of I'm tightening my belt."

TiVo I could live without, but designer bangles? "That's terrible. Don't worry. I'll work something out. Listen, doesn't having a room A imply that we also have a room B?"

"Technically, yes. But it could also imply that we're being optimistic and looking toward the future. As in a penthouse suite, complete with rooms A to Z and a media room so that we can keep up with current trends."

"And *CSI?*"

She grinned before the look faded into confusion. "So why *do* we need to know about the orgasms?"

She waved a clipboard at me. "Not to mention, what is a fertility rating? Because one of the women from earlier today asked me about it, and I told her it was the reading from this new scale that they just came out with. You know how some measure body fat? Well, I told her this one measures a man's percentage of fertile sperm. He just steps on and *bam,* he knows just how many loaded bullets he's ready to fire."

"Clever." I flew around my desk and snatched the clipboard from her hands. "Wrong questionnaire." I retrieved a set of the newly drawn-up questions for humans from my file cabinet and handed it to her. "This is the one you should be giving out. This other one was just a . . . a joke. Yeah, my girlfriends and I were sitting around last night, and we came up with these joke questions. I guess we had too many apple-tinis."

"That'll do it." She started to turn. "Oh, and by the way, your mother is holding on line one."

"Tell her I'm not here."

"I already told her you were here."

"Tell her you made a mistake."

"She can't be that bad. She really sounded sort of nice. She said she wants to invite you and Wilson for drinks on Saturday."

"Tell her I can't make it."

"What about Wilson?"

"He can't make it either."

"No, I meant who is Wilson?"

"A client."

"Your mom said he was your significant other."

"He's a client." A very impatient client. He'd already called my cell phone twice to see if I'd found him a prospect and I'd only made the deal with him last night. "Just tell her we can't make it because . . . I don't know. A prior engagement or something."

"Why don't I tell her he doesn't drink?"

"I don't think she would buy that."

"Sure she would. Lots of people don't drink."

People being the key word. Vamps were a different animal altogether.

"Tell her he cheated on me and we broke up," I said. "Tell her it was really ugly and I'm too upset to talk and I'll have to call her back later." I read the doubt racing in her mind. "Please. I really can't talk to her right now. I'm in a hurry and she makes me crazy."

"Okay, but I'm agreeing only because I have my own mother and I understand the crazy issue completely. You're doing your own dirty work next time."

"I promise. Oh, and can you call Nina and give her this address?" I handed her a piece of paper.

"Which Nina?"

"Either. They'll pass it on to the other one. Just tell whichever to be at that address in exactly half an hour." I moved past her and nearly collided with the petite redhead who'd just exited the storage closet aka room A.

"Are you the matchmaker?" the young woman asked.

"I'm Lil." I juggled my purse and Gucci carry-all to one arm and held out my hand. "Lil Marchette."

"I'm Melissa."

As if I didn't know. Her eyes were deep brown and they said it all. Melissa Thomas. Born December 27, 1978. Capricorn. Allergic to peanuts. Prone to bad relationships. Most hated body part: hips. Second most hated body part: thighs. Third most hated body part: arms. Fourth . . .

I blinked and forced my attention to the small mole on her left temple. "Thanks for coming in, Melissa. I'd love to chat, but I've got an important meeting. Just relax and be as detailed as you can with your answers. When you're finished, we'll enter your information into the computer and see if we can match you up."

"How long will it take? I need a date by Saturday night. My oldest sister is getting married in Jersey, and if I show up without a date, my mom—who's flying in from Philadelphia—will start to worry. The last thing I need is her worrying over me. She didn't want me to move to New York in the first place. She wanted me to live in Jersey near my oldest sister, which I wasn't about to do because my sister, Marjorie, is just as bad as my mother."

"I understand completely." While Max was younger and hipper, when it came to Moe's he could be just as anal as my father.

"When my youngest sister moved out to California," Melissa went on, "my mom got so worried that she started flying out once a month to 'keep her company.' Instead, she killed her social life and her sex life and almost got my sister fired from her job on account of my mom insisted on telling off her boss because he'd passed her over for a promotion. Katie's back in Philadelphia now. She works in the shoe department at the local Wal-Mart, and she's gained thirty pounds. I seriously think she's trying to eat herself into a coma as a means of escaping her crappy life."

"Say no more. Been there, done that." Hey, I had a meddling mother, too. Even more, I had a serious aversion to faux leather footwear and was one paycheck away from the whole crappy scenario myself. "I'll certainly do my best to find that perfect someone."

"Oh, he doesn't have to be perfect," she blurted. "I mean, eventually I do want to meet someone perfect who likes dogs and doesn't mind that I still haven't found the perfect career—I'm waitressing at this little hole in the wall in the Village until I can find something more permanent."

"As a waitress?"

She shrugged. "Maybe. The tips are pretty good—Daisy and I aren't about to go hungry or anything like that—but I haven't decided if I really like it or not. Right now I'm just trying different things."

"Who's Daisy?"

"My dog. She's the only thing I brought with me from Philadelphia. Anyhow, right now I don't give a crap about meeting someone for the long term. I'll gladly settle for a warm body. Just so that I don't have to go alone and my mom doesn't think I'm navigating the big city all by my lonesome, which I am. Except for Daisy, that is."

"Got it." I smiled and patted the young woman's shoulder. "It was wonderful meeting you. Evie will help you finish up. And remember, happily ever after is just a question away."

Okay, so it was another lame slogan, but I'd had so much on my mind that I hadn't had the leftover brainpower to come up with a brilliant ad logo yet.

"Lock up for me, would you?" I asked Evie as I headed for the door. "After I meet The Ninas, I have to head down to SoHo for my meeting with Francis, so I doubt I'll make it back tonight."

"The dorky guy?"

I'd already filled Evie in on Francis. Rich. Eccentric. Lame. I'd left out the vicious bloodsucker part, of course. Not that it mattered. A dweeb was a dweeb was a dweeb.

"Good luck," she told me. "If he's half as bad as you said, you're going to need it."

"We're at the library," Nina One declared when I met her outside the New York Public Library. The clock had just struck seven in the evening, which meant we had exactly thirty minutes to get some work done before closing time. "The *library.*"

"And?"

"I thought we were going to hand out cards to singles like we did Saturday night."

"We are."

"Here?"

"Lots of single people come here. Lots of single, intelligent, successful people." I glanced at a man in a three-piece suit who walked past us. He was carrying a thick volume on tax law in one hand and a leather briefcase in the other. "Case in point. A single, successful lawyer."

"How do you know he's successful?"

"Hello? He's wearing a Cartier watch. Not to mention, I'm a vamp and can actually read some of the case load currently swamping his brain. Namely a five-million-dollar lawsuit that he's *this* close to winning."

"So he's successful. Libraries are boring."

"It's a half hour out of your endless existence." I handed her a stack of cards. "You take the fifth floor."

"To think I gave up a date with Adrian for this." Nina slid the cards into her Fendi bag.

"Adrian's a self-centered, pompous ass."

"True, but he's great in bed. I could be having an orgasm right now."

An image of Wilson the CPA rushed at me, and I eyed Nina. "How many orgasms?"

"Six."

"Minimum or maximum?"

"Minimum. I can go eleven on a really good night."

I smiled. "I think I love you."

*   *   *

"So what sort of female are you looking for?" I asked Francis after I left The Ninas, and several dozen business cards, at the library.

We stood neck deep in silk shirts and hand-stitched suit jackets at Pierre Claude's, an exclusive men's boutique. Pierre was one of the trendiest new designers in Manhattan (and a mega-hot born vampire), and so he kept much later hours than everyone else. He'd gone to the back to unearth a few casual classics from last season while we cruised the front of the elegant storefront. It smelled of champagne and money and new clothes, and I took a deep, rejuvenating breath. Ahhh . . .

"What's your ideal?" I prodded.

"Well." Francis rounded a rack of suit jackets Pierre had just finished for an up-and-coming runway show. "I'd like someone who's nice."

Francis might be a total dweeb, but he was a sweet dweeb. Unfortunately, sweet wasn't an attractive quality when it came to male vampires.

"I was thinking more in terms of an orgasm score? You want a three, four, or a five? A ten? Don't be afraid to dream big."

"I don't know." He shrugged and bypassed a bright orange box cut.

Atta boy. Despite Pierre's great design, he had the crazy notion that he was going to bring back shoulder pads. Not!

"A one would be okay."

"*One*? Don't you think you're underestimating yourself? I mean, sure, you're nothing to look at now." I pulled out a silk navy blazer with pinstripes and held it out to him. "But once we're done, you'll be a hot commodity."

"Maybe so, but that's not going to change my fertility rating. It's sort of low."

"How low? On second thought"—I shook my head and handed him a pair of navy trousers, the color a slightly darker shade than the jacket, and a fitted crimson button-up—"I'd rather not know." The odds were already stacked against us, and I didn't want to give myself yet another thing to worry over. "So what if you have a low fertility rating? That's all the more reason to aim high. If we can find you an eight or nine, she should balance out that low rating."

"You might need to look a little higher if you really want to balance." He eyed the clothes as if I'd handed him a girdle and a pair of support pantyhose.

"How high?"

"A fifteen or so."

Fifteen? I was not going to freak. I had known this would be difficult from the start. That's exactly why I'd decided to do it. The higher the degree of difficulty, the more impressive when I found Francis an eternity mate. "Okay," I said as I pointed him toward the fitting room. "A fifteen orgasm quotient it is."

"Or above," he called back over his shoulder.

"Or above," I added, doing my best to keep the tremble from my voice.

"And she has to like dogs," he said from behind the curtained area. "Specifically smaller dogs with shrill barks. No way am I bringing anyone home who can't get along with Britney." Several minutes passed before his voice floated from behind the curtain. "I don't know about this. It really isn't me."

"That's the point. Come on. Don't be such a wuss. Lemme see."

"Okay." A few more seconds ticked by. "I feel sort of weird."

"Vampires don't feel weird. They're in control of the situation. Speaking of which"—I took control and shoved the curtain aside—"they also don't cower behind dressing room curtains. They seize the moment to strut their stuff and . . ." My words trailed off as I stared.

He glanced up and his nervous gaze collided with mine. "What do you think?"

"I think . . ." Actually, I couldn't think at the moment. The shock I'd experienced at seeing Francis naked didn't begin to touch what I felt right now.

The navy blue jacket molded to his modest but well-shaped shoulders. The trousers shaped his trim waist and thighs. The color brought out the blue in his eyes and made them seem more vivid and penetrating. And the red shirt was just . . . red. Vivid. Stimulating.

My stomach hollowed out, and I smiled. "You look great."

A sheepish expression crept over his face as he glanced down. "You really think so?"

"Yes, but it's not about what I think. It's about what you think. No suit in the world can make you look good if you don't believe it in your gut. You believe it, don't you?"

He glanced down again and flexed his arms to test the fit. "I guess I do look sort of nice."

"Puppies are *nice*, Frank." I stepped back and swept my gaze from his head to the tips of his toes—okay, so we definitely needed to add a pedicure to our To Buy list, along with some expensive Italian leather loafers and trendy socks. "You, on the other hand, are *hot*. Definitely Matt Damon with a hint of Brad Pitt."

"What about Bob Barker?"

"Excuse me?"

"The guy on *The Price Is Right*. He's my favorite television personality."

"He's old."

"He hasn't always been old. He was something back in his day. I've watched him for years. Really snazzy dresser. He's my idol."

That explained a lot. "Listen, whatever floats your boat. If you want to look like Bob, that's your choice. But women tend to find younger, more trendy men attractive, so I wouldn't mention anything about him being your idol when you're talking with prospective mates."

"What about the show itself? I never miss it. Not once in the past twenty-five years. Can't I at least talk about that?"

"No."

"Then what am I supposed to talk about?"

"We'll build you up as the strong, silent type so you don't have to do much talking at all. You'll seduce them with your eyes and wow them with your moves."

"Moves? I don't have any moves."

I smiled. "Lil to the rescue."

Fourteen

♥ ♥ ♥

Ty wasn't just a mega-hot made vampire, he was also early.

Two things clued me in on this all-important fact when I walked into Dead End Dating at six-thirty on Tuesday evening (by the way, a huge high five to the genius who came up with Daylight Savings Time).

One—Evie was sitting at her desk, a dreamy smile on her face and a tiny rivulet of drool coming from the corner of her mouth. Okay, okay, she wasn't actually drooling, but she was close. Two—and this was the biggie—I could *feel* him.

My skin prickled as I set Evie's extra-large mocha latte on the corner of her desk. My thighs trembled. My knees felt suddenly weak. My nipples went on high alert. And my . . . Ugh, we are *so* not going there.

Made. Born. Big no-no.

I knew that, but knowing and remembering were

two very different things when I walked into my office. He was sprawled in the chrome chair in front of my desk, his back to me.

"You're really early."

"I'm staying nearby."

"So I guess the myth isn't true."

"What myth is that?" He pushed to his feet and turned. His blue eyes caught and held mine, and I actually forgot to breathe. Not that I need to breathe, mind you. But after five hundred years, it's become sort of a habit. So forgetting it *just like that* is a big friggin' deal.

Made. Born. *Humongous* no-no.

"What's the myth?"

"What?"

"You said something about a myth."

"I did? Oh, yeah. I did."

"Which was?"

"That made vampires can't get it into gear as fast as born vamps."

"It's true for some. But it really depends on the made vampire. I don't have trouble turning anything on."

It figured.

"You said you needed to talk. So talk." He eyed me as I walked around the desk and sank to the edge of my chair. Only when my ass had actually touched the seat did he sink back down into his own. "What's up?"

"Well." I set my purse in the bottom drawer, folded my hands in front of me, and eyed him. "So how's the city treating you? Are you getting around okay?"

"I've been to New York before. Several times, as a matter of fact."

"You're not having any trouble finding anything? Landmarks, police stations, shopping. You've got it all covered."

He gave me an odd look. "Yes."

"Then you don't really need any assistance."

"Are you volunteering your services?"

I smiled. "Actually, I am."

"So the myth isn't true."

"What myth?"

"That born vamps are incredible snobs who only hang out with their own kind." He grinned. "You want to hang out with me. Show me around. Assist me."

"With a date," I blurted. Not that I didn't want to *assist* him with a heck of a lot more, but I didn't want him to know that.

"When's the last time you actually went on a date?" I rushed on, eager to keep my lips busy forming words. Otherwise, they might be tempted to act on their own.

"Excuse me?"

"A date. You know—two people sharing the same space while participating in some sort of activity together. A date."

"I know what it is. What I don't know is what it has to do with my case."

"Nothing."

"Then why did you drag me here?"

"You should really consider softening up a bit.

Maybe being more open to new experiences. See, I have this client—a made vampire—who would be perfect for you—"

"You asked me here to fix me up?"

"I figured you weren't getting much action on your own—not with that attitude—and since things on the New York kidnapping scene have been pretty quiet, I thought you might have some time to kill."

"Now I know why we keep our distance."

"Excuse me?"

"From you born vampires. You're not just a group of elitist snobs, you're also a crazy-ass bunch."

I thought of my own family. I wasn't about to argue the crazy-ass part. "For your information, *we* keep our distance from *you*."

"Sweetheart, if you were so distant, there wouldn't be an *us*. How do you think made vampires came into being in the first place?"

"A few rotten apples in the bunch."

"Aren't we all?"

"No, I meant we had a few rotten apples in our bunch and that's how you came into being." He kept staring at me and my lips kept twitching, and so I rushed on to keep them busy. "I wasn't implying that I'm a rotten apple. I mean, based on your comment, it sounded like you thought I was saying I was a rotten apple and you—"

"I already knew that." He grinned, the expression slow and easy and dangerous to my peace of mind. "Rotten apples don't smell like cotton candy."

The words washed over me, dusting over my skin and stirring it as if he were actually touching me.

But he wouldn't. He couldn't.

Made. Born. *Gargantuan* no-no—

To hell with it.

"How do you know what I smell like?" I asked him.

"Because I can smell you. Crazy, huh?"

Damn straight. Made vampires couldn't smell born vampires. The "scent" was strictly a mating thing, and he was a different breed entirely.

His gaze drilled into me and his nostrils flared, and I could practically feel him breathe me in. "Warm. Fluffy. Sweet." He seemed both surprised and pleased at the observation, and I had the sudden urge to lunge across the desk and feel his lips move against my own.

But then he shook his head and the look dissolved into his usual come-on-and-make-my-day expression. He pushed to his feet.

"If you come across any *real* information, call me."

"She's really nice," I blurted as he started for the door. *Nice?* What was I saying? "Her orgasm quotient is out of this world." He gave me an odd look, and I realized that (a) made vampires couldn't procreate which meant (b) orgasm quotients meant doo-doo. "She's really cold-blooded and bloodthirsty." Way to go, Lil. Much better.

What can I say? I was frantic. Scrambling for words. Nervous. *Me.*

Because of Ty Bonner.

Not.

Because of Esther, I reminded myself. I really wanted to find her someone, and Ty was my only hope at the moment. It only made sense that I would start grasping at straws and act like a complete idiot when watching my only viable prospect walk out the door.

"Wait—" I moved so fast that I grasped his arm before he could reach for the doorknob. "It has to get really lonely living out of a suitcase."

"I like living out of a suitcase. I like being alone." His hand closed over mine. "I don't like someone meddling in my life."

"I wouldn't call it meddling."

"What would you call it then?"

"Business. My business. I'm a matchmaker."

"You're a vampire," he pointed out.

"Tell me something I don't know." Please, a voice whispered, my gaze fixed on the tiny scar.

"You're nuts." He grinned. "Cute, but still nuts."

"I already knew that," I called after him. "The cute part, I mean." *Cute?*

Kittens were cute. Baseball sleep jerseys with matching socks were cute. I, on the other hand, was a red hot, sexually potent, fashionably vibrant *vampere*.

I smiled.

Okay, so it wasn't the description I was used to, but it was . . . nice. Sort of.

"Your mother's on line one," Evie's voice came over the intercom.

My smile faded.

I considered several options as I walked back to my

desk. I could just not pick it up and leave her on hold until she gave up and hung up. Or I could pick it up and hang it back up again and swear the phone line went dead. Or I could just stab myself with the letter opener and put an end to the lame excuses. Or I could act like a grown-up and tell her exactly how I felt— namely that I liked my life and I didn't need an eternity mate (at least not one she picked out) and she should just butt out.

I drew a deep breath, sank down into my seat, plastered on my brightest expression (just in case there was something to the whole Big Brother thing and my mom was the head honcho), and reached for the phone.

"We can't make it for drinks," I blurted the minute I picked up the phone. "Because there is no *we*." I heard only a dramatic pause on the other end as she waited. I don't like him. Just say it. "I don't like him." There. That wasn't so bad. Except the pause continued, expectant and frightening, and before I could stop myself, I added, "I don't like him because he's a low-down, two-timing cheater. He's seeing someone else."

"Wilson?" The name was little more than a gasp. "Since when?"

Since tomorrow night. "It's been going on awhile."

"Dear, you know perfectly well there are some men who keep sheep."

"She's not a sheep, Mom. She's his . . . She has an astronomical orgasm quotient. I can't even begin to compete."

"Well. I guess that saying is true. If you don't use it, you lose it."

"I use it, Mom." What was I saying? This was my mother. Can you say *yuck*? "I'm fine in that department. This just wasn't meant to be."

"Ah, well."

"Sorry about drinks. I'll talk to you later."

"Actually, I didn't call to talk to you about Wilson."

"You didn't?"

"No. It's about Louisa. She's getting very anxious about the Midnight Soiree. I assured her that you wouldn't let her down, but since she hasn't seen a suitable vampire from you yet, she's seriously considering asking for a refund."

"But she can't." Namely, because I'd already spent the money on several must-haves. Office supplies. The telephone bill. A new Hermès scarf. "I'll find her someone."

"She doesn't like to wait."

"I'll find her someone by this weekend. I'll bring him with me to Sunday's hunt. She can meet him there."

"Excellent, dear. I'll see you then."

"I'm heading out now." Evie ducked her head into my office. She took one look at my suddenly pale complexion and frowned. "Are you all right?"

"Yes."

"Are you postal upset, or a box of Godiva upset?"

"I'm appletini upset."

She grinned and crooked a finger at me. "Then come with me."

"You should be happy," Evie told me an hour later as we sat at a nearby bar. Several empty martini glasses sat at the center of the table. "Things are starting to take off. Slowly, but surely."

"I know that." I lifted my latest glass to my lips and sipped the tart drink. "But slowly and surely aren't in Mrs. Wilhelm's vocabulary."

"I've got a single great-uncle." Evie popped a cherry into her mouth and chewed. "Bernie Kopecki," she said after she swallowed. "He's a retired loan officer. Widower. He doesn't get out much on account of he has a bad memory and keeps forgetting how to get home."

Despite the appletini haze surrounding me, I perked up. "Exactly how old is he?"

"About ninety, but he's in excellent health. For a ninety-year-old, that is. You said Mrs. Wilhelm was old. They ought to hit it off."

There were two things wrong with the scenario taking shape in my head. First, the great-uncle was human, and Mrs. Wilhelm wasn't. Second, while they *were* close to the same age (she was a younger vampire who'd just turned one hundred and nineteen), he looked ninety and she looked about twenty-nine.

On the other hand, my choices were limited.

"Do you think he would be interested in going on a date?" Not that I was agreeing to it. But with Sunday looming, it was worth discussing at least.

"I'm sure I could get him to go along with it. He's

really sweet and it's been forever since he's had any-one to share a tapioca with. Does Mrs. Wilhelm like tapioca?"

"I seriously doubt it." This was crazy. They had nothing in common save the fact that they were old. But he looked old and she didn't. He acted old and she didn't.

They had zero in common.

"That's Uncle Bernie's favorite food," Evie went on, sipping her newest appletini. "He's lost some weight and his dentures don't exactly fit the way they should, which means they come out when he actually bites into anything solid. He usually sticks to soft foods and liquids. He's big on liquids. Didn't Mrs. Wilhelm say something about a liquid diet?"

I smiled. It wasn't much, but I was willing to take what I could get. "Let's make a match."

"For the last time, I'm not going," Nina One told me.

I sat in the penthouse suite at the Waldorf and watched her primp in front of the mirror the next night. "But I already set up the date. You're meeting him in two hours."

"No, I'm not." She brushed her flawless skin with a hint of sparkle dust. "I'm going to Alain Ducasse tonight for dinner." She smiled, revealing her straight white teeth and slightly protruding incisors. "I'm in the mood for French."

"In particular, a cute French waiter named Jacques." Nina Two sat on a nearby sofa, a glass of wine in one hand. "She's been feeding off him for the past few weeks." She shifted her attention to her blond friend. "If you're not careful, you're going to drain the poor boy dry."

"I'll do no such thing." Nina One licked her lips. "But he *is* delicious."

"You can't do the waiter tonight. You're going out with Wilson." I bolted to my feet and paced around the coffee table. "I already told him you would be there."

"That's not my problem. I told you I didn't want to go. I'm not looking for a mate right now." She shuddered. "I'm having too much fun to devote myself to one man."

"You don't have to spend eternity with the guy. Just a few hours. Meet him and act a little interested. That'll buy me more time to actually find him a real mate."

"No."

"Please."

"No."

"Please, please."

"I'll go."

My head swiveled toward the sofa. Nina Two shrugged and smiled. "He sounds like an okay guy, and I haven't been out with an actual vamp in forever."

"Because they're all a bunch of chauvinistic narcissists," Nina One said.

Nina Two shrugged. "Aren't we all?"

"I might be a narcissist, but I believe in equal rights for all female vampires."

"Which is why you're still single," I told Nina One.

"I have commitment issues." She fluffed her blond hair. "That's why I'm still single. Why devote yourself to one man when there are so many?"

"It's called procreation," I said. "As in survival of the species. Speaking of which"—I turned to Nina Two—"what's your orgasm quotient?" *Ten,* I silently begged. *Just say at least ten and we'll be in business.*

"Five."

"Close enough."

Fifteen
❤ ❤ ❤

"Frank?" I came up short when I walked into my office Saturday night and found my latest project pacing a hole in my ultra-favorite Persian rug.

Okay, it was my only Persian rug, and had been a present from The Ninas to wish me well in my new business venture. Either way, I liked it and I wasn't in a big hurry to have to replace it. "What are you doing here?"

He stopped. His head snapped up, and his watery blue gaze collided with mine. "What if she doesn't like me?" he asked in a small, pitiful voice that made my chest tighten.

Or it would have tightened, if I wasn't a badass, cold-hearted V-A-M-P.

"She's not supposed to like you." My own voice went soft despite the whole V-A-M-P thing. "You're her

warm body—sort of—and she's your practice run." I
figured I needed to break Francis of all the blushing,
and the best thing to do was send him out and get him
used to social situations. Hence, my fantabulous idea
to pair him up with Melissa Thomas, the human who'd
come to Dead End Dating to find a date for her sister's
wedding. "Nobody has to like anybody. You should
be charming enough so that everyone will think that
she likes you and that you like her, but there's no genuine *like* involved." I stepped closer and my eyes narrowed. "Why aren't you wearing the contacts?"

"They make my eyes itchy. You want me to be calm,
and I can't be calm with itchy eyes."

Okay, one mountain at a time. He was wearing one
of the outfits we'd picked out. His hair was styled—or
it had been before he'd run his hand through it about
a zillion times while pacing my rug. Now it looked
windblown. Casual. *Reckless.*

I smiled and set my purse on the desk, along with
the latte I'd picked up for Evie. I'd forgotten that she
was leaving early tonight—her TiVo was misbehaving
and she didn't want to miss a *Lost* rerun, which she'd
originally missed before I'd given her enough of a raise
to have the TiVo reconnected.

Reckless was definitely a mesmerizing vamp trait.

"What?" he asked when I continued to stare at him.

"Just admiring my handiwork." I came around to
stand in front of him. "Even without the contacts,
you look really good. Wrinkled"—I noted his new
Dior tie which now looked ragged and limp because

he'd tugged on it one too many times—"but good. How do you feel?"

"Nauseous."

"Vampires don't get nauseous. We have an iron constitution." Unless you accidentally sank your teeth into a werevamp, but that was another story entirely. "Did you feed?"

He shook his head and started pacing again. "I couldn't. I was too nauseous."

"Frank, Frank, *Frank*." I gripped his upper arm to keep him from delivering any more torture to the Persian. "You've got to remember our objective. We're trying to hook you up, not get you arrested for attacking some poor innocent because you're starved to death from nerves."

"But you said this wasn't a real hookup." He turned a stricken look on me.

Good going, Lil. Now he looked panicked *and* nauseous.

"It isn't a real hookup," I assured him. "I'm speaking figuratively. Tonight is just a chance to flaunt your new look, make eye contact, and get you used to being a hot commodity." I added another soothing pat to his shoulder, and my palms cheered from the wonderful feel of his new shirt. What can I say? I've got a weakness for silk. "Even so," I told him, "you have to feed. Otherwise, while everyone else is chowing down on wedding cake, you'll be draining the maid of honor in the nearest linen closet." I shook my head. "Dead End Dating rule number one: no biting. At least not tonight. *Nada.* Zip." I walked around to my desk, retrieved a bottle of the imported stuff I kept in my office mini-fridge for desperate moments—Evie had her Godiva, and I had my O positive. I uncorked the bottle and handed it to him. "Don't be shy. Drink."

He hesitated and I motioned him on until he took a tentative swig. His cheeks instantly pinked and his breathing seemed to slow. "There." I took a sip of the latte. "Now, don't you feel better?"

He shrugged. "A little."

"Good. Now take another drink and stop worrying. You'll do just fine. Just be yourself."

He took another quick gulp and nodded. "I can do that."

"Sure, you can. Whatever you do, just remember to make eye contact with every female. And try not to use that whiny voice you use when you're nervous. And don't talk about Bob Barker or *The Price Is Right*. Or Britney. Or the twins. And whatever you do, don't talk about scrapbooking." I eyed him. "On second thought, nix the whole 'be yourself' idea."

"What do you mean?"

"Let's try a little role-playing. Who's your favorite actor?" When he opened his mouth, I added, "He's a game show host, not an actor."

His mouth snapped shut and he seemed to think. "John Wayne."

"Too old."

"Jerry Lewis."

"Too funny."

"Rock Hudson."

"Too gay." I motioned him to take another drink and tried to quench my own thirst with another mouthful of latte. As if. I hadn't fed yet, and the sight was making my tummy tingle. Francis did look positively yummy tonight.

Francis and yummy in the same sentence?

I shook away the disturbing thought. "Think of an actor who wasn't around during the Great Depression," I went on. "Someone who's been popular in the last decade. Someone who epitomizes the good-looking, successful, sexy, alpha male."

He shrugged. "I don't know. I don't really watch a lot of action-type movies." He seemed to think and his gaze lit. "I did see *Blade*, though."

"Which one?"

"All of them."

"Perfect. We'll use Wesley Snipes. Tonight, you're not Frank. You're Blade. Now let me see your Blade face."

He made an expression that looked like a cross between a smile and a snear, and I started to feel a little nauseous myself.

"Okay, so forget the face. Let's focus on the walk. You're dangerous and cool and aloof. A real badass. Men fear you. Women lust after you. Now go." I watched him strut across the carpet and did my best not to cringe.

"How was that?"

"Forget the walk. Let's focus on the talk. Just keep your voice low and to the point. Can you do that?"

"I'll try, but—"

"To the point," I cut in. "The less said, the better." He nodded and I smiled. "Now get going." I steered him through Evie's office and outside to the curb. I signaled for a cab and turned back to Blade.

He looked ready to throw up.

"Stop worrying," I told him as he climbed into the cab. "She'll like you." Okay, okay, I fell off the big, bad V-A-M-P bandwagon. So sue me.

I gave his shoulder a reassuring squeeze. "Just relax and try to have some fun." He actually smiled then, and I waved him off. "Go on and get out of here. DED rule number two: never keep a woman waiting."

It wasn't actually a rule, but I was sort of making things up as I went along, and it sounded good.

I sighed, sent up a silent plea to that Great Big Vamp in the Sky, and turned to walk back into my office.

I was just about to reach for the door when I felt the human a few feet away. He was staring at me—hey, I hadn't worn my pink chenille tank top and boot-cut, low-rise Fornarina jeans for nothing.

The thing was, he wasn't thinking about me or what he'd like to do to me. He wasn't thinking about anything except a hot dog. To be more specific, a chili cheese dog with extra heavy onions and sauerkraut and—ugh. No wonder this guy couldn't get a date on his own.

"Welcome to Dead End Dating." I held the door for him, and he followed me inside. "I'm Lil Marchette, your Dead End Dating diva." I'd learned from watching several marketing videos that it was best to mention your business name as often as possible. "And this is the Dead End Dating headquarters."

"I'm Jerry. Jerry Dormfeld."

"Well, Jerry, I'm glad you could come in and fill out a profile. That is why you're here, isn't it?" Normally, I wouldn't have to ask, but I couldn't read anything off this guy. Except the hot dog, that is. I could see him chowing down on a foot long, chili dribbling down his chin . . . I closed the window—actually, slammed it shut would have been a more appropriate description. "So, you're looking for Miss Right?"

He nodded. "I'd really like to meet someone special."

"You've certainly come to the right place. Let me show you into room A, and you can get started filling out the personality profile." I ushered him in, retrieved a clipboard and the appropriate paperwork, and returned just as he slid into his chair.

"Wow, you're fast."

Duh. "What can I say? I'm on top of my game. So, Jerry, what are you looking for in a woman?"

Redundant question, I knew. Guys like Jerry—clueless, dateless, lonely guys like Jerry who lived for hot dogs and hot dogs—had but one criteria when it came to the opposite sex: a pulse.

He shrugged. "Oh, I don't know."

"Someone nice?" I prompted.

He nodded. "Nice would be good." He picked up the pencil and attacked the clipboard with the same determination I'd seen him use on the chili dog. "And she should be a redhead. With shoulder-length hair. Straight, not curly. And brown eyes. And no previous marriages or children. I don't want anyone with extra baggage. Come to mention it, I'd prefer it if she didn't have a lot of family hanging around. They can really get on your nerves what with calling all the time and showing up unannounced and butting in. I don't like people who butt in."

Okay, so I wasn't as sharp as I thought. Jerry—one. Dating diva—zero.

"Just jot it all down in the Must Have section and I'll do my best to pair you up in no time."

"Good. Time is precious, you know."

Yeah, yeah. Tell that to someone who didn't have a few centuries to kill.

Sixteen
❤ ❤ ❤

"He's human." My mother took a long gulp of her prehunt Chardonnay and eyed the old man who sat on the imported Belgian sofa next to Louisa Wilhelm. "*Human.*"

"Mrs. Wilhelm didn't specify that she wanted a vamp."

"I would think that much would go without saying."

"Not necessarily. For all I know, she could swing both ways. Besides, she's not looking for an eternity mate. She merely wanted an escort for the soiree." I let out a little of the breath I'd been holding. At least she hadn't commented on his age.

"True, but the term *escort* usually implies accompanying someone somewhere. Didn't you have to help the man onto the sofa?"

"He was a little stiff after the long ride."

"Dear, he's stiff because he's just this side of rigor mortis."

"He's not *that* old."

"He's human, dear. If he's over thirty, may he rest in peace." She shook her head and took another huge gulp of her wine. "What were you thinking? Louisa is the chairwoman of this year's event. She can't attend the soiree with an old, decrepit human on her arm."

"She won't. This is all part of the process. There's a trial-and-error period involved in making a perfect match." *Not,* but my mother didn't know that, and I was grasping. "That's why I offer three free dating prospects. Third time is a guaranteed charm."

"At least he isn't a made vampire. Did I tell you that Kendra St. Claire has taken up with one? The next thing you know, she'll be making one of her own."

A serious no-no among upper-crust born vamps as far as my parents and their hoity-toity friends were concerned. See, made vampires were a liability since they fit the stereotype of a vampire.

It was a made vamp who'd inspired *Dracula*. And *Blades I, II* and *III*? Made. The *Underworld*? Ma-ade.

"I can't imagine what she's thinking. Made vampires are all stragglers. The whole pathetic lot. And they certainly don't know the meaning of the phrase *low profile*. They'll be the reason for our demise. You mark my words."

"Sounds a little hypocritical if you ask me. I mean, made vampires wouldn't even exist if it weren't for us. It's not their fault." I know, I know. I had to be crazy to say such a thing to my M-O-T-H-E-R. She gave birth to me, for Pete's sake. She labored and toiled for hours and hours. She endured *mucho* pain and suffering and for what? So that the object of all that pain and suffering could call her a hypocrite?

What can I say? I had the guilt thing down to an art.

My mother's gaze narrowed. "What did you just say?"

"I said that I worship and adore you and I totally appreciate your sacrifice. Mrs. Wilhelm!" I cried before my mother could say anything more. I turned my brightest smile on the woman who glided toward me on a pair of black patent Dolce and Gabbana pumps. "It's so wonderful to see you."

Louisa Wilhelm looked like a walking poster girl for vampires. She had long, straight black hair and eyes as black as obsidian. In my opinion, she needed a bronzer in a major way and a little neutral lip gloss to kill the whole crimson thing she had going on with her mouth, but then I seriously doubted she gave a fig what I, or anyone else, thought. She wore a fitted black dress and a diamond choker and a look that said she was royally pissed.

"Is this some sort of joke? Because if it is, I have to warn you that I don't have a sense of humor."

I never would have guessed.

"This is the ice-breaker prospect. See, a lot of clients who come to me aren't really socially inclined." When she frowned, I added, "Not that you have that problem, but Dead End Dating has a foolproof system by which we match up all of our clients." I repeated the whole spiel about the trial-and-error period, and I added a line about the first prospect being someone with whom the client could relax. "Tonight is all about letting your guard down and just enjoying yourself. Talk. Reminisce. Bernie was stationed in Europe during World War I. You love Europe."

"That is true." A faraway look touched her eyes. "But I can hardly take him to the soiree." She glanced back at the old man who sat on the sofa, his head tilted back, his mouth open. His nostrils flared as he snored softly. "He creaks when he walks, so dancing is completely out of the question. And I certainly can't bite him. Stale blood gives me cramps." She let loose an exasperated sigh. "I guess I could wake him and inquire about the Louvre. Do you suppose he's been there?"

"Hasn't everyone?" I smiled. "Just have a seat and visit and rest assured that you'll have the perfect escort for the soiree."

"When do I get to meet him?"

"Soon. But it's the third time that's the charm, so that means you have two prospects to go through first. It's sort of like skulking the countryside for a rare blood type." When hanging by the skin of one's fangs, it was always good to throw out a hunting analogy. "You have to bypass a few O and AB positives to get to the really good stuff. Not that it's time wasted, because you've sharpened your skills."

"True."

I poured her a glass of wine and handed it to her.

"Now head back over there and practice your conversation technique."

"Oh, all right. But I expect results."

"And I guarantee them." I smiled, and then I frowned as my mother came up next to me, a good-looking male vamp on her arm.

"I hope you don't mind, dear, but I invited Jon Naples to join us for the hunt. He's been wanting to meet you. His fertility rating is off the charts."

Ugh. Here we go again.

"He's not really my type," I said into my cell phone later that evening as I walked up the steps leading to the front door of my building.

"He's got fangs, a penis, and a bloodline that can be traced back to Napoleon I. What else do you need?"

I paused on the top step and rummaged in my purse for my keys. "Nothing. It's just . . ."

"Just what?"

"I don't know. He sort of smells funny."

"Funny?"

"Like bourbon-soaked sponge cake."

"Actually, the bourbon part is your father's fault. They had a few drinks while we were waiting for you."

Which left the second half of the equation. Sponge cake and cotton candy? *Ewwwwwwwwwwww.*

"He's a little too tall," I blurted, eager to fill the expectant silence. I felt for my keys and promised myself for the umpteenth time that I would trade fashion for one of those compartmentalized bags my mother carried.

"So you'll wear your shoes a little higher. You like high heels."

"True, but I still don't think he's right for me."

"Why not?"

"He's got brown eyes. I hate brown eyes."

"You have brown eyes, dear."

"Uh—yeah, and I happen to wear contacts."

"I've been meaning to talk to you about that. I don't think this infatuation you have with the Barbie image is healthy."

"I'm not infatuated with Barbie."

"Of course you are. The blond highlights. The blue contacts. We all know that humans can't resist falling victim to society and peer pressure, but we're different, dear. We're strong. We're superior. You're embarrassing yourself. Embrace who you are."

"I do embrace who I am. I just like to tweak a little."

"Born vampires don't tweak."

"Mom, I really need to go."

"You're embarrassing us all," she repeated again. "Me. Your father. Your brothers. The entire Marchette family."

"I *really* need to go."

"Luckily, Jon is willing to look the other way and ignore your eccentricities in the interest of making a good match."

"That's admirable, but unnecessary. I can make my own match."

"Another ninety-year-old human who keeps losing

his dentures? That's hardly appropriate son-in-law material."

"Actually, I've got a totally good-looking prospect standing right next to me." Sort of. My nostrils flared and the scent of leather spiraled through my senses. "He's tall, dark, and handsome, and he's definitely got a penis." Not that I would ever make that acquaintance firsthand, but a girl could dream.

Excitement filled my mother's voice. "What about his bloodline?"

"What?"

"His bloodline? How old is he and where is he from?"

"You're breaking up, Mom." I made a few crackling sounds for good measure. "I'll . . . you . . . to . . . evening . . ." I said in a garbled voice and hit the end button before she could reply.

I slid the phone into my purse and tuned my senses to the man standing nearby. "Do you mind not breathing down my neck?"

"First off, I don't breathe, sugar." The deep timbre of his voice vibrated inside my head. "Second, I'm a good ten yards away from your neck."

Unfortunately.

I squelched the thought and tried to calm the sudden pounding of my heart.

"Do you make it a habit of sneaking up on unsuspecting women?"

"You're a vampire. Unsuspecting doesn't touch you."

No, but you could.

Another squelch.

I turned and gazed down the sidewalk. He stood several houses down, his back against a tree, his arms folded as he stared in my direction.

"So what brings you to the neighborhood?"

He grinned, slow and easy, and I felt a quiver down south.

Major squelch.

"You." He pushed away from the tree and, in the blink of an eye, stood directly in front of me, his gaze dark and mesmerizing as he stared deep into my eyes. "I need you, Lil."

Seventeen
❤ ❤ ❤

"**I** need to talk to you," he corrected once he realized what he'd said.

Thankfully, I told myself. Otherwise I would have had to send him on his way because I didn't *do* made vampires, even ones who needed me. Even tall, good-looking ones who smelled like fresh air and freedom.

I was about to drop to my knees and cry when another thought struck and I smiled. "You changed your mind."

His brows drew together. "About what?"

"Letting me hook you up. You realized how right I was and how lonely you were and you decided to stop being so stubborn and let Fate work her magic."

His gaze narrowed. "You *are* a vampire, aren't you? Because if I didn't know better, I'd swear you were one of those wannabes."

"These fangs are the real thing, buddy." I gave him

my best offended look despite the strange warmth bubbling deep down inside. Of course I was a vampire. Always had been. Always would be. *Always.*

I ignored the depressing thought and focused on Mr. Tall, Dark, and No-No. "You need a social life."

"And you need to keep a watchful eye on your clients."

"What are you talking about?"

"Wanda Ellen Shriver. Twenty-nine. Single. No children. Moved here from Wisconsin last year to take an entry-level job at a publishing house. She went out on a date set up by Meet and Match on Wednesday and hasn't been heard from since. Her boss thought she was sick, but when he stopped by to check on her this morning, she wasn't at home. He alerted the police."

"Meet and Match?" I recognized the name of the Lower East Side dating service I'd seen advertised in several of the local papers. "They are *so* yesterday's news. They don't even use a personality profile. They just invite a bunch of singles to these meet-and-greet parties and let the clients match themselves." I shook my head. "If people were good on their own, they wouldn't need a dating service."

"You're missing the point."

"Oh, no I'm not. They just throw everyone together, no rhyme or reason, and see who clicks. Talk about old school. That's why I've spent weeks perfecting the Dead End Dating questionnaire. To save my clients the time and trouble of pairing up with losers. Or, in this case, a kidnapper/possible murderer wanted by the FBI."

He looked like he wanted to strangle me almost as much as he wanted to smile. "You took the long route, but I think you got it."

"You were right. This guy *is* targeting the most populated cities."

He nodded. "The local authorities aren't as convinced. Since the MO is a little different—he used a dating service instead of the singles ad—they're telling themselves this might be an isolated case."

"That's why he did it. To throw them off and keep them from calling in the big boys."

"The big boys?"

"You know, the feds."

He grinned. "I know. I'm a bounty hunter, remember? But you're not and so it sounds a little funny coming from you."

"Hey, I catch *CSI* every now and then." Usually more then than now. It had been months since I'd tuned into anything other than reruns of *America's Top Model* on UPN and *Dr. Phil*. But Ty Bonner didn't know that, and I wasn't about to clue him in, particularly with him smiling at me as if he were slightly impressed. "I also watch the news."

His gaze narrowed as if he didn't buy *that*. Smart guy. "You should be very careful. It's even more important now that you take a close look at everybody who comes into your place."

"I always do that."

"I'm talking about looking into their head, not at what they're wearing."

"For your information, I do that, too." Not on

purpose, mind you. I couldn't help myself. It came with the vamp territory. "So far, the only thing I've got are women obsessed with the size of their thighs and men infatuated with chili dogs. No crazed kidnappers."

"Good."

"I am." I didn't mean to flirt, but in the face of so much testosterone, I couldn't help myself. Obviously my poor hormones couldn't differentiate the good testosterone from the bad.

"I bet." His hand came up then, and his fingertips trailed over my cheekbone.

Then again, maybe they could.

The rough feel of his skin was so different from that of any other vamp in my past, and I tingled from my head to my French-tipped toes. Born vamps didn't get calluses. Rather, their skin felt cool and smooth and *perfect*. But not Ty. He was far from perfect. My gaze riveted on his scar, and I couldn't help myself. I reached up and felt the puckered skin against my fingertips.

"What happened here?"

He shook his head. "It was a long time ago."

"Duh." I let my hand fall away, and if I hadn't known better, I would have sworn he actually looked disappointed. But that would mean that he liked my touch. And judging by the way he frowned, he didn't like too much about me at the moment.

The frown deepened. "Anyone ever tell you that you're damned nosy?"

Yes. "Geez, it's just a question. What's the big deal?"

"I don't like to talk about my past."

"I don't like to talk about mine, either." At his questioning glance, I added, "Flapper dresses. Not my proudest moment."

He stared at me a few more seconds before a grin touched the corner of his mouth. He shrugged. "A bottle of whiskey. I got into a bar fight in this little Mexican border town around the turn of the century."

"What was the fight about?"

"It doesn't matter."

"Tell me anyway."

Another shrug. "It was over a girl. One of the girls who worked there at the saloon."

"You had a thing for her?"

"She had a thing for me."

"But did you have a thing for her?"

"What does it matter?"

"It doesn't. I'm just curious."

"Why?"

It was my turn to shrug. "Because I am, that's all. You were human then, right?" He nodded. "I just think it's interesting, that's all."

"So sayeth the bear when he shoved his nose into a beehive and found himself a world of hurt."

"Excuse me?"

"Just something my ma used to say when I was a kid." A faraway light flashed in his gaze. "A long, *long* time ago." He seemed to shake off the melancholy, and his look grew intense as it drilled into mine. "I'm serious about being on the lookout. You have an advantage because you're a vampire. Use it. If you notice anything suspicious—*anything*—call me. No matter how small." He turned.

"Wait." I reached out, eager for more sizzling contact. My hand closed over his upper arm. The smooth leather of his jacket felt cool against my skin. "So what about the girl?"

He stared at the point of contact. I barely ignored the urge to smooth my palm up over his shoulder and, instead, let my hand fall away.

"I liked her, all right," he finally said. "But not enough to marry her."

"She was in love with you?"

"She was in love with my horse." When I gave him a puzzled look, he added, "She wanted out of that town, and I was the first thing to come riding up. When I refused to marry her and take her with me, she sicced her brother on me. We fought."

"And you won?" He nodded and I smiled. "Good-looking and tough. You would definitely make a good match for someone." He stared at me as if I'd grown two heads. "You really should let me set you up."

He shook his head. "I don't think so."

"What about friends?" Surely you have some date-less buddies who were turned around the same time as you? A few country boys who've yet to be influenced by modern society's twisted view of beauty?"

That earned me a small smile. "No buddies."

"Acquaintances?"

"None."

"Relatives?"

"All dead."

"But I need a made vampire."

He stared at me for a long moment, and I had the sudden feeling that he was going to touch me again.

If only.

I saw the lust and longing and regret so bright and vivid in his deep blue gaze before he slammed the window shut and shielded himself from me. Suddenly, a great big chili dog flashed in my mind, the weiner swimming in enough cheese to make a cow wince.

"Funny. Really funny."

He grinned and my tummy tingled. "You've got the equipment, sugar. If you need a made vamp so bad, make your own." He winked and blended into the darkness.

"Brilliant idea," I called after him. "But that won't work because I need someone made around the turn of the century." Someone Esther could relate to.

Not to mention pulling some poor schmuck in off the street, draining him to the point of death, and sharing my blood with him wasn't part of the Dead End Dating mission statement.

First off, I didn't do schmucks. Second, I had never actually drained anyone to the point of death—my mother would have had the granddaddy of all fits. And third? While I don't get all creeped out at the sight of blood (I *am* a vampire), there's just something extremely icky about slicing my own wrist and passing it to the next guy as if it were a shrimp appetizer.

Which meant I was back to cruising made vamp hangouts if I wanted to find Esther a date.

And if I wanted to find my own date?

I didn't. I was a busy woman with a blossoming career and a really great wardrobe. I was completely and totally fulfilled at the moment, even if I did feel this strange emptiness in the pit of my stomach.

Suspicious, I reminded myself. I had to be suspicious to pick up the phone and give Ty a buzz. Not thirsty. Or desperate. Or horny. Or empty.

I turned and walked up to my apartment. I tried to ignore the way my nipples rubbed against the lace of my bra and the way my knees trembled with each step and the way my skin felt itchy and tight and alive.

I paused outside of my apartment and tuned in to the early morning news drifting from my neighbor's television. But they were doing the weather, not local disappearances, and so I didn't hear anything about the missing woman.

Inside, I bypassed the blinking answering machine, peeled off my clothes, and retrieved a bottle of blood from my fridge. I didn't bother with a glass, much less taking the time to nuke it. Rather, I popped the cork and raised the bottle to my lips. It wasn't very couth and my mom would chew me a new one if she saw me drinking straight from the container, but I couldn't help myself.

I was suddenly more thirsty than I'd been in a very long time.

And desperate. And horny. And empty.

Squelch.

I drank half the bottle before shoving the cork back in. I turned on the television and tuned in to CNN. Killing the lights, I checked the blinds and crawled into my ultra-soft bed with the remote.

I didn't close my eyes and give in to sleep, despite the fact that I was exhausted. Instead, I watched until a picture of the missing girl finally flashed. She wasn't a raving beauty, but she knew how to play up her best features. I had to give her props—no lip liner or harsh color. She wore a pale beige lip gloss and minimal eye makeup. She was a strawberry blonde, with rich red highlights and nice teeth and a glint of hopelessness in her brown eyes that said she knew what it felt like to sit home alone on a Saturday night.

I thought of my own growing client list. There were men and women from a variety of backgrounds. They differed in shape and size; some blond, some brunette, some redheaded. But they all had one thing in common: lonely with a capital L.

I swallowed against the sudden lump in my throat and forced my eyes closed. Sunset would come soon, and I needed to rest and regroup. Even more, I needed to escape the image of Ty Bonner that lingered in my head and made my chest ache.

Okay, so it wasn't just my chest that ached. The feeling gravitated a good twelve to twenty-four inches south.

Regardless, Ty was off limits.

No thinking about him.

No fantasizing about him.

No wanting him.

Nada.

I know, I know. I'm delusional. But at least I'm trying to keep my priorities straight. Definitely an A for effort.

Eighteen
♥ ♥ ♥

"**Y**ou're early," Evie declared when I walked into the office just after sunset that evening and handed her the usual steaming latte.

"I had a rough day." Rough? More like unbearable. Horrific. Disastrous.

I hadn't slept a wink.

I still couldn't believe it. In five hundred years, I'd yet to have a restless day. You would never find a born vampire popping Ambien. It just wasn't necessary. When it was time to sleep, we conked out and slept like the dead (ahem). Neither sickness nor stress nor worry could interfere with a vamp's sleep. I'd slept through several plagues, a couple of world wars, and hoop skirts.

Until today.

I'd tried to close my eyes, but every time I'd seen the missing girl's face.

All right, all right, so not *every* time. A few of those times (quite a few), I'd pictured Ty. And felt his fingertips on my cheek. And imagined that touch traveling down my body, over my breasts, between my legs and my—

"Are you all right?" Evie's voice disrupted my train of thought.

Way to go, Evie.

"I-I'm fine. Just a little tired."

"You need this more than me." She handed me back the hot drink and bounced up from her desk. "Jeanine Booker is in room A—she's one of the people who got your card at the library the other night—and Connie Laramie is due any minute to fill out a profile—she's another library connection. The two of them will make a total of twelve new clients today—all courtesy of the library except for a couple à la Moe's. And not a one of them came in just for the freebie profile. They're actually paying for our services." She handed me a small stack of checks. "Retainer fees for various packages."

"No way!"

She smiled. "Total way. Of course, a few have stopped by for the free coffee and dessert."

"What free coffee and dessert?"

"The free coffee and dessert I mentioned in the ad that you took out in all those local singles magazines." Worry lit her face. "I hope you don't mind. When they sent over the copy, it just looked so blah. It needed some spice. Some sort of incentive to get people to come in and see what we have to offer. I thought about offering free Trojans—a friend of mine works over at The Pleasure Chest on Seventh and will give them to us at cost—but I figured that might send a mixed message. We're all about finding Mr. or Miss Right. Not Mr. or Miss Right Now."

"Good thinking."

Evie smiled and reached for another stack. "You've got twelve messages."

My face brightened. "More clients?"

"Eight are from your mother. Esther Crutch called. And there was one lady who wanted to sell you life insurance. And Melissa called twice with an update on her sister's wedding." She smiled. "We're on a roll, so you should definitely cheer up."

"What about Francis? Any calls?" I'd tried him several times yesterday, on the way to the hunt, during the hunt, after the hunt, but had only gotten his machine.

"No."

Okay, I was starting to get worried. Two calls from Melissa, zero from Francis. She was no doubt ready to chew me a new one, and he was definitely hiding out.

"You want me to try him for you?"

"I'll try myself. I'll be in my office." But first I ducked my head into room A and introduced myself to Jeanine, who sat eating scones and free coffee. Code for "I used my vampire skills to scope her out and make sure she wasn't the kidnapper/possible murderer in drag."

Sinking down into my chair, I inhaled the scent of

latte and let the aroma clear away a few of the cob-webs. Then I turned my attention to the retainer checks. I endorsed each one and filled out a deposit slip in less than sixty seconds. I buzzed Evie and she came into my office.

"Can you drop these in the bank's night deposit box on your way home?"

"You're already done?"

"What can I say? I'm excited." She gave me a curious look, which I ignored by reaching for the stack of messages.

"I'm heading out then," she told me. "Don't forget the client in room A."

"Got it. Be careful." Evie disappeared, and I shoved the messages from my mother to the side while I dialed Francis. His machine picked up. "I know you're there. I can hear you breathing," I told him. Nothing. "If you don't pick up, I'll just keep calling and then I'll start hanging out on your doorstep. You can't avoid me forever." Nothing. "If you don't pick up, I'll call your cable company and have them disconnect your game show channel."

Click.

"You wouldn't," he said.

"No, I wouldn't, but it got you to pick up the phone. Now what's up?"

"Have you talked to Melissa?"

"I'm talking to you first." I didn't tell him she'd called. Twice. Not a good sign.

"I totally suck at this," he said after a long pause during which I could envision him turning every shade of red, from blistering to crimson. "Not literally," he rushed on. "I remembered what you said about no biting and I didn't suck on anyone, so we don't have that to worry about. Not that I would have even if you hadn't told me the rule. I don't really like to eat in social situations but—"

"You're digressing. Get to the point."

"It was terrible. *I* was terrible. I just can't do this."

"What exactly happened?"

"Nothing. I just sat there and it was terrible. Everyone was staring at me. Except for Melissa. She wouldn't even look in my direction. I even tried to talk to her."

"You didn't."

"I know I was supposed to be the strong, silent type, but it was so quiet and we weren't dancing or anything so I had to do *something*. I figured it was better to talk than try to waltz. I don't dance very well."

"I never would have guessed. So what did you talk about?" *Please, no scrapbooking.*

"I told her about my latest scrapbook."

Ka-boommm! "You didn't!"

"I couldn't help it. We were sitting there and everyone else was having fun and we weren't doing *anything*. I opened my mouth, and it just came out."

This was not the end of the world. It didn't matter if Melissa had had a horrible time. All that mattered was that she'd had a date. An attractive date, I reminded myself. He *had* looked pretty hot, even if he hadn't perfected the attitude to go with it. And she'd just contracted for a date. Any old date. In her own words, a warm body.

"I'm sorry," he said. "I really didn't mean to mess things up. I bet she hates me."

"I'm sure she doesn't hate you."

"She certainly doesn't like me."

"She's not supposed to like you, remember?"

"I know. I just thought . . ." His voice trailed off. "You're right. It doesn't matter if she likes me. Or if I like her. I'm not doing it again."

"Of course you are—you like her?"

"Sure. She's nice."

"She's human, and totally inappropriate. You're letting this failure make you crazy. Just calm down," I said, despite the ringing in my ears and the frantic beat of my heart. "Everything is going to be okay."

"No, it's not. That's why I'm not doing it again. Our deal . . . Let's just forget it. I'm terrible when it comes to women."

"*Human* women. You haven't tried a female vampire yet." Just the thought made my heart pound that much faster.

"You think I'll be any smoother?"

"Most definitely." Hopefully. "Especially after Saturday night. The whole point was to give you a chance to get the screwups out of the way with someone who isn't a potential eternity mate. You did, which means you're ready to try someone who is."

"I don't know about that."

"You didn't throw up, did you?"

"No."

"You didn't talk about *The Price Is Right*, did you?"

"No."

"You didn't mention Britney or the twins?"

"No."

"Then I'd say you did pretty good. So you slipped up once? You'll do better next time."

"You really think so?"

"I know it. You're growing, Francis. Evolving. Getting comfortable in your vamp skin. A few more training sessions and you'll be right at home with the opposite sex."

At least that's what I was desperately hoping.

I talked Francis up a few more seconds until my second line rang—yay!—and I had to let him go.

"Stop beating yourself up. Before we're through, you'll be total vampiric beefcake," I told him before disconnecting and punching the blinking button for line two. "Dead End Dating. Where happily ever after is just a date away."

"Lil? It's Melissa."

Three times. Yikes! "Melissa! I was just going to call you." *Not.* "No need to thank me for Saturday night. I'm just glad I could help."

"Thank you? I have no intention of thanking you."

"It's really against our policy to give refunds when we've fulfilled our part of the deal—"

"A thank-you isn't nearly enough. He was wonderful!"

"While we pride ourselves on making a perfect

match, we can't realistically be expected to hit pay dirt the first time—what did you just say?"

"I said he was wonderful. Great. Fantastic."

"Who?"

She laughed. "Who do you think? Francis, silly. He's the most handsome man I've ever met. And such a good conversationalist. And he's got a great sense of humor."

"Francis?"

"He's like a dream come true."

"*Francis?*"

"I have to go out with him again."

Just as the words registered, the conversation with Francis replayed in my head. "I, um, don't know if that's such a good idea."

"He didn't like me?"

"Sure, he liked you." Okay, if I totally failed at the dating business, I could always find work at Liars-R-Us. "He thought you were, um, really great."

"He didn't like me, did he? I knew it. It's the story of my life. No decent guy is ever interested. I'm a bum magnet. If there's a loser within a fifty-mile radius, he'll be knocking on my door. But the good ones . . . They run the other way."

"You are *not* a bum magnet," I heard myself say. "You're a beautiful, vibrant woman with oodles to offer the right guy."

"So you think he'll go out with me again, then?"

"I haven't actually spoken with him, but when I do, I'm sure he'll be itching to see you again."

"You're the best, Lil. I really had zero expectations when I went to you. I just wanted off my mom's radar. But now I'm actually starting to think that I may have met The One. And it's all because of you. You've totally changed my mind about love."

"Glad I could be of service." I said good-bye, slid the phone into place, and resisted the urge to impale myself with the letter opener sitting on the corner of my desk.

What had I done?

I'd just given Melissa false hope and set her up for an even bigger heartache.

Then again, maybe she was a drama queen and she hadn't really liked Francis half as much as she'd made out.

I turned to my computer, pulled up her file, and did a search for "overly dramatic."

There are zero matches . . .

Ugh. I was definitely having the vampiric equivalent of a bad hair day.

Nineteen
♥ ♥ ♥

I craved a fix in the *worst* way.

The thought ambushed me when I rounded the corner a half hour later and spotted the guy standing at the entrance to a nearby alley.

Okay, so I don't usually go ga-ga over anyone or anything in the general vicinity of so much garbage and muck (see *New York City alley* in your handy *Webster's*). But I'd been having a hellacious evening, and it had been sooooo long since I'd fallen off the wagon.

I was definitely ready to take a nosedive.

Remember your priorities, I told myself. Namely, I had a client in room A and I'd run out of coffee. A major emergency thanks to Evie and her "sit back, relax, and enjoy complimentary coffee and dessert while filling out your Dead End Dating profile" addition to our local ad. Which meant I desperately needed a bag of Starbucks gourmet roast, enough scones to make it through the rest of tonight's appointments, and some extra packets of sugar. End of *must have right now or will be sued for false advertising* list.

I didn't need *this*.

My nostrils flared at the familiar scent, and my mouth watered. My ears perked, and I heard the steady sound of his breathing and the *thump thump* of his pulse. My gaze traveled the length of the guy, from his Knicks cap, down past his beat-up leather jacket, his slouchy jeans, to his high-dollar tennis shoes, and back up again before my attention zeroed in on the gold creation in his meaty hand. A Prada clutch like the one I'd seen at Barney's just last week.

"Can I touch it?" I breathed.

"Sure thing, little lady."

"It's amazing." My fingertip traced the smooth buckle, and I practically orgasmed right there on the spot.

"It's a bargain at fifty bucks."

"*Fifty* bucks? Are you crazy?" Okay, so I was the crazy one. Fifty bucks should have started some major alarm bells, but I was so desperate that I didn't see past the shiny gold clasp and sequined material. "That's a steal."

"Hey, keep your voice down, lady. This stuff is totally legit."

Which totally explained the alley showroom.

"I don't know if I have that much on me." I whipped open the wallet I'd pulled out of my purse before starting my mission for . . . Now, what was it I'd been after? The handbag reflected the neon sign across the street and glittered a thousand shades of gold and pink and blue. "I don't suppose you'd take a check?" I shifted my attention from the purse to the man, and my gaze clashed with his.

"Are you fuckin' insane? This ain't motherfuckin' Macy's—" The words seemed to stall in his throat, and he swallowed. His brown eyes glazed over, and a hungry, desperate light fired in the dark depths.

I recognized the look even though it seemed ages since I'd seen it. I couldn't help but smile.

"I've got a twenty," I told him. "Otherwise, I have to use my checkbook."

"Yeah, yeah. Sure. Whatever you say."

"So you'll take twenty? Or do I write the check for the full amount?"

"Sure. I mean, no. I mean, you take it." He thrust the bag into my hands. "If you like this one, I've got another right here. It's silver. And a black leather one, too. And brown crocodile—"

"That's okay. This is fine." I held the bag close and let the feel of all that mesh sink into my skin. "Thanks so much."

"Thank *you*."

"No, really." I smiled at him. "It's way hot. I absolutely love it."

His eyes gleamed with sincerity. "I love *you*."

Uh-oh. I fixed my most intense stare on him. "You don't love me," I said in my most persuasive voice.

"You like me. Got that? *Like*. Just think of me as your sister."

"I don't have a sister."

"Then consider me a good friend."

"I don't have any friends. Unless you count Jimmy down at the chop shop. But he'd sell his own mother out if the price was right, so I have to watch my back. But you're different. You're *really* hot."

He took a step forward, and I took a step back.

Not out of fear, mind you. I could have broken him in two if the need arose. But I'm really more of a lover than a fighter—like you don't already know *that*— and, geez, it's not as if the poor guy could help himself.

"What about your grandmother?" I blurted, eager to distract him from whatever lusty, demented road his brain was currently cruising down. I needed a totally nonsexual person to compare myself to. "A guy's gotta love his grandma."

"Died before I was born."

O-kay. "An aunt?"

"Only one."

He seemed to pause, and I took the opportunity and ran with it. "I bet she's very sweet and maternal. You're lucky to have her."

"She sold my Tonka truck when I was a kid to buy a rock of cocaine."

"Oh. I'm so sorry."

He shrugged. "Life's a bitch, but you keep going." Another step forward. Another step back. "You ever play with a Tonka truck?"

"I can't say that I have."

"They're really cool. I've got an entire collection back at my place. Wanna see 'em?"

I'd heard a lot of pickup lines in my five hundred years. This, I had to admit, was a definite first.

I had to give him kudos for originality.

But that was all I was giving him.

"You know." I smiled, and he practically salivated. *Bad smile*. I drew my forehead into a frown. "I'd really like to, but I'm sort of in a hurry." I turned. "Nice doing business with you."

"Wait!" His voice followed me as I darted back around the corner. *Mucho gracias* to the Big Vamp Upstairs for preternatural speed. "Can I go with you?" he called after me.

But there was no place to go because I'd already made it safely back to my office while the guy still stood around the block, too lovestruck to move.

Thankfully.

A stalker I did not need. Been there, done that. Which was why I tended to refrain from using my vamp abilities to wow anyone except in dire circumstances: war and famine and tanning emergencies.

I closed the door, peered past the blinds, and waited several seconds just to make sure he hadn't tailed me. A couple strolled by, followed by a businessman in a suit, a group of giggling girls, and a woman being pulled along by several monstrous dogs. No seedy-looking guys carrying a stash of designer purses.

I let out a deep sigh and walked over to Evie's desk. Sinking down into her chair, I fixed my attention on my new purchase. I heard a deep sigh coming from room A, followed by the squeak of a chair as my newest client readjusted her sitting position, and I remembered I'd forgotten the coffee and the scones.

Not good. At the same time, I was beyond the point of panic. I was riding a Prada high and feeling no pain.

It *was* a beautiful purse.

I trailed my fingertips over the mesh and smiled. I could see myself strutting down the street in matching shoes and something ultra slinky. Of course, I didn't have matching shoes, which meant that I'd have to make time for a shopping trip ASAP. I had slinky in my closet at home, but I didn't have *ultra* slinky. At least not anything from this season. I ran through the fantasy a few times with various things I already owned. No. Nah. *Never.*

The phone rang while I was contemplating a black miniskirt and a leather halter I'd gotten for a steal six months ago. I pressed the blinking button.

"Dead End Dating," I said. "Where we turn your dating disasters into blissful moments of exquisite bliss." Ugh. Can you say American *and* Swiss? With a side order of Gouda?

"I'm calling for Lil Marchette," said a familiar voice. "This is Esther Crutch. E-S-T-H-E-R Crutch. Spelled like Dutch, but with a C instead of a D. That's C-R-U—"

"Es, it's me," I cut in. "Lil."

"I thought it was your answering machine."

I made a quick mental inventory of my greeting.

Nope, no *please leave a message after the tone*. "It's really me."

"Well, I'll be. It *is* you. Your enunciation is wonderful. I've been calling the psychic hotties line since we had our talk, and you'd be surprised at how garbled the operators can sound."

"Don't you mean psychic *hot* line?"

"That's just to find out what's going to happen in the future. The psychic *hotties* line hooks you up with someone who has a compatible sign so you're not spending that future completely alone. I know you said I should try to get out more, but I really hate going places by myself. Social places, that is. So I thought I'd try some of the phone hook-up lines being advertised on the TV."

"And how's that working for you?"

"It's not. I've called the singles network, too. And Guys, Guys, Guys. You know, you really should think about doing phone work. You have the perfect voice."

True, but I hadn't invested a small fortune in cosmetics to hide behind a receiver. "I like a more personal approach. Speaking of which, I'm this close to finding someone for you." Now why had I said that? Because she was calling the psychic hotties line. Talk about desperate. And pathetic.

I was a total sucker for both.

"Really?" Hope infused her voice. "I mean, I know you said you'd work on it, but I didn't expect anything this soon. Is he, you know, like me?"

My thoughts shifted to Ty. In a purely professional

sense this time. No whipped cream or neck biting or toe licking . . .

As if that would ever happen.

"He's tall, dark, and handsome"—the words flowed out before I could stop them—"and one hundred percent made. And he wears a cowboy hat."

"He's a cowboy?"

"Once upon a time. Now he just wears the hat out of habit. And boots, too."

"Do you think he'll like me? Don't answer that. I have to focus on my positive attributes."

"You have taken our little talk to heart."

"It's all I've been thinking about. I even bought a couple of books at the bookstore. *Love Yourself. You Got It, So Flaunt It.* Anyhow, I've got a good eye for detail. And brains. And I've scheduled one of those messotherapy sessions to work on the neck down. They smooth out your cellulite without any invasive treatment."

"You mean the thigh wrap didn't work?" *As if.*

"For about twenty-four hours. Then it was back to square one. Story of my life. But a girl has to try. So do you think he'll think I'm interesting? I was pretty popular back in my day, but in a nice, sweet, settled sort of way. Maybe he's one of those cowboys who goes for the saloon-girl type."

I remembered Ty's comments about his past. "Trust me, if he sees another saloon girl, it'll be too soon."

"So he prefers a good girl?"

"Definitely." All men wanted their women good at

something. Didn't they? Anxiety rushed through me and made my hands tremble. I fidgeted with the Prada nameplate on my new purse. "I'm sure he'll be totally blown away by you." If I managed to get them together. "It's just a matter of laying the groundwork before the introduction." I trailed my fingertip over the signature metal, and panic fled as I focused on my elite piece of handbag couture. A thrill raced up my spine. It felt so cool and slick and *loose* . . . Loose?

I fingered the edge. The plate popped off and flew over the desk. A soft *plink* echoed in my ears as it hit the floor somewhere to my right.

"Oh, no." I blinked back a sudden swell of tears. My purse. My beautiful purse . . .

"So you really think he'll find me interesting?"

"I do," I said as I shoved back my chair and dropped to my hands and knees.

"Why?"

"Because you are." I cradled the phone between my chin and shoulder and felt around. "You two have oodles in common. You're a country girl, he's a country boy."

"True. So when can I meet him?"

"Soon. Listen, can I let you go? I've got an emergency."

"But—"

"I'll call you back ASAP." I hit the off button, set the phone on the corner of the desk, and crawled toward the spot where I thought the plate might have landed.

I know, I know. Hot, happening vampires didn't crawl around on the floor, but I was on edge. Sleep-deprived. Hormonally repressed. *Desperate*.

I wasn't sure what I intended to do. It wasn't like I was going to glue the plate back on and carry the darned thing around as if nothing had happened.

Okay, so maybe I was *thinking* about it. Other than the glob of glue where the plate had been, it was a brilliant knock-off. It looked like Prada. Even more, it *felt* like it. At least for the few moments I'd let myself forget about the guy in the alley and the fact that I'd paid zilch for it.

"Hello? I'm out of coffee here." The statement followed the slow creak of the door as the client in room A ducked her head out and waved her cup. She made a visual search of the outer office before her gaze dropped to the spot where I crouched near a potted palm. "I need a refill."

"I, um, was just on my way to get some more. We've had a busy day." I forced myself to my feet and ignored the urge to shove my hand into the planter and feel around in the soil. I'd heard the plate hit the floor, which meant it had to be on the floor.

Unless it had bounced.

"Excuse me a second." I shoved my fingers into the moist dirt and felt around while my newest client stared at me as if I'd grown a halo.

"What are you doing?"

"Plant massage." I pulled my hands free and did my best to dust off the dirt. "It's the latest thing in gardening. Makes the darned things double in size just like that." I took her coffee cup. "Let me just get you a glass of ice water instead."

"I don't want a glass of ice water. I want a coffee. And another scone."

I forced a smile. "I'll just dash over to Starbucks." Taking the long way, of course. I wasn't in any hurry to run into my stalker again.

On the other hand, he'd had an armful of other knock-offs that had looked just as wonderful as the gold mesh. If I were extra careful around the nameplate, the thing would hold together and, *bam*, I'd be riding my Prada high once again.

"Mimi Moseley over at Match Me has donuts."

"Excuse me?"

"Not the glazed either. We're talking *filled*. Strawberry filled, with powdered sugar on top."

"Meaning?"

"I think I'd be a lot more relaxed sitting next to an overflowing box of my favorite donuts instead of drinking ice water and *waiting* for scones. This thing's too complicated anyway." She waved her questionnaire at me. "Christ, it's dating, not rocket science. I'm out of here."

"Wait. I can get Krispy Kremes. I can get anything you want." Desperation welled inside me. It was crazy. She was just *one* client. One itty, bitty, teeny, tiny single in a city over four million strong. At the same time, a good businesswoman valued every client, and I needed all the help I could get. "Don't go."

"This place is lame."

"No, it's not. It's the latest and greatest. Hands on meets high tech. Guaranteed."

"You can't even guarantee coffee. How are you going to follow through with a soul mate?"

Good question. "But—" My words drowned in the tremble of the bell that shook as she pushed through the door.

I barely ignored the urge to rush through the door, tackle her on the sidewalk, and drag her back inside. *One* client would not make or break me. My business wasn't down the drain. Okay, so technically it was, but I was unplugging things slowly, but surely. I'd be floating to the top in no time.

Besides, most clients weren't after the freebies. If the woman was that picky with her donuts—strawberry filled with powdered sugar? pulease—I didn't stand a chance in hell of hooking her up with a guy. Picky I didn't need. I needed clients who were more desperate than picky. Lonely. With zero expectations.

They were out there, and any second one of them would waltz through my door. He or she would be drop-dead gorgeous, with an open pocketbook and zero expectations. He/she would whiz through the application, and I would match 'em up in no time. Score one for Lil, zero for the picky, donut-loving Antichrist.

Okay, so maybe drop-dead was setting the bar a little high, I decided a half hour later when the doorbell trembled and a man walked in. I had to settle for clean-cut. And bald. With lousy taste in clothes.

"Welcome to Dead End Dating. Scone?" I'd zoomed out and restocked while licking my wounds.

He shook his head, and I smiled. "I'm not really hungry. I just want a date," he said.

"How are you with questionnaires?"

"If you've got a pencil, I'm good to go."

My night was definitely looking up.

"Let's see . . ." I stared at the carefully filled-out questionnaire a short fifteen minutes later—the guy was fast—and read some of the specifics. "You really want someone who enjoys long walks in Central Park and Italian food."

"That's right."

"It says here that you like action-adventure flicks."

He nodded. "This past Christmas my buddies at work got together and gave me a year's worth of AMC movie passes as a present."

But he wasn't half as anxious to use his freebies as he was to whip out the new pair of handcuffs stashed in his briefcase.

The thought struck as I stared into his hazel eyes with my ultra-vamp vision. I stiffened as an image rushed at me. While I couldn't see an overall picture—just an arm here, a leg there—I knew it was a woman by the way she gasped as the cold steel bit into the soft flesh of her small wrists.

My nose wrinkled against the sharp scent of oil.

Wait a second . . . Handcuffs. Oil. Cold steel and soft flesh and . . . *No way.* No friggin' *way.*

The kidnapper?

Definitely.

Probably.

Maybe.

There was only one way to find out.

"You've come to the right matchmaker. I've got the perfect woman for you."

Twenty

❤ ❤ ❤

"I've got the perfect woman," Evie declared the next evening.

It was barely eight o'clock, and we were sitting in my office on either side of my desk. Mocha latte steamed from a Starbucks cup near Evie and sent wisps of white curling through the air between us. Since I'd walked in an hour ago, we'd been searching our current list of clients for the perfect match for Hunka-hunka-handcuffs. In between fielding phone calls, setting up room A for the evening's client appointments, and admiring each other's accessories—rhinestone bangle for me and bohemian beads for Evie—that is.

I know. If I thought he was the kidnapper, what the hell was I doing?

The whole point was to prove his guilt. Which

meant fixing him up, following him, and nailing him
to the wall before he actually hurt anyone.

Evie didn't know this, of course. To her, we were
just setting up an eager client.

She set aside the stack of paperwork she'd been
leafing through. We'd had a mini client rush over the
past few days, and so she hadn't had time to put
everything into the computer. I say *she* because my
typing skills are right up there with my knack for
dealing out death and destruction to helpless humans.
Not happenin'.

"Get this," she told me. Bohemian beads clicked
together as she held up one of the questionnaires.
"Her name is Roxie. She's a bungee-jumping fanatic
who loves Thai food. She's had a total of ten broken
bones *and* two concussions, and her favorite actor is
Vin Diesel." Her excited gaze collided with mine. "If
that doesn't say action-adventure, I don't know what
does."

I gave up my own search and reached across the
desk to have a closer look. I scanned the questions
and answers, and a smile lit my face.

"Looks like we have a match." I handed her the information on last night's Most Wanted. "Get them on
the phone and let's set up a date."

That's *date*, not felony. I valued my clients far too
much to let one of them get dead. Especially one
who'd forked over an obscene amount—thank you,
Roxie—for the cream of the crop hook-up package
that included personalized service from yours truly

and a free groom's cake should she tie the knot with a Dead End match.

But while I wasn't going to let her get hurt, I *was* going to use her for bait. I had to. I wasn't exactly the picture of vampiric nutrition. I'd been bottling it for so long that I'd forgotten what fresh-from-the-vein blood tasted like, and how keen it kept the senses. There was a big possibility that I was no longer the sharpest knife in the silverware drawer and that I was way off base about the handcuffs.

Yeah, right.

Who am I kidding? I knew I wasn't *that* far off. But I wasn't making that phone call to Ty Bonner until I was one hundred percent sure. I didn't want him thinking I was an idiot. No, I wanted him desperately in debt to me for saving his ass. Enough so that he would gladly agree to a date with Esther. One date would lead to two. Two to three. Three to matching coffins and a joint account at the local blood bank.

Hey, it could happen.

On top of my professional reasons for wanting to nab the kidnapper, I couldn't seem to forget the face of the latest missing woman. I'd spent another sleepless day, tossing and turning and thinking about sordid, twisted serial killers.

And Ty.

And hot sex with Ty.

That was *so* not happening.

I was through with dead-end relationships. I wanted happily ever after. While I couldn't have my own at this moment due to an extremely demanding career and a totally happening social life, I was still one hundred percent committed to helping others find romantic bliss. Also, if I hooked up Esther and Ty, I could totally cross him off the hot sex list. I didn't do committed vamps any more than I did made ones. Ix-nay any and all ideas about stripping Ty bare and licking him from head to toe.

No, I had my duty as Manhattan's latest and greatest to sacrifice my own fleeting sexual gratification for the good of all vampkind. And so I was going to set up a date, follow Hunka-hunka-handcuffs, and wait for him to make a move. Then I would save the day, forget the missing girls, match up Ty and Esther, and get back to sleeping like the dead again.

"Surprise!"

I'd just settled down to check my e-mail when I heard the familiar female voice.

At least I thought it was a female voice. But when I turned toward the doorway, I saw what looked like a gigantic flower arrangement with legs.

"Melissa?"

"I hope you like flowers." A hand parted the arrangement and a familiar face stared back at me. "I know you're probably busy, but I just had to thank you again for the date with Francis. It was a night I'll never forget."

"That's great. Really great." *Not.* "But you didn't have to go to so much trouble."

"It's nothing compared to what you've done for me."

"But I really haven't done anything."

"Of course you have. Matching up soul mates is a huge deal."

"About that . . . How do you *really* know that he's your soul mate?"

"I felt a connection with him like nothing I've ever felt before. It grabbed me. Right here." She touched her chest.

"Maybe it was indigestion. Sometimes catered food can really get to you. Especially the Swedish meatballs." Not that I knew firsthand, but I'd watched enough episodes of *Bridezilla* to know the complete lowdown when it came to waltzing down the aisle.

"True." She looked thoughtful for a moment before shaking her head. "No, I'm sure it was Francis and not the meatballs. You said he liked me. He did, didn't he?"

"Sure, um, yeah, he did."

"Then he's probably just too busy to call." She glanced at her own watch. "Speaking of which, I really should be getting home. I've got a ton of things to do, and I really don't want to miss his call if he feels like talking tonight. If you happen to talk to him, tell him . . . just tell him I had fun. That is, if he says he had fun. If he doesn't say anything, don't bring it up." Her anxious gaze collided with mine. "Unless you think you should bring it up. You are the expert, so you probably know just the right way to approach these things. I'm sure you're a genius when it comes to reading body language."

"I wouldn't say genius." *I* wouldn't say it. But that

didn't mean that I had a problem hearing it from someone else. "In my line of work, it pays to be intuitive. Don't worry about a thing. I'm sure he's dying to call, but there's some life-or-death issue keeping him busy right now."

"You think?"

"Of course." I know, I know. I should have stomped her hopes and dreams into my new Persian rug right then and there. But experts/geniuses didn't snuff out dreams, particularly when they were wearing a pair of three-inch Christian Louboutin slingbacks.

On top of that, she looked so hopeful that I couldn't bring myself to tell her she would have better luck marrying Brad Pitt.

"Don't worry about a thing. Go home, put it out of your mind, and just let things happen."

"I owe you, Lil. And once we get married, I intend to pay you back in full."

"Excuse me?"

"Our firstborn, silly. We're naming her after you. Unless it's a he. Then it'll be Francis, Junior. But otherwise, you're going to have a namesake."

"I don't know what to say. That's so . . ."— irrational, unrealistic, delusional—"sweet," I finally said, blinking frantically against the moisture that sprang to my eyes. "That's really sweet." Well, it *was*.

"It's the least I can do." She closed the door before I could say another word—and dig the hole even deeper—and I found myself staring at a slightly wilted red rose.

My earlier high seemed to deflate.

Marriage? Kids?

Shit, what had I done?

I spent the next thirty seconds mentally kicking my own ass. But ass kicking didn't do much when it came to solving problems. And that's what I needed. To solve this problem. Now.

I figured I had only three options. One, I could actually encourage Francis to meet with her again. He could use his elite vampire skills to "suggest" that they'd had an awful time at the wedding and that she hated him.

The thing was, Francis wasn't too savvy in the vamping department (remember the Italian grandmother?), which meant I couldn't totally trust that another meeting would kill the attraction. It could backfire. Melissa might be so overwhelmed by lust for Francis (go figure) and jump his bones before he could so much as say boo, much less vamp her. Talk about undermining my entire project. The point was to find him an eternity mate, not get him laid.

Possibility number two: I could simply put the poor girl out of her misery before she fell any harder for a vamp she absolutely, positively could not have. I was a vicious bloodsucker, after all. But as I've said, murder and mayhem weren't really my lifestyle choices. Which left the third possibility: find Melissa another match and make her forget all about Francis.

I browsed my database and leafed through the questionnaires Evie had left on my desk until I'd singled out two possibilities—a guy who researched preservatives for a local food corporation and one who mapped out sewer routes for New York City. I hoped Melissa would be so distracted by their total hotness—they were both *really* cute—that she wouldn't notice the lack of personality.

"Melissa," I said to her answering machine a few minutes later (apparently she hadn't made it home yet). "This is Lil. I know you had a wonderful time with Francis, but as owner and quality control president of Dead End Dating, I'm obligated to provide at least two more matches for you. We guarantee three, after all, and because you're one of my favorite customers, I'm going to pick up the tab for both dates. Just my way of saying thanks for being such a good client. All you have to do is show up, and your charm and smile will do the rest." I left the dinner dates and times for two of New York's top restaurants and informed her that her dates would be eagerly awaiting her arrival. "When it comes to the future, a girl can't sell herself short by falling for the first warm body she meets." Or lukewarm, in Francis's case. Hey, he was a vamp. "You owe it to yourself to explore all of your options. Have fun." I hung up.

Problem solved.

"I've got Roxie, the Vin Diesel fan, on line one," Evie said from the doorway. "She says she's busy all this week. She can't make a date until next weekend at the earliest."

I thought about the missing girl and my desperate hormones. "Tell her to cancel. This is urgent."

"Urgent?" Evie gave me an odd look.

"You've heard the saying . . . Love waits for no man. Or woman."

"That's time. Love is patient and kind."

"What are you? An inspirational calendar?"

She grinned. "I love those things. My uncle Bernie gives me one every year." Her expression faded. "And speaking of Uncle Bernie, Louisa Wilhelm called and said she's ready for prospect number two. I told her not to worry and you would be calling her ASAP. You will be calling her ASAP, won't you?"

"Probably."

"And we do have a prospect number two, don't we?"

"Sort of."

"That's what I thought. Why don't you deal with line one and I'll go fill out our application for bankruptcy?"

"Remind me to give you a raise for unyielding optimism."

I knew Evie was joking, but I couldn't shake the fear that niggled deep down in my gut. But it went beyond the worry over falling flat on my face and tending the counter at Moe's night after night. I was afraid that maybe, just maybe, my mother was right. Maybe true love was just a crazy idea thought up by humans to sell books and movie tickets and celebrity perfume. Maybe there was no real emotional bond between two individuals. No cosmic connection. No true soul mate.

Maybe it *was* all about the sex and orgasm quotients and fertility ratings.

I forced aside the dismal if slightly titillating thought. I had a much more pressing issue at the moment. I had to convince Miss Action-Adventure why she simply had to drop all and rearrange her schedule to meet a man.

As if he might be The One who would totally and completely change her life.

He couldn't.

But he could change someone else's if I didn't expose him in time.

I reached for the receiver, pasted on my most persuasive smile, and punched the blinking button for line one.

If I hadn't been dangling just this side of sanity thanks to another sleepless day, the Melissa dilemma, and a useless search for Louisa Wilhelm's next prospect, the forty-five-minute cab ride with Francis would have pushed me right to the edge.

It was Thursday evening, and I'd picked him up at his place for the next step in his metamorphosis.

"You've got the look nailed," I told him as the cab rolled to a stop in front of our destination—an enormous Colonial-style mansion that sat next door to my parents' estate in Fairfield, Connecticut. I adjusted the slightly crooked collar of his black silk Gucci shirt and smoothed the edge. My fingers brushed his jaw, and his ears turned a bright pink. "From here on out, it's all about attitude. The way you perceive yourself. Your charisma."

"I don't have charisma."

"Exactly, and you won't ever develop any if you don't stop with the blushing."

"I can't help it."

"Of course you can't. You're completely and totally uncomfortable around the opposite sex. But all that's going to change tonight. Keep her running," I told the cabdriver before reaching for the door and climbing from the backseat.

"Do you really think this will work?" Francis asked as he followed me up the stone walkway to the front door.

"It can't hurt."

"Actually, it could. In case you haven't heard, werewolves are the enemy."

"It's not the Middle Ages, Francis. Werewolves have evolved. They own property and pay their taxes and put their pants on one leg at a time just like the rest of us."

"Unless it's a full moon."

"We all have our flaws. Stop being so negative. This is going to work." It had to work. No way was I going to hook up Francis if he looked ready to self-combust every time a woman glanced at him. I came to a halt at the massive double doors and pressed the doorbell. A belled version of "Born to Be Wild" by Steppenwolf echoed from inside the house. A few seconds later, a tall, attractive woman with long, brown hair and equally dark eyes pulled open the door.

Viola Hamilton looked like any other filthy rich werewolf living in Connecticut. She wore a flaming red Christian Dior pantsuit, reeked of Chanel No. 5, and had a RE-ELECT MAYOR BRADLEY LIVINGSTON sign perched on her lawn.

Bradley Livingston was a werewolf and a liberal, and both equaled the Antichrist as far as my conservative father was concerned.

I, myself, rather liked the Cher impersonation Bradley had done at the annual Founder's Day Dinner and Dance. You gotta love a man who can pull off fishnet and thigh-high boots.

"Can I help you?"

"It's me, Miss Hamilton. Lil. Lil Marchette from next door."

Her bright red lips drew into a tight line. "If you're here with another one of your father's petitions, you can take it and stick it straight—"

"I don't have a petition," I cut in. "Just a meat loaf." I held up the foil-covered dish. "The best in Manhattan."

"A meat loaf." Her nostrils flared, and a look of euphoria glazed her eyes for a brief moment. "I'm afraid I don't understand," she finally said.

"I know you and my father don't actually get along, but—"

"He called the pound last week and reported a wild pack of strays terrorizing his property," she cut in. "First off, they weren't strays. I was having a dinner party that included two senators and a chief of police. Second, we didn't go within five feet of his precious property."

"Maybe he was just playing a joke. He's always been a prankster."

"He's crazy."

I started to protest (he *was* my father), but then I remembered the color scheme he'd picked out for the Moe's uniform. I shrugged and nodded. "That doesn't mean we can't be friends, does it? I would never call the pound on anyone. Live and let live. That's my motto." Liar. But I didn't think Viola would be nearly as impressed by "shop 'til you drop." "We're all stuck here together, so we might as well get along and help each other out."

Her gaze narrowed. "What exactly do you want?"

"This is Francis." I tugged him up beside me. "He's an ancient vamp who's never met his eternity mate. In fact, he's barely had sex. Overall, he's just not all that comfortable with women. He's always been more of a hermit, living alone, avoiding social situations. He really needs to get out more."

"And you're telling me this because?"

"He wants to join the NUNS."

She eyed him for a long moment. "He's a vampire."

"A small technicality."

"A male vampire."

"Barely, on both counts."

She smiled, and the tension that had coiled in the air seemed to ease. "My dear, we call ourselves a sisterhood because we're all women."

"Vibrant, exciting, sexy women," I added. *And naked.* "Which is why I'm bringing him to you."

"What do you have to do with this anyway?"

I pulled a card from my sequined clutch. I was

banking on the whole honesty's-the-best-policy theory. "I've just opened a matchmaking service and Francis is one of my clients. He's eager to find an eternity mate, but that's not going to happen until he stops purring like a kitten and starts roaring like a lion. But he can't roar since he's too busy blushing. It's a terrible habit he has because of his lack of interaction with the opposite sex. I would drop him off at my mother's huntress club, but those are the very women I'll be trying to hook him up with later. Human women aren't much help because they're too easily wowed by all vamps."

She nodded. "Such weak creatures."

"Since female vampires and werewolves are alike in that we gravitate toward the king of the jungle when it comes to mating," I went on, "I thought being around a group of women like yourself might help Frank get over his awkwardness."

"And why would I want to help?"

Honesty, I reminded myself. *Just be open and up front and honest.* "Because it's the neighborly thing to do?" She frowned. "Because you appreciate a good meat loaf?" She seemed to think about that one before her frown deepened. "Because I'll guarantee that my father will stop cutting down the eastern bushes?"

"Those are *my* bushes. They're on my side of the property line, and your father has no right to hack them to nothing."

"He thinks he does."

"He needs to learn how to read a property survey." She eyed me. "How are you going to guarantee such a thing?"

"I have my ways."

"Coercion?"

I was thinking more along the lines of begging and pleading, but instead I said, "Exactly."

She stared at me a moment before she finally nodded. What can I say? While honesty's nice, bribery (with a side of meat loaf) gets results.

Her gaze shifted to Francis, and she eyed him. "Nice shirt," she said, and watched as his face turned as bright as her lipstick. "It usually takes a good feeding to get the cheeks that color."

"Tell me about it," I said.

"It's a full moon this weekend. Which means we won't be our usual selves." Her eyes glittered, and Francis swallowed. "We'll be better. Do you think you can handle it?"

"No."

"Which is the very reason you have to try," I told him.

"I don't know about this," he murmured, as Viola stepped back and motioned him inside. "I really think I should go home. I may have left the stove on."

"You don't cook." I glared at him. "More importantly, you don't eat."

"But where will I sleep? It's not like they have coffins."

"You don't sleep in a coffin."

"That's not the point. The point is, they're"—he lowered his voice to a whisper—"different."

"I heard that," Viola said.

"They're not *that* different. They're just a little . . . ferocious."

"Exactly."

"Vamp women are ferocious, too." He'd never seen me at a Macy's two-for-one. "Stop being such a wuss. I'm sure Viola has a nice wine cellar where you can crash."

"That, or he can take his pick of the walk-in closets."

"See? You'll be fine." I gave him a forceful shove. "I'll pick you up Sunday night."

Viola winked at me before turning a hungry smile on Francis. "Provided there's anything left to pick up."

TWenty-one
❤ ❤ ❤

A thrill raced up my spine as I stepped out of a cab on East Twelfth Street in the West Village. I'd made it back from Connecticut just in time for the meeting between Action-Adventure Girl and Hunka-hunka-handcuffs. The site of tonight's rendezvous? The Gotham Bar and Grill.

It was Friday evening, and activity buzzed all around me. People climbed in and out of the subway entrance near the corner. Cabs zipped up and down the street. The blare of horns filled the air. The fresh aroma of bread drifted from a bakery just across the street and mingled with the sharp scent of cigars that came from a nearby tobacco shop.

I'd had the driver drop me a block up—the key tonight was to watch and wait, which meant keeping a low profile—and my heart beat faster as I strolled toward the restaurant. Casual. Unhurried. Just a well-dressed, attractive woman out for an evening of fun.

Who was I kidding?

This was New York.

I picked up my steps, dodged a fire hydrant, and ignored the whistles of a group of teenage boys and a "Come to Daddy" from a white-haired old man who looked more like my great, great-granddaddy.

It was a half hour after the scheduled meeting time. Which meant the couple had already met and were probably in the middle of the first course. I was just a few feet shy of my destination when a cab pulled up just ahead and a familiar woman climbed out. I recognized Action-Adventure Girl from her photograph and dove behind a businessman who was walking just to my right to avoid being seen.

"Hey, watch it," he said when my hand closed over his shoulder and my preternatural strength (just call me Popeye with fangs) brought him to a jarring stop. "You shouldn't—" His words stalled as he turned and his annoyed gaze captured mine.

I gave him my brightest smile. "Jake? Jake Abernathy?"

"The name's Phil."

"Really?" I shook my head. "Why, you look just like Jake. You could practically be his twin." I glanced past him to see Miss A-A pay the cabdriver and start up the walk toward the restaurant's entrance.

I made a mental note to check *punctuality* off her list of character assets and pencil in *desperately late*.

"It's been ages since I've seen Jake. I certainly couldn't let him get away without saying hi. But since you're not him . . . Sorry."

He smiled. "Any time." He started to turn, but Miss A-A stopped just outside the restaurant doorway. She stood out front and glanced up the street before her gaze swept my direction.

"Since you offered." I pulled Tall, Dark, and Anytime directly in front of me, his thick build no match for my superduper vamp strength. Surprise registered in his gaze before the expression seemed to fade into one of pure bliss. "Could you just stand here for a second?" I asked just to be polite, but I didn't have to bother. He wouldn't have moved to save his life. He couldn't have.

What can I say? I'm total man candy when I want to be.

"There's someone I know whom I'm trying to avoid," I added. Just because I was man candy didn't mean I had to be rude man candy.

"Jake?" His look grew ferocious as if he meant to rip the guy apart.

"Just a friend. Now calm down. Just stand here for a second." *And don't move,* I added silently. *Don't try to hug or kiss or touch me, either. Just stare adoringly at me and keep your mouth shut.*

He did. He stood stock-still, his body shielding mine as I stared up at him with an adoring expression. To the world, we looked like a couple happily into each other.

I ticked off the seconds as I waited for the woman to go into the restaurant.

Endless moments passed before another cab pulled up and Mr. Hunka-hunka-handcuffs crawled out. Obviously, he wasn't any more punctual than she was.

I was definitely on top of my game when it came to this matchmaking thing.

They introduced themselves, shook hands, and did the usual small talk before finally walking into the restaurant.

"You sure are beautiful."

I breathed a sigh of relief and turned my attention to my human shield.

"Excuse me?"

"You're gorgeous."

Duh.

"You're sweet, but this just isn't going to work. I need good looks and fangs, and a decent fertility rating. I'm afraid you're only one out of three." He gave me a dumbfounded look, and I smiled. "Not that it's your fault, but it's just not meant to be." Before he could respond, I stared deeply into his eyes and willed him to forget all about me.

He didn't; not that I could blame him. The man candy thing again. But he did space out long enough for me to dart past him and head into the restaurant.

I slipped inside, found a nice spot at the end of the bar where I could sit discreetly and sip ice water while listening to the conversation, or lack of, at the small, quaint table on the far side of the room.

"So do you like music?" Hunka-hunka-handcuffs asked.

"Not really," replied Action-Adventure.

"What about dancing?"

"Sort of. I mean, I do aerobics. And Pilates. There's always music playing in the background, so that sort of counts. What about you?"

"I don't do Pilates."

"I meant dancing. Do you?"

"I like dancing, but it doesn't like me."

"Sorry."

"Me, too."

Forget a matchmaker; these two needed divine intervention.

I ordered a club soda and tried not to grimace at the raw oyster appetizer being sucked up by the woman next to me. For the life of me, I couldn't figure out the appeal of the slimy, mucuslike seafood. And people actually got queasy at the sight of blood? Give me a break.

I turned my attention back to the couple.

"So I heard that you like Vin Diesel?"

"Well, I don't actually like him. Just the sunglasses. And the leather pants. I really like leather pants."

"Really? I have a pair of leather pants."

"No way!"

"And a matching vest."

"Wow."

"I thought I lost you." The deep voice sounded right in my ear, and I jumped.

"What? Where?" I whirled. My elbow bumped the

platter of oysters and sent them flying over the edge of the bar.

"I'm so sorry," I told the woman. Not. I signaled the bartender to bring her a new platter, on me, before I turned toward the man towering over me, a smile on his face and lust in his eyes.

"You haven't changed a bit," Phil told me. "You still look every bit as sexy as I remember."

"It's only been fifteen minutes since I last saw you."

"The longest fifteen minutes of my life. Let me buy you a drink."

"I've already got a drink."

"Then let me buy you another."

"Mine is still full."

"Then I'll just sit here with you until you finish and then I'll buy you another." He whipped out his wallet, tossed several twenties at the oyster sucker until she gave up her seat, and then settled down in her spot. He tugged at his tie to loosen it and stared longingly at me. "You're really pretty."

"Thanks." I stared deep into his eyes and willed him to leave me alone. He stiffened, and I knew the message had registered in his brain. And then he blinked, and out it went.

"Would you like something to eat to go with the ice water? I'd be happy to buy you some oysters. Or steak. Or lobster. Or lobster and steak . . ."

His voice faded as I shifted my attention back to the couple across the room.

". . . *love Madonna, too.*"

"*I'm a total Madonna fan. Pre-Marilyn phase.*"

"I actually liked her during the Marilyn phase. And the stuff after—"

"Come on," Phil said as he took my hand and snagged my attention again. "Tell me what you'd like to eat."

"Trust me," I told him. "You really don't want to know."

He obviously thought I was flirting because he smiled, leaned in front of me, and blocked my line of vision. "I'd love to buy you dinner. Or we could just go straight for the dessert."

"All right, all right." I leaned toward his right and peered around him. "You can buy me another drink."

"But you're not done with the first." He indicated my full glass that sat on the bar.

I turned and downed the ice water in one gulp. "There. All gone and ready for number two."

"Great." He smiled as if I'd just opened up my cookie jar and handed him a great big double-stuffed Oreo.

As if.

I ordered another ice water and watched Hunka-hunka-handcuffs pull out his wallet to reveal an official Madonna Fan Club card. Oy.

"So what do you do?" Phil asked me. He braced his elbow on the bar, rested his chin on his fist, and stared at me as if he'd like to take a big bite. "What's your claim to fame?"

I thought of a dozen responses all intended to scare the crap out of the average heterosexual male—from

Grim Reaper to proctologist—and blurted out the most terrifying. "Wedding consultant."

He didn't so much as blink. "No way." Excitement infused his voice. "I love weddings."

Nix average heterosexual male. This guy was a workaholic, which meant socially deprived, which meant lonely. Which meant he didn't just want to boff me. He wanted to *talk* to me.

"So how long have you been coordinating weddings?" he went on.

"For a long, long time." I shifted my gaze back to the couple and tried a human tactic. Ignore him and he'll go away.

"How long?" Phil persisted.

"Too long." So much for ignoring him. *Shut up*, I willed. *Shut. Up.*

"*. . . never actually joined her fan club, but—what did you just say?" The smile faded from Action-Adventure's face as she stared across the table at her date.*

"*I've been a member since I was sixteen.*"

"*Not that. After that. You told me to shut up," she said accusingly. "You did.*"

"*No, I didn't.*"

Uh-oh. Multitasking was definitely not my strong suit.

"*Really, I didn't say that. It must have been somebody else. I'm interested in what you have to say. Very interested. Please go on.*"

"*Really?*" She eyed him uncertainly and he nodded.

"Please."

"Well, okay. So I thought about joining the fan club after 'Material Girl' came out, but I was busy in high school and my babysitting money was tight and I just didn't get around to it . . ."

"How did you know you wanted to be a wedding coordinator?" The deep voice pushed into my thoughts again.

Get out of here. The command flew from my head before I could stop it.

". . . she wasn't half bad as an actress, either. She's an all-around dynamite performer . . ." Action-Adventure's words stumbled to a halt as she frowned. *"Fine, I'll go."* She tossed her napkin down while Hunka-hunka scrambled to his feet.

"Wait. What's wrong?"

"I appreciate your honesty. This obviously isn't working, and you're in no hurry to prolong the pain. Fine by me. You don't have to say it twice." She snatched up her purse and started for the door.

"But wait—" He bolted to his feet and tried to follow. The tip of his shoe caught the chair and sent it tumbling as he raced after her. *"Wait up."*

I practically jumped off the bar stool.

"Where are you going?" Phil caught my hand.

"Out of here." I tugged free, which really didn't require much tugging at all since I might as well be wearing a great big SV on my chest—Super Vamp in the house. "Alone."

"I'll go with you—" His voice died as I whirled on

him and did something I don't normally do in mixed company: I flashed him a little fang.

"I'm leavinth," I told him, the words cold and deadly and slightly slurred—you try talking with two gargantuan fangs hanging out of your mouth. "And you'll thtay here if you know whath good for you."

His eyes widened and he sank back down to his bar stool. He looked as if I'd kicked his favorite puppy.

Okay, so he looked more like I'd eaten his favorite puppy, and a pang of guilt shot through me.

"I *have* to go," The fangs retracted. My voice lost its frosty edge and the speech impediment. "But call me sometime." I handed him one of my business cards and his fear vanished at the brush of my hand against his. "I'll hook you up with someone. Not with me," I rushed on. "But someone else. Someone just as nice." When he didn't look all that excited, I added, "Someone just as nice, and just as hot."

What can I say? I'm a softie. In the interest of good business, of course. Lonely? *Check*. Desperate? *Check*. Well-dressed professional with lots to offer but not enough finesse to meet the right woman? *Check*. This guy was a matchmaker's dream come true; therefore, I couldn't leave him with the impression that I was Queen of the Damned.

"We'll talk later," I promised.

"But—"

I was already pushing my way to the door before he could say anything else.

"Excuse me." I tapped the maître d' on the back as I shouldered my way through the entrance. "Did you see a couple just leave here? Tall guy, sort of balding? He was with a redhead with a Madonna fetish?"

He pointed to the left, and I swiveled my head in time to see the duo disappear into the back of a cab just up the street. The door slammed, the brake lights dimmed, and the yellow Chevy swerved into the flow of traffic.

I spent the next ten minutes trying to hail a cab of my own before I finally gave up and decided to go it on foot. I wasn't sure where they were going, but I knew that if my hunch was correct and he did turn out to be the kidnapper, he would have to take her someplace private. That meant his place. Or hers. Or a third, undisclosed location where he took his victims, in which case I was out of luck because the Dead End Dating profile didn't list a blank for PLEASE LIST A THIRD, UNDISCLOSED LOCATION PERFECT FOR SLICING AND DICING VICTIMS. As for the first two . . .

I decided to head for Action-Adventure's SoHo apartment as fast as my shoes could carry me—pretty fast considering I had the whole preternatural speed thing going for me and I'd actually toned down my look—low profile, remember?—and worn a pair of low-heeled Christian Louboutins I'd gotten on sale at Barney's.

Okay, *okay.* So Barney's didn't actually put Christian Louboutins on sale, but they were very moderately priced considering the designer, and so I hadn't been able to pass them up.

But that's neither here nor there. The point was, I

couldn't leap any tall buildings in a single bound, not without kissing my low-profile image good-bye, but I did make quick work of the sidewalks and give new meaning to the phrase *power walking*.

I arrived to find the street empty. Which meant they'd beaten me here and Action-Adventure had already gone inside. Or they'd opted for his address.

I walked up the front steps and buzzed her apartment and waited. Nothing. She obviously wasn't home.

I'd just turned to head back down the steps when I heard the peel of tires. Yellow flashed in my peripheral vision, and my head swiveled. I saw the cab catch the far corner and barrel up the street toward me. My heart jumped into my throat, and I glanced frantically to my left. I leapt over the railing and dropped to the ground. Fading into the shadows of the next building, I watched as the cab peeled to a stop.

The door opened and both Action-Adventure and Hunka-hunka climbed out. Obviously they'd resolved the whole "get out of here" issue, because both seemed happy. They laughed and smiled as they climbed the steps to the front door of her apartment building. They held hands until they reached the top step.

Hand-holding? Laughing? Smiling? *Kissing?*

I watched them embrace and started to think that maybe I'd been wrong. Maybe this guy wasn't the kidnapper. Maybe the handcuffs I'd glimpsed when I'd looked into his eyes had just been some sort of leftover impression from a freaky movie.

Maybe.

Probably.

"You have the prettiest eyes."

Okay, so it was the cheesiest line ever invented, but with the moon so full and bright overhead—so romantic—it actually sounded kind of sweet.

Awww . . .

No way was this sweetheart of a guy—however unoriginal—a cold-blooded kidnapper.

"I really had a nice time," Action-Adventure murmured when they came up for air.

"So did I." He leaned in and kissed her again, tenderly, as if he had all the time in the world and he wanted to spend it with her.

Deep sigh.

"I would love to do it again," she told him. "That is, if you want to."

"Actually"—he slid his hand up her back to the nape of her neck and threaded his fingers into her hair—"I *would* like to do it again." His grip tightened, and she stiffened. "But I'm done with nice." He urged her backward into the building. The door slammed shut.

Ohmigod. OHMIGOD. OH. MY. GOD.

This was it. He was it. He was the guy and he was going to . . . And I was going to . . .

I had to stop it. First, I had to call Ty, and then I had to stop it. No, first I had to call Ty, wait for him to get here to catch the guy just this side of a felony, and then I had to stop it. Yeah, that was it. That was the plan.

I whipped out my cell phone, punched in his number, and waited for him to pick up.

"Get over here right now," I said the moment I heard his deep *"Hey."*

"Who is this?"

"It's Lil, and I've got your kidnapper. He's right here, and he's about to nab another one." Nab? Since when did I say nab? Oh, yeah. Since I'd decided to lurk in alleyways in order to catch serial kidnappers in the interest of my business. "Hurry!" I gave him the address, punched the off button, and racked my brain for some way to stall what was happening until Ty could get here.

I rummaged through my purse and pulled out a miniature can of hairspray to use as a weapon if things got too out of hand.

Hairspray? I had fangs, for Pete's sake. What kind of evil creature of the night was I even to think of using a can of aerosol?

Duh. The materialistic kind, of course. I was wearing my new Guess mini tee with the rhinestone etching. Not major dollars, but we're talking *rhinestones,* which require dry cleaning. Nix any spewing blood and flying body parts. While I could subdue him with my superduper strength, I wanted some backup in case he whipped out a weapon of his own.

Can in hand, I willed my feet to leave the ground and floated up to the eighth floor.

I'd peeped into all the windows on one side and was just about to round the corner of the building when I heard the deep, familiar voice behind me.

"Where are they?"

I whirled to find Ty looking as dark and delicious

as ever in a pair of black leather pants and a black T-shirt. He was minus the duster tonight, and I wasn't sure whether to be happy or worried.

I could see the ripples of muscles in his upper arms. The soft material of his T-shirt framed his broad chest and narrow waist. Forget dark and delicious. This guy was positively mouthwatering.

Crazy, considering he was a *made* vampire. It wasn't as if he had even one thing to offer me. Except maybe some really hot sex. He definitely looked capable of that.

"Hello?" His brows drew together into a tight frown that snapped me out of my trek down into the gutter where raunchy sex reigned supreme and fertility ratings didn't mean a hill of beans.

"You're fast." *Waaay original, Lil.* Of course he was fast. He was a vampire.

"Where are they?" he asked again.

"Somewhere on this floor." I moved around the corner, and he followed. Several windows later, at the very rear of the square structure, we hit pay dirt.

"I knew it," I said as I stared through the window and watched Hunka-hunka knot a black blindfold firmly over Action-Adventure's eyes. Her hands were secured behind her back with the handcuffs I'd glimpsed in his thoughts. He held a menacing-looking leather belt in one hand and a large black vibrator in the other—wait a second.

"I don't think he's kidnapping her." Ty said a few heartbeats later while we watched the scene unfolding before our eyes.

"No, he's definitely not kidnapping her," I managed to croak out the words despite my suddenly dry throat.

He was doing something a hundred times more pleasurable. And I was watching with Ty Bonner, of all vampires.

Hot, hunky, I-wish-he'd-touch-me-like-that-and-do-even-more *Ty*.

Yowza.

Twenty-two
❤ ❤ ❤

Like, I know I should be concerned with being spotted hovering outside someone's eighth-story window, but I'm not.

We're talking in-your-face and the reason Bigfoot and his buddies no longer exist. My dad had raked in the big bucks betting with colleagues on how many pictures it would take for SOB to find the colony and take the poor furry things out (SOB being Snipers of Otherworldly Beings aka vamp/were/anything-that-goes-bump-in-the-night hunters). All in all, the Bigfeet had been annihilated in a matter of minutes and all because a few of them had been suckers for the paparazzi.

Sure, I was on the backside of the apartment complex with nothing but an alleyway beneath me. But I was floating in full view of the surrounding buildings, not to mention the bondage duo on the other side of the window. Talk about scary. Or it would have been if my radar had extended beyond the made vampire who was hovering directly behind me.

There was nothing sweet or sugary about the man. He smelled of fresh air and raw, rugged strength, and leather. The mix was musky and potent, and I breathed it in. My stomach grumbled in response. A crazy reaction, I knew. I was supposed to get off on rich and decadent and *born*. Sweet scents, I reminded myself. There was nothing remotely sweet about Ty Bonner.

No wonder I wanted him.

Want?

Okay, so I did want him. In a bad way. Not that I was acting on it. There were a zillion reasons why Ty was not the vamp for me. He wasn't born. I'd given up wasting my time with temporary flings. He didn't even know what a fertility rating was. I'd given up wasting my time with temporary flings. He could care less about my orgasm quotient. I'd given up . . . Wait a second? What was it I'd given up?

I tried to remember, but my brain was fogged with Ty's essence. Suddenly, I couldn't seem to concentrate. I trembled and my body swayed, and my balance took a nosedive.

"Easy," Ty murmured. One large hand slid around my waist, and he pulled me back up against his hard length. His lips brushed my ear, and a shiver went down my spine. "What's wrong with you?" he murmured. "Did you feed tonight?"

"No." I did, of course. But I wasn't about to tell him that because then I would have to tell him why I'd lost my balance. *You just smell so good and it's scrambling my brain.* Not! "I've been really busy tonight. I was going to get a bite later after I managed to catch up on things."

"Most vampires feed first and work later." His palm settled fully against my tummy and held me firmly against him. "Then again, you're not most vampires. At least none I've ever met."

The comment sent a rush of tingles through my body. I had the overwhelming urge to turn in his arms and press my body up against his. My nipples tightened and my mouth went dry. My ears prickled and the frantic *zip, zip* of cars on the nearby streets faded into the steady thump of his pulse. Slow and sure and mesmerizing. Hunger gnawed inside me. I wanted to taste him almost as much as I wanted to touch him.

Almost.

I swallowed against the urge and tried to get a grip on myself. *Think! Remember what's important.*

Oh, yeah. Fertility ratings, wasn't it? I had to think of the future. It was all about finding the perfect born vamp with the highest fertility rating and making perfect little baby vamps.

Or was it? I drew another deep draft of air and breathed Ty in, and, suddenly, I wasn't so sure. In fact (another deep breath), I'd take sexy over fertile any old day.

"We should go," Ty murmured. "I don't think there's a law against getting your ass spanked." I followed his gaze to the couple and watched as Hunka-hunka bent a very naked Action-Adventure—with the exception of the blindfold and handcuffs—over the bed. He proceeded to swat her with a black feather boa he'd pulled from her nightstand drawer.

She let loose a low, stirring moan, and my stomach quivered.

"Isn't there something on the books about unnecessary force?" I didn't want to go. Not just yet. Not when Ty felt so close and so strong and smelled so delicious.

And, let's face it, it had been *so* long since I'd been close to any male that I was starved for contact.

Hey, that was my story at the moment, and I was sticking to it.

"He's not using force." Ty's deep voice stirred the hair on my neck. "She's provoking him, and he's giving her what she wants."

Action-Adventure struggled against her restraints and let loose a string of curse words that made my ears burn. (A first since I've been around *forever* and have heard every expletive known to man thanks to my three brothers. Heck, I've said most of them a time or two. When provoked, of course.)

"If you keep giving me attitude, I'm going to make you pay," Hunka-hunka told her. "You know that, don't you?"

"Yes," Action-Adventure breathed before she called him a dozen names that brought a smile to his lips.

"If you insist on being a bad girl, then I have no choice but to punish you appropriately. Do you know what happens to bad girls?"

My guess would be another swipe of the black feather boa.

Ty and I both watched as the feathers slid across the pale white flesh of the woman's back. She gasped and moaned, and my skin tingled where Ty's hand rested just above the waistband of my DKNY hip-huggers. I felt his hips press against me from behind, and I could tell he had a hard-on (boy, did he ever). More moaning and panting echoed in my ears—some of it my own, I realized, when I felt his lips graze my ear—and his fingertips curled around my rib cage. His thumb brushed the underside of my breast.

Okay, so vamps didn't really need air. We drew it in and out like everyone else, but it wasn't crucial to our life force. Our hearts kept our rejuvenating blood pumping, and so it was the only truly vital organ in our bodies.

Yet here I was and I couldn't seem to get enough air into my lungs. My breaths came short and shallow. *Panting*, of all things. Every nerve in my body stood at full alert, aware of every scrumptious inch of the man holding me close, screaming for more than the closeness. I wanted naked closeness. Followed by a spectacular orgasm. Followed by another, and another and . . .

"We should leave."

"We should do a lot of things, but leaving isn't one of them." The thought flew out of my mouth before I could stop it. "That is, I mean, unless you want to."

"Not at the moment. At the moment, I'd rather stay right here." He nibbled at my earlobe, and I tipped my head to the side to give him better access.

His own cool breath rushed over my skin a split second before he pressed his lips to the spot. His tongue darted out, and he licked a path from the base of my jaw down the slope of my neck.

It felt so good that I didn't think it could get any better. But then I heard his deep hiss, followed by a low, throaty rumble, and I felt his sharp fangs glide across the tender flesh.

He wanted to bite me. I knew it deep in my gut. Even more, I felt it in the tension that held his body so rigid and the erection pressed up against me.

He wanted me bad.

So why didn't he bite me, already?

Instead, he ran his open mouth up and down the length of my neck, tasting and touching and grazing until I couldn't stand it any longer.

"Are you going to kiss me or what?" I breathed.

And just like that, he was.

He whirled me around and his mouth covered mine so fast that my head went light again and I actually felt myself floating higher and higher.

His lips nibbled at mine before he slid his tongue into my mouth. It was the best kiss of my life, and that was saying a lot since I'd had many kisses and been around for one heck of a long time.

But there was just something about the way he held me and the way he tilted his head as if he couldn't get enough, and the way he tasted, that made me forget all those other times with all those other men.

It was just him. And me.

". . . stop, stop! There's someone outside the window."

Make that him. And me. And the bondage duo.

Ty was pulling away just as my eyes snapped open. Our gazes swiveled toward the window in time to see Action-Adventure scramble out from under a very naked Hunka-hunk.

"See," she shrieked, her eyes widening as she pointed at me. "I told you there was someone out there . . ."

The rest of her words faded as Ty gripped my hand and pulled me to the ground with one fell swoop.

I landed in a greenish-looking puddle that had dripped from a nearby trash can, which would have killed the romantic moment if being caught spying hadn't already done the trick.

"Do you think they'll call the police?" I asked as I examined the gunk on my shoes.

"And tell them there were a couple of vampires levitating outside their eighth-floor bedroom window?"

"Good point."

We stood there a few more moments, an awkward silence stretching between us. "I should really get going. I was in the middle of a ride-along with a homicide detective from the Seventh Precinct. He's up against a murder investigation he can't seem to get a break on. I thought I'd help him out while I'm in town. Never know when I'll need to call in a favor."

"I get it. You scratch his back and he scratches yours."

"Right."

"Right."

I licked my lips and tasted him. My tummy flipped and my heart did a double thump. I had the sudden urge to rip off his shirt and do a little back scratching of my own. Maybe if I scratched his, he would be inclined to scratch mine and then we could—

"Look, this is wrong on so many levels," I blurted before I could venture any further into the land of the crazies. "You . . . me . . . It just isn't going to happen. You know that. I know that. It can't happen."

"You're right. It can't." He winked. "At least not tonight."

Not ever, I wanted to add, but I couldn't seem to make myself say the words. Not with him smiling that little half smile, as if he knew something I didn't. His neon blue eyes crinkled at the corners, and a dimple cut into his dark, shadowed cheek.

Just like that, the expression faded and he frowned. "You shouldn't have set this up yourself," he said, his voice cool and clipped and totally pissed. "If he had turned out to be the kidnapper, you could have made the situation worse. He might have ended up with two victims this time instead of just one."

I managed a sarcastic laugh even though I wanted to (a) punch him in the nose for even suggesting that I couldn't take care of myself and (b) pull him close and kiss him until he smiled at me again. "I can take care of myself and anyone else who comes along." I gave him my best holier-than-thou imitation. "I *am* a vampire, remember?"

"I'm not the one who keeps forgetting." He stared

down at the can that had fallen to the ground when he'd floated up behind me. He bent down and retrieved the small container. "What were you planning to do with this? Give him a makeover?"

"You can't prove that's mine."

"True. It probably belongs to that homeless guy over there. He can't afford a place to live, but he can drop a quick twenty for designer hairspray."

"It was twenty-five and just because I wasn't going to tear Hunka-hunka to shreds if he'd really been the kidnapper doesn't mean I can't." I bared my fangs for a quick moment and snatched the can from him. "This must have fallen out of my purse while I was levitating."

"Sure it did."

"Don't you have a back to scratch?"

"Call if you suspect anybody else."

The *if* niggled at me as I watched Ty disappear down the street. My body trembled, and my nipples stood at attention. My skin felt itchy and tight and needy, and I'd never been so thirsty in my entire life.

Just one drink and I would feel better.

My gaze swiveled to the homeless guy whom Ty had mentioned. He was leaning back against the building, his eyes closed, an empty wine bottle in his hand. The steady beat of his pulse filled my ears. The warm, inviting scent of blood overpowered the smell of stale beer and old tuna fish, and drew me closer.

Ka-thump. Ka-thump. Ka-thump.

I knelt down next to him and willed his eyes open.

His eyelids fluttered. His gaze focused, lit with recognition, and then widened in fear.

"What the . . ." he sputtered.

But then I touched him, just the light press of my fingertips on his arm, and his fear faded. His expression eased into one of pure bliss.

I leaned toward him, and he leaned toward me and . . .

"Come on," he slurred, wanting me more and more with each moment that passed. "Do me, baby."

Do me, baby? The cheesy line pushed past the bloodlust that fogged my senses and jerked me back to reality and the fact that I'd been about to feed off this poor soul.

Even worse, I'd *wanted* to feed off him. To sink my teeth into his neck and feel his life force rush into my mouth. My nipples tingled at the notion, and a wave of remorse washed through me.

Forget matching up everyone else. I needed a date of my own in the worst way. Otherwise . . .

My gaze zeroed in on the smelly drunk, and my stomach did a somersault. I turned and left the alley as fast as my Christian Louboutins could carry me. I headed back to the office with only one thought on my mind: finding someone for myself.

Okay, so I had two thoughts on my mind: finding someone and having mad, passionate, monkey sex with him.

But first things first.

Twenty-three

❤ ❤ ❤

I spent the next two hours reading through various profiles. While I came up empty-handed for *moi,* I did get *très* lucky and come up with a viable date for Mrs. Wilhelm—he was human and only thirty-three, but he appreciated older women and enjoyed ballroom dancing. Not eternity mate material, but good enough for a second "practice" date—which would buy me more time before I had to produce a real prospect.

I also matched up three other clients, including a bank teller from SoHo and a graphic designer who enjoyed jogging in Central Park and eating tofu. I *know.* Talk about hitting the jackpot. Who would think there would be two tofuans in the world? Much less that they'd wander into the same matchmaking service. The third? Jerry Dormfeld aka the guy with the chili dog on the brain who, as it turned out, seemed perfect for Melissa. Even more so than the other two men I'd sent her way to distract her from Francis. *Bingo*.

You would think that several hours of work would have put a serious damper on my libido. But we born vamps aren't sensuous, amorous sexual beings for nothing. By the time I'd left instructions for Evie to finalize the details for tonight's trio of matches—time, place, and what not to wear—I was still thinking about Ty Bonner and his kiss and how I really needed another.

Not with him, mind you. That would be like licking a drop of blood all the while knowing that you couldn't down the entire glass sitting right in front of you. In human terms—settling for one itty-bitty piece from a giant-size box of Godiva chocolates.

Painful.

I just needed someone to help me take the edge off. Someone to distract my thoughts from Ty. Someone who had really great lips and knew how to use them.

"Don't we all?" Evie asked when I called her just before midnight and explained my dilemma. She was in the middle of a *CSI* rerun and a pint of Ben & Jerry's Cherry Garcia. "Nothing comes to me at the moment, but I'll look through the database first thing tomorrow and see if I can find someone for your friend."

Okay, so I didn't exactly explain *my* dilemma. It was one thing to admit to myself that I was beyond desperate, and quite another to blab it to someone else. Besides, I had an image to maintain and I didn't want Evie to think I wasn't all that.

I listened for a few minutes while she went on and on about the current episode she was watching and then filled her in on the matches I'd made.

"That's a shame Mrs. Wilhelm wasn't interested in my uncle. He had a really excellent time."

"He slept through most of the date."

"At ninety-three that's an excellent time."

"Good point."

We talked a millisecond more before she had to hang up—the commercial was over (her TiVo still wasn't cooperating, and so she was watching regular TV) and she needed more ice cream.

Work, I reminded myself. Forget Ty. Forget the kiss. *Forget.*

Not a problem.

I checked my e-mail, salivated over this cute little A-line skirt from Ann Taylor I'd been eyeing online, and brainstormed a few more possible match markets to add to my ever-growing list—all-night deli, ATM, movie theater.

Okay, so maybe I still had a tiny problem. I came to that conclusion when I closed my laptop and grabbed my beaded MUDD jean jacket (not major bucks, but sooo cute). My lips *still* tingled.

Oh, and I had some major tingling going on in other places that shall remain nameless.

"Where to?" the cabbie asked me when I folded my tingling body into the backseat and tried to ignore the delicious way his pulse thumped against his neck.

*Hello? The neck is thick. And it's attached to an
even thicker, fiftyish head with a bushy gray mustache
and stained teeth. Are you crazy, girl? Don't even
think about it.*

But I *was* thinking it.

"Hoboken," I choked out. *"Now."*

I don't usually do Jersey any more than I do Brooklyn, but I *really* needed to talk. If I'd needed to shop,
I would have headed over to the Waldorf and stolen
Nina One away from her job. But linguistics and a
decent amount of sympathy required Nina Two. I
tamped down my panic and tried to keep myself busy
during the cab ride to the sanitary products plant
where she headed the accounting department.

"It can't be healthy to work at a place like this," I
told Nina when I walked into her office an hour later.

For the record, I'd managed to keep my fangs to
myself and *not* molest the cabbie.

Barely.

Nina Two glanced up from where she'd been
hunched over her computer screen. Her brown hair
was pulled in a simple ponytail. She wore minimal
makeup and her usual serious expression. "We don't
release any toxins into the air. We only stock, package, and ship here." She sounded as if she'd read one
too many PR pamphlets. "All of the manufacturing is
done at our facility in Philadelphia, and then everything is shipped here for the final round before being
introduced to the public."

"I'm not talking about the air. I'm talking about

the decor." I glanced around and made a face. "It's beige."

"Oh." She followed my gaze. "I like beige."

"And plaid. Nobody does plaid anymore."

"It's yellow and orange plaid. Our signature colors." She pushed up from her desk. "What are you doing all the way out here?" Panic lit her eyes. "It's not Nina, is it? Tell me she didn't buy another Tiffany bracelet."

"She bought a Tiffany bracelet?" I forgot all about my hormones, and my heart did a double thump. "When?"

"Two days ago. Hasn't she told you about it?"

"I've been sort of busy and haven't had a chance to really talk." I smiled. "So what does it look like? What's she going to wear it with? How much did it cost?" I spent the next few minutes getting the complete lowdown on Nina One's new acquisition. "It sounds totally cool," I declared once I had a clear mental picture of Nina's new baby. "And expensive."

"Too expensive," Nina Two said. "She could have invested in three different mutual funds and bought a five-year CD. Who wouldn't want a five-year CD that pays *eight* percent?"

"Beats me."

Nina sank back in her chair and eyed me. "Give. What's really up with you?"

I kissed a made vamp.

It was there on the tip of my tongue, but for some reason I couldn't seem to push it any further.

Hello? This is Nina. You give her the dish on all of your kisses, made or otherwise.

The thing was, I'd never kissed a made vampire before, and I wasn't sure how I felt about it, much less how one of my best friends in the world would feel. What if she thought I was the scum of the earth and no longer fit to be in her company?

Okay, so I knew she wouldn't think that. Even so, I didn't have near the urge to dish about this bit of personal info the way I usually did. I was still too busy replaying it in my mind and trying to file it away into the drawer marked MOMENTS OF COMPLETE AND TOTAL INSANITY.

Instead I said, "I've been thinking that maybe work isn't all it's cracked up to be. That maybe I need some downtime."

"I've got work up to my armpits. I don't have time for a trip to Madison Avenue."

"I prefer Fifth Avenue myself, but that's not what I'm talking about." I cleared my throat. "See, the thing is, I've been feeling very isolated and . . ." Let's see. How could I put this without sounding totally needy and insane? "That is, I've been uptight, and I think if I could just blow off a little steam, I might be able to get my head back on straight."

"O-kay." She stared expectantly at me.

"See, I have a lot of frustration, and I need an outlet for it."

A knowing light filled her eyes, and she smiled. "Why didn't you say so?" She reached into her drawer. "You need a stress ball." She tossed me a yellow, squishy round ball with WELLBURTON FOR WOMEN in bright orange script. "You can't go wrong with one of these. We had them printed up for clients, but the employees love them, too. I've personally gone through several this year alone."

"I don't really think I need a stress ball." I set the thing aside.

"What about a pressure clamp?" She pulled out what looked like a pair of pliers and squeezed. "I know this company that makes heavy-duty ones especially for vamps, so you can squeeze until your eyes cross."

"I don't need a pressure vise."

"What about tick-tock balls?" She reached toward the contraption sitting on the corner of her desk. Silver balls hung suspended in a row from a wooden bar. Pulling one ball to the side, she sent it rocking against the others. "These can be very soothing. I know it doesn't seem that way at first. The noise is sort of annoying, but if you watch the motion and concentrate, it can be soothing. *Tick-tock. Tick-tock. Tick-tock. Tick—*"

"I NEED TO HAVE SEX," I blurted, grabbing the balls with both hands. The noise stopped and my nerves eased enough to pull me back from homicidal to the land of misdemeanor. "I need it in the worst way."

"Oh." She swallowed, and a strange look came over her face. "Listen, Lil, I would love to help you out. Really I would. You're such a good friend, and I really value our relationship. And it's because I value it that I have to say no." She shook her head. "I just can't do it. I mean, I've thought about it. What woman hasn't? But not seriously. I like men."

"Not with *you*. I'm speaking figuratively. I miss sex. I miss falling asleep with someone. And waking up with them. And . . ." I shook my head. "I just miss it."

"What are you going to do?"

We both knew what I could do. I could pick up someone, have a little fling, and be done with it. But I'd been there and done that, and as tempted as I was, I knew it would only be a temporary fix. I'd be in the same boat six months from now. Or sixty years. Or six hundred . . .

"Maybe I've been too hard on my mom." I told you I was desperate. "She *has* introduced me to some decent prospects. This last guy—Wilson Harvey— wasn't too bad. Okay dresser. Decent-looking. Low fertility rating, but my orgasm quotient could more than compensate. We could make a decent match. You went out with him." I eyed her. "What do you think? Speaking of which, thanks again for doing that. You saved my ass."

"No problem."

"So what do you think? Me and Wilson? Wilson and me?"

"Maybe."

She didn't sound very convinced, and my desperation kicked up a notch. "I know, I know. He's boring as hell, but there has to be more to him. He can't be a complete dud, can he? Maybe he's just got boring exterior. Maybe underneath lurks the heart of a real hottie, and I'm going to miss out because I refuse to take the time to look beyond the surface."

"Maybe."

"Help me out here. I know what he's like on paper, but you spent time with him. Tell me, is he that bad?"

"Actually, he's very smart."

"See there."

"And attractive. He's very attractive in a fierce, Pierce Brosnan way."

"They can't all be Brad Pitt."

"And he really knows his opera."

"Everybody has some flaw." As soon as the words left my mouth, I remembered a key point. "You like opera."

"I adore opera." A strange gleam lit her eyes. "It's so passionate. Wilson thinks so, too. And he's not just one of those I-like-opera-because-I-should-like-it types. No, he truly appreciates it as a quality form of dramatic expression."

"You like him," I said.

She stiffened. "Do not."

"Do too."

"Do *not*. I just think he's a great guy, that's all. If I were in the market for a great guy, then I would definitely consider him."

"Since when *aren't* you in the market for a great guy?"

She shrugged. "Since the great guy in question isn't in the market for someone like me."

I remembered Wilson's number-one must-have—a

high orgasm quotient—and suddenly the situation made sense. "You like him, but he doesn't like you."

"There's no *like* involved. He wants an eternity mate, and I'm not what he has in mind."

"Did he say that?"

"He didn't have to. I know. Besides, I feel the same way. He isn't exactly my top pick either. With such a low fertility rating, he's a far cry from Old Faithful." She shook her head. "We don't make a good match, and we both know it."

"So the coast is clear for me then?"

"Wide open," she declared before glancing at her watch. "But not tonight. I'm diversifying my portfolio, and he's offered to give me some investing tips. We're meeting in a half hour for a nightcap."

"I see," I said, all the while my brain chanted, *Wilson and Nina sitting in a tree . . .*

"It's not like that." Obviously it wasn't just my brain doing the chanting. "I don't have designs on this guy, and he certainly doesn't have any designs on me. Our relationship is strictly business."

"Then you really won't mind if I call him up?"

"Of course not."

"Good."

"Good." She tried to look disinterested as she logged off her computer and reached for her purse. She pulled out a tube of lipstick and swiped her bottom lip before she seemed to notice my smile. She shoved the lipstick back inside and stood. "So where are you off to?"

"I thought I'd pay a visit to a couple of health clubs

before heading home. You know, Crunch Fitness. The Sports Zone." I'd racked my brain for possible made vamp hangouts that didn't include alcohol and a dance floor. A crowded place where a nice, decent, respectable made vamp (if any existed) could go to scope out decent dinner prospects. Since low fat, low carb was all the craze among humans, why not made vamps? If I'd had to go out and find dinner on my own, I'd certainly want someone healthy as opposed to, say, a drunk passed out in an alley.

I forced the image away. I wouldn't have bitten him.

Or kissed him.

Or taken advantage of him in any way, shape, or form.

I was horny. Not crazy.

At least that's what I told myself.

"Happy hunting," she said, as she reached for a black leather coat that hung near her desk.

"Yeah, you, too." I smiled and she stiffened.

"I told you." She pulled on the coat and straightened the collar. "It's not like that."

"Of course it isn't." I came around the desk and pulled the band that held her ponytail in place. I fluffed. "Just because it isn't *like that* doesn't mean you can't look ultra hot and show him what he's missing out on."

"I couldn't care less what he thinks so long as he gives sound financial advice."

"And I've got this great little condo in Hawaii smack dab on the beach that's screaming your name."

She made a face. "You're a real pain in the ass sometimes."

My smile widened. This was the most fun I'd had all night—that didn't involve a hands-off vampire and lots of tongue action, that is. "It's a tough job, but somebody has to do it."

Twenty-four
♥ ♥ ♥

I spent the next night combing Laundromats for the perfect mate.

Not for myself, of course.

I'd given up that idea last night. Once I'd taxied home from Jersey and handed out cards at four different twenty-four-hour health clubs, I'd gone home, crawled into bed, and come to the realization that I'd totally overreacted. The eye-opener? Two words: multispeed vibrator. (Technically we're talking three words, but if memory serves me, I distinctly remember my tutor Jacques saying something about the hyphen serving as a sort of wedding ring . . . forever and ever and all that jazz.)

Imagine *moi* actually *considering* one of my mother's prospects just because I needed a good orgasm. Or a good dozen.

Talk about the deep end.

With the midnight soiree a little over a week away, I needed to drum up some business in a major way. Not only did I have Mrs. Wilhelm breathing down my neck, but my mother had sent a handful of her other friends to Dead End Dating to find a date for the annual event.

Luckily, no one really wanted an eternity mate. The entire club consisted of much older female vampires who had already gone the commitment route. They'd had their children and contributed to the survival of the race and had now kicked back to enjoy life. Some were widows, and some just had an agreement with their significant other to dabble with other men. Overall, they wanted a good time, which meant I didn't have to fix them up with a born vamp with an off-the-charts fertility rating.

"You're paying me mega overtime for this," Evie said after a twenty-minute conversation with a not-so-cute guy debating the merits of liquid bleach versus powder. She had the business casual look down pat—with a small side of trendy—in a Rebecca Taylor denim pencil skirt, a cotton sweater, a denim jacket, and (what really pulled it all together) a beaded ribbon pendant.

I was keeping it real with an embroidered Vivienne Tam skirt, a silk shell, and a pair of Nancy Geist leather stilettos. And a Furla leather hobo bag.

I know, I know. So *not* on my current budget, but luckily Nina One and I were the same size and she was a total sucker for begging.

"Just think of it as a night out on the town with your best girlfriend."

"This isn't Avalon." She referred to one of my favorite dance spots over in Chelsea. "It's the Fold-n-Dry on Seventy-sixth."

That's what Nina One had said when I'd invited her after raiding her closet. (While I was back on the I-don't-need-a-mate-to-validate-me bandwagon, I wasn't in any hurry to be alone.) Nina Two had had another financial powwow with Wilson; that's right, Saturday night, drinks at the Bubble Lounge, strictly business—I'm not touching *that* one. With The Ninas both busy, that left Evie.

"It's still fun." When Evie gave me a pointed look, I added, "Or at least educational."

She shrugged. "That is true. Who would've thought you could tell so much about a person by what's in their laundry basket? Whether they're single or married. If they have kids or not. How many kids they have."

"How many times they change their underwear." I eyed a guy who'd just walked in with a minuscule laundry bag. He made a beeline for the nearest washing machine, up-ended the canvas sack, and three T-shirts rolled into the washing machine. "Or not."

"You think?" Evie eyed the guy as he fished quarters out of his pocket. He stood well over six feet. Decent build. Dark hair. He wasn't exactly a fashion guru in a plain T-shirt and jeans, but he did have good taste in running shoes—Nike. "I would have made him for a boxer guy."

I stared the man up and down before focusing on his butt. "Trust me, he's flying solo at the moment."

"How do you know this stuff?"

"Sixth sense." Aka super vamp X-ray vision. I walked over to him, introduced myself, and handed him a business card. Turns out his name is Jeff, human, works construction, doesn't date much but he'd like to, and he doesn't wear underwear on account of he's allergic to elastic and the waistbands make him itch.

Okay, that last part was a tad more than I needed to know, but at least the guy was friendly. And excited. He promised to give me a call when his current project slowed down and he had some free time.

Meanwhile, Evie handed out three cards and had two thrown back at her. One from a born-again virgin who was taking a lengthy hiatus from the opposite sex. The other? A divorcé still hopelessly in love with his ex. The single pair of women's panties mingled in with his socks should have clued her in, but she'd given him the benefit of the doubt and chalked it up to a fetish.

Hey, we all had to learn.

We were about to leave our eighth location when Evie's voice stopped me just shy of the door.

"Hey, isn't that one of our clients?"

I turned and followed Evie's gaze to the large television that sat bolted high on the far wall. It was tuned to a rerun of tonight's local news which, of course, I'd missed. As usual.

A woman's familiar face stared back at me, and my stomach hollowed out.

"She was almost one of our clients," I told Evie. Before I'd chased her away during the fake Prada incident. I'd run out of freebies and so she'd run across town to Match Me for the complimentary strawberry-filled donuts (with powdered sugar).

And now she was missing.

". . . police are asking for witnesses to step forward." The announcer's voice rose above the steady whir of the washers and dryers. "If you've seen this woman or have any information regarding her whereabouts, please call our tips hotline posted at the bottom of this screen."

With trembling hands, I pulled out my phone and punched in Ty Bonner's phone number.

"I knew this woman," I told Ty a half hour later. I'd dropped Evie off at her apartment and headed back to the office to find him waiting for me. "I *knew* her."

"Then you know this guy is sticking to his MO." He wore black jeans, a black and silver San Antonio Spurs T-shirt, and boots. His black leather duster lay draped over the back of the chair where he sat. He had his legs stretched out in front of him, his ankles crossed. He was all hard muscle and dark brooding looks, and he watched me from beneath a black cowboy hat tipped low on his forehead. His neon blue eyes followed my every step as I walked from one end of the rug to the other. "While he's changed location, he's still after the same type of female. Laura Lindsey fit the bill to a T."

"Laura?"

"The woman he just abducted. She was divorced. No children. She's got a grandmother back in Kentucky, but no other family. She came here on a job transfer last year and hasn't made many friends since. She worked at the Metropolitan Life Building, went to the library twice a week, and liked her coffee with sugar and extra cream."

"Okay, so I didn't *know* know her. But I knew about her. She filled out a profile."

His facial expression didn't change, but a gleam lit his eyes. "Did you set her up with anybody?"

"I didn't get a chance." I explained the freebie ad incident and how I'd run out of goodies. (I was still going for the hot, unattainable born vamp image, so I figured it best to leave out the crawling around on the floor over the lost Prada nameplate.) "She got mad and acted like a total bitch. Still, she didn't deserve this." I paused midstep and my gaze met his. "You have to find her. Or at least find out what happened to her."

"I will." He pushed to his feet and crossed the distance that separated us.

I had half a mind to run. Unfortunately, the other half had its own ideas (which involved a lot more touching than running), and so I stayed put.

"What?" I asked when he simply stared down at me, a funny look on his face.

"You're too much."

"Meaning?"

He tipped his hat back, as if to get a better look at

me. "You're scared, aren't you? That's why you called me and asked me to meet you here. Because you're really *scared*."

"I am not. I called you because I thought you might want the inside scoop on the latest victim."

"I already know the inside scoop."

"You didn't know that she'd been here."

"No, but I don't see as how it's relevant in this particular situation."

I didn't see how, either, but it had seemed relevant when I'd seen her picture flash on the television screen and I'd felt this overwhelming sense of loss. I'd wanted to do something. To say something. "Okay, so maybe it's not. But you never know where a lead might turn up. I just thought you could get an even better picture of her if you knew she'd been here. And that she's into freebies. And that she's lonely enough to visit more than one matchmaking service."

"Actually, she was lonely enough to visit three, not counting this one. They all set her up on dates. We're investigating all of them."

"You're kidding. Do you think the kidnapper has been to all three?"

"Maybe."

Which meant there was a really good chance that he might end up at Dead End Dating.

The notion didn't make me half as excited as it had before I'd kissed Ty Bonner the night before. I told myself it was because the danger had become that much more real. No way was it because I no longer wanted to save the day and set Ty up with Esther. Or with anyone, for that matter. Or that I was saving him for myself.

No *way*.

He eyed me. "You're scared, all right."

"I'm a vampire. I don't get scared. I'm just concerned."

"Vampires don't get concerned."

Good point. "Look, I've already told you, I have a business to think of. If my clients start disappearing, it will destroy everything I've built." I knew we'd had this discussion before, but it sounded much better than *You're right. I'm scared shitless.* It was one thing to see an anonymous picture on the television—like the first victim—and quite another to have actually met someone face-to-face and then have her disappear. It made it all seem so . . . *real*.

"Business, huh?"

"That's right."

"That's why you've been pacing since I walked in the door. Because you're worried about business?"

"I have not been pacing."

"You've been moving so fast your shoes are smoking."

I glanced down to see white wisps circling my ankles. "All right, I've been pacing. From frustration, not fear." He started to point out the obvious—vampires didn't get frustrated—but I held up a hand. "Don't say it. Just don't." I nailed him with a stare. "So what are you going to do?"

"What I've been doing. I'm going to keep tracking him until he slips up."

"What if he doesn't?"

"He will. They always do."

"But what if he doesn't right away?" I persisted. "What if he keeps getting away with it? What if he kidnaps another woman? What if he decides to go after one of my clients? He could walk away with Melissa or Action-Adventure, or any of the other nice women who've come to me for help."

I wanted him to say it wasn't going to happen. That he would find the guy first and kick his ass, and all that other macho bullshit that most men dished out like pizza at a Super Bowl party.

Instead, he simply stared at me. "That's a very real possibility."

His words sank in and settled into a tight knot in the middle of my chest. "Shit, he could, couldn't he? He really could." The truth weighed on me for a long, silent moment. I shook my head. "No, he couldn't. Because that means he would have to get by me, and that's not going to happen."

He grinned. "Atta vampire." He touched me then, his cool fingertips stroking my cheek. "If there's one thing I've learned in the last one hundred years, it's patience. It may take a while, but I always get what I want."

"Is that so?"

He leaned down. His mouth moved closer to mine. "Always." The word was a soft rush of air against my lips, and I felt a rush of electricity zip up my spine.

Hello? Is this the wrong guy or what? Made vamp,

my conscience reminded me. *Zero fertility rating. Bottom dweller. Low end of the food chain . . .*

Yeah, yeah.

Here's the thing. I wasn't going to kiss him. *He* was going to kiss *me,* which put an entirely different spin on things. I couldn't very well do the wrong thing (and beat myself up over it) if I wasn't the one making the decision. I was an innocent bystander. A rose just waiting to be plucked. A ripe strawberry ready to burst—

Okay, so *wrong* analogy, but you get the idea.

Now back to the good stuff. He leaned into me, his eyes fierce and gleaming and hot. Mmm . . . I felt the rush of his breath against my lips. He was going to kiss me, all right. He was going to—

"Just keep your eyes open for anything suspicious." His deep voice penetrated the steady *thump, thump* of his pulse, which echoed in my ears.

My eyes snapped open to find that we were nose to nose. But he wasn't puckering. He was grinning.

I frowned. "You're not going to kiss me, are you?"

He shook his head and the tip of his nose brushed mine. "Not this time."

Darn it.

"The way I figure, sugar, it's your turn now."

Meaning I was going to have to kiss him or it just wasn't happening.

He didn't budge. He waited, his body taut and close. Waiting.

I licked my lips and remembered last night. How good he'd tasted and how much I'd wanted him.

Enough to get myself all worked up and actually consider my mother's advice. I'd gone so far as to picture myself with Wilson. I'd even pictured the two of us with a half-dozen little Wilsons.

Eee—ewwww.

I swallowed and searched for my strength. "I think I'll pass. Um, thanks for stopping by."

I thought I saw a flash of disappointment, but then his smile widened and I was left thinking it was just my own hormones on the chopping block.

"Any time, sugar." And then he turned and walked away.

It's for the best, my conscience whispered. (Yeah, I know vampires aren't supposed to have those either, but get over it.) *You shouldn't have let him kiss you last night. And you shouldn't have called him earlier when you freaked. And you certainly shouldn't have stood there just waiting for him to make another move—*

"Oh, shut up," I growled. "Just shut the hell up."

I listened until his footsteps and the delicious thrum of his blood disappeared, and then I snatched up my purse, killed the lights in the office, and headed home.

Another Saturday night bites the dust.

Twenty-five
❤ ❤ ❤

"**P**lease tell me this isn't what I think it is." My gaze shifted from my mother to the most handsome vampire I'd ever seen, which was saying a lot on account of all vampires are usually super-duper handsome.

It was Sunday night again. Another family hunt. *And* another fix-up.

Tonight's prospective mate looked as if he'd stepped off the cover of a romance novel. He had long, flowing black hair, a strong jaw, piercing green eyes, a sinful mouth, and a body to absolutely *die* for. Whew . . . Was it hot in here, or was it just me?

Certain, ahem, body parts tingled with excitement, and a small flutter of hope went through me.

Hope?

Ack. I *was* desperate.

I shifted my attention to the guy standing next to

him—a mirror image as far as features go. But number two had flowing blond hair and rich chocolate brown eyes.

There were *two* of them.

"They're fraternal twins," my mother voiced my thoughts.

Okay, so we're talking only a smidgeon of what I was thinking. Thankfully.

"Both fantastic," she went on, "yet different enough to satisfy all tastes. I figured since you're being so picky that I couldn't go wrong with two fantastic men—each with an extremely high fertility rating—who are handsome, yet different. If Thirston's hair is too dark, then you have Theodore, here, who's a blond. If Theodore's eyes are too brown, then you can liven things up with a bit of color and go for Thirston. What more could you want?"

"That's, um, nice, Mom, but I really don't think I'll be going for either of them."

"Why not?" She looked so clueless that I found myself seriously contemplating the existence of pod people. There was an entire world of supernatural beings in existence, why not aliens? That would explain so much about the woman staring back at me. My mother wasn't my mother. She was a deaf, stubborn pod with one purpose on Earth: to make her only daughter's life a living hell. Today me, tomorrow daughters everywhere, until pushy mothers singlehandedly ruled the world.

The thought was enough to calm all tingling body parts.

"You have to stop with the pickiness, Lilliana. You're not getting any younger. Besides, do you have an escort for the soiree?"

"I don't need an escort. I'm perfectly capable of flying solo."

She shook her head. "You can't fly, dear, until after midnight. It's against soiree rules."

"I didn't mean *fly* fly. I meant that I'm perfectly capable of attending on my own. Without a man."

"Why ever would you want to do such a thing when these two are more than eager to accompany you? They're both handsome and virile, not to mention Thirston owns a paper products plant and Theodore is big in the domestic waste industry."

Did she just use *virile* and *domestic waste* in the same sentence?

"They're perfect, Lilliana. Absolutely perfect."

"One makes toilet paper and the other takes out the trash."

"Not just toilet paper," Thirston chimed in. "We also make paper towels, napkins, and we've just revamped our line of disposable eating utensils. We make the super duty plate."

"The what?"

"The super duty. Guaranteed not to bleed, break, or fall apart, or your money back."

"That's really . . . nice." My attention shifted back to my mother. "So, um, where's Dad?"

"He's in the library talking business with Wilson."

"Wilson's here, too?" My eyes rolled to the back of my head, and I groaned. *"Mom."*

"I didn't invite him. He just showed up. He said he needed to talk to your father about one of the new investments he's adding to our portfolio. And it's a good thing; otherwise, your father would still be sulking."

"Why?"

"That woman stole his lucky golf ball during this evening's game." *That woman* aka Viola "the werewolf" Hamilton.

"You're kidding, right?" She hadn't struck me as the petty thief type, but then what did I know? I'd met her for all of five minutes.

"I wish I were. He was a little off on his aim, and the ball went over the hedges. Viola and her bunch thought your father was instigating a game of fetch. Needless to say, she won't even think of returning it. Your father is devastated. He prizes that ball above everything, except his autographed Knicks cap. It was given to him by a golf legend."

"Tiger Woods?"

"Tiger's dad's chiropractor's daughter." She smiled at the two male vampires. "So how about a little drink to whet everyone's appetite?" Both men nodded, and she smiled. "Lilliana, why don't you visit with Thirston and Theodore while I pour?"

"I would love to, but I really should go and find Max. He's doing some color brochures for me, and I need to talk to him about the setup."

"He's not here yet."

"Well, uh, I sort of need to speak to Jack, too."

"He isn't here yet either."

"Rob?"

"Probably en route."

"You mean they're all late?" Jack I could see. He was always late. But Max was just a younger, more hip version of my father, and he was *always* on time.

"I told them to come a half hour later."

"You didn't tell *me*."

"Because I wanted you here at the usual time. I wanted to give you a chance to meet Theodore and Thirston without any interruption."

Which added an additional half hour to an evening that was already way too long in the first place.

She handed both men a glass of bourbon on the rocks and motioned them over to the sofa. "Lilliana, you should join them." She indicated the space on the sofa between them, but I quickly sank down in an armchair on the opposite side of the Queen Anne coffee table. "There. Now everyone's settled." She smiled at me. "Hold down the fort, dear. I need to go down to the cellar and pick out a bottle of something ancient and imported for tonight's dinner."

"But I'd really rather—" She disappeared before I could finish the sentence. The *click click* of her high heels on the tiled marble floor echoed down the hallway and quickly faded to nothing.

The trash king gave me a serious expression while the toilet paper guy pulled a BlackBerry from his suit pocket.

"You don't mind if I take a few notes, do you?"

"I guess—"

"Good," he cut in, a serious expression on his face. "So what's your orgasm quotient?"

Ugh. Here we go again.

I drew a deep breath and searched for a tactful reply that didn't include *None of your friggin' beeswax*. "Zero," I replied.

Both men exchanged puzzled looks. "You're kidding," he finally declared. "A sense of humor." He shook his head. "That's not really important, but I guess it can't hurt," Theodore told me while Thirston made a few frantic notes on his BlackBerry.

"I do have a sense of humor, but I'm being serious." I gave him a somber expression to back it up. "I have this horrible affliction that totally inhibits my sexual appetite so much that I don't even like sex."

Theodore looked relieved. "You don't have to like it. Just so long as you can pop out an egg."

Oh, *no* he didn't.

He leaned closer. "So can you?"

I leaned closer. "Yes." He smiled and I smiled. "Not that it's going to help in this particular situation." His smile disappeared, and mine widened. "No offense, Theo, but when I picture my dream guy, he's a pilot or a Navy SEAL or a half-naked construction worker." Or a bounty hunter, a small voice added. *Bad voice*. "He isn't mopping up spills with a roll of Bounty." Harsh, I know. But, come on, *pop out an egg*? Pu-lease.

"That's the other paper towel. We make the Spill Slurper."

"It was a figure of speech. And while I do the trash thing, too"—I turned to his brother—"ditto on what I just said to him. Not that you dudes aren't totally hot or anything, I just don't think we're compatible. *But*"—I smiled—"I'll bet I can find you someone who is . . ."

I was this close to the pool house—my chosen hideout for tonight's hunt—when I heard Wilson's voice.

"How goes it with the hunt?"

I whirled to find him standing behind me. He looked as handsome as ever in a three-piece suit, his expression dark and brooding and very vamplike. Sort of. He did have an inkstain on his tie, and I could see the bulge of a calculator in his coat pocket. "Actually, it's going pretty well." I'd let it slip that our next-door neighbor on the east was an uncommitted born female vampire who'd recently made the vamp book of world records for having the highest orgasm quotient in the history of the race. That had sent Theodore and Thirston off in her direction while I'd headed for the pool house. "I'm not *it*. Max has the pleasure tonight, which means I just lay low until it's over."

"I meant the hunt for an eternity mate. For me. Have you found anyone?"

"But I thought you and Nina . . . I mean, you *did* see each other last night."

"I thought she was just a warm-up. For the real thing."

Okay, so she had been. I'd needed to hook him up and Nina had volunteered so I wouldn't look absolutely inept. But then they'd hit it off and now she liked him.

Case in point, *she* liked *him*.

"She's an intelligent woman," he said. "Very intelligent. And I don't think I've ever met anyone who knows more about IRAs. She's also very attractive. But let's face it, she doesn't come close to meeting the requirements I've set forth."

"But you've seen her more than once," I pointed out. My throat burned, and my chest felt tight.

"Well, yes. But it's just business. We enjoy talking about the latest financial news, but it's not as if I can take her home to my family. Come on, they'd all have a great big laugh."

For the second time that evening, I found myself seriously rethinking my position on the violence issue. If ever anyone needed a good ass kicking, it was Wilson Harvey. And maybe the vamp twins. And every other chauvinistic born male vamp out there.

Hello? That's most all of them.

True, but at the moment, I was really pissed, and I felt up to the challenge.

"Let me put it this way, *Wilson*. I wouldn't hook you up if you were the last born male vampire and the survival of our entire species depended on you. And what the hell kind of name is *Wilson* anyway? It's a last name, that's what kind it is. What sort of guy has a last name for a first name?" I was ranting, I knew, but I was doing it on behalf of one of my dearest friends, as well as all born female vamps everywhere. "A boring guy, that's who. A guy who carries a calculator and gets ink spots on his tie. What was I thinking letting you within five feet of Nina? You're not fit to lick her conservative but tasteful shoes."

"Excuse me?"

"No, excuse *me*." I turned, stomped toward the pool house, and slammed the door. And then I sulked for the next two hours until the whistle sounded.

When I walked back into the house, I noted that Wilson had left. Lucky for him. While I'd stopped shaking, I was still wound up and not in the mood to take any crap.

Jack had been rewarded with five extra vacation days after pouncing on Max near the pecan orchard—following one heck of a chase. My youngest brother sat on a nearby sofa celebrating his victory with his latest minion—Dolly something or other, a buxom bartender from Greenwich. Rob stood across the room with my father. My mother had gone off in search of a fresh bottle of AB negative.

"What's up with you?" Max asked as I settled on the sofa next to him.

"Why do you men have to totally suck?"

"What?"

I shook my head. "Never mind." I pinned him with a stare. "Thanks for taking so long. I could be back in Manhattan by now."

He grinned. "I had to put up a fight. What sort of prey just rolls over and surrenders?"

I nodded toward Jack and the woman holding his wineglass. "Dolly?"

"Okay, but she's human. I had to give Jack a run for his money. You're just jealous because you got caught in the first fifteen minutes." He winked before turning to my mother, who handed him a glass of AB negative.

"So what happened to Delphina?" my mother asked him.

Delphina was my oldest brother's current live-in. She taught human sexuality at NYU, and she was— you guessed it—human.

"We're taking a break. We're tired of each other."

"Of course you are." She cupped his cheek. "You're too young to be tied down, dear, much less with a human. This is the time for you to spread your wings. To soar. You'll have plenty of time for commitment later with a born vampire who's more suited for you."

Yep. I was jealous of Max, all right. But not because he made a better *it* person.

"So where are Thirston and Theodore?" My mom's gaze met mine as she handed me a glass. "I haven't seen them since we started the hunt."

"They, um, left. Something about business."

"On a Sunday night?"

"Probably some super-duper emergency. Say, Mom"—I pointed past her—"is that a new vase?"

"Why, yes." She smiled and walked over to pick up the large ornate container. "My club had an auction, and I picked this up. It's from a very small village near the Riviera . . ."

She gave us the full history of the vase before going to retrieve another glass.

"You are so lucky," I said once she was out of earshot.

"There's no luck involved. It takes practice to be as cunning as me. I think. I concentrate. I *blend*."

"You also pee standing up."

When my meaning hit, he winked. "What can I say? I've got it going on."

"Going?" My mother returned with another glass and handed it to me. "Who's going somewhere?"

"I didn't say . . ." His words trailed off as his stare collided with mine. "Actually, um, I really should get going. I had a delivery of ink toner that came yesterday, and I haven't had a chance to check in any of it."

"But it's early."

"Which gives me plenty of time to get those ink toners organized. Lil offered to help."

"You did?" My mother's gaze swiveled to me.

"I did?" I glanced at my brother. "Oh, yeah," I said when realization hit, "I did. Just for tonight. I'm not working there," I added when I saw the excitement light my mother's dark eyes. "I'm just helping my big brother out this once because he desperately needs me. Don't you, Max?"

"I don't know if I would say desp—*ouch*!" He rubbed his arm where I'd pinched the hell out of it. "Yeah, I need her."

"Desperately?" I smiled.

"Hey, I'm the one helping you—yeah." He grunted and rubbed his thigh this time. "Desperately."

"I ought to make you walk back," he told me when we climbed into the black Hummer he'd bought last year by selling his free vacation days back to my father. "You're vicious, you know that?"

"Am not. You're just a big sissy. And speaking of sissies, can you do me a favor?"

"No." He keyed the ignition.

"Thanks. I need to stop off at Viola Hamilton's."

"Are you shitting me? In case you haven't heard, she's the enemy. Dad's so wound up about the golf ball that he actually talked about hiring a professional sniper to go in, retrieve the ball, and take out anyone who gets in his way."

"Dad overreacts. He should try asking her nicely."

"Yeah, right."

"I don't know. She seemed like a decent enough woman."

"And when did you get this impression?"

"When I brought her a peace offering the other day."

"As in money, gold, your firstborn?"

"A meat loaf, doofus."

"So what? Did you leave the pan or something?"

"Actually, I left a client." I fastened my seat belt and settled back into the leather seat. "And I need to get him back."

Twenty-six
♥ ♥ ♥

"He looks . . . different." I stood in Viola Hamilton's marbled foyer and stared at Francis.

"Don't we all?" Viola waved her hand. She looked immaculate in a clingy black Christian Dior dress that hugged her from breasts to midcalf. High-heeled black sandals completed the outfit. Bright red lipstick shaped her plump lips, and dark eyeliner rimmed her eyes.

"He looks really different," I said. Francis could barely stand up. He slumped against the wall. He had huge shadows beneath his eyes as if he hadn't slept since I'd dropped him off. His shirt had been buttoned up all wrong, and his khaki trousers were wrinkled.

"To hell with different," Max said, peering over my shoulder. "He looks *orange.*"

Bye-bye, pasty face; hello, Tony the Tiger.

"Camille, I told you you used too much bronzer," Viola called down the hall. "See"—she shifted her attention back to me—"he kept turning such a bright pink every time one of us got too close or, heaven forbid, tried to talk to him."

"He doesn't do interaction well."

"That's an understatement if I've ever heard one. Anyway, I swear, we all thought his face was going to explode. Since nothing seemed to stop the blushing, we thought maybe we could camouflage it. Camille—that's Camille Rhinehart of the New England Rhineharts— just bought this new do-it-yourself spray tanning gun, and so we thought we'd try it out. But I told her she was using too much bronzer and not enough base tan."

"Tan?" Max scratched his head. "He's *orange.*"

"He's Tahitian," Viola corrected. "Tahitian Sunrise. It's a great shade provided you get the base right." She raised her voice toward the end of the sentence and we heard a faint "I got it right. I didn't have much to work with" from somewhere inside the house.

"So he's still blushing?" I asked.

"Well, technically we haven't actually seen him blush since last night. But I would be willing to bet he still is. That, or he's traded one bad habit for another. Leona Stallenburk—that's the Philadelphia Stallenburks rather than the ones out of Chicago—peeled off her clothes a few hours ago and paraded around in front of him to sort of test the waters. To make it even more difficult, she challenged him to a game of poker. While we didn't see any actual color change, he started blinking. And then they started to actually play and that only made it worse." She leaned in front of him, whispered a few seductive phrases, and licked her lips suggestively.

Sure enough, he started blinking as if he were sending Morse code with his eyelids.

"Oh, no." The blushing was bad enough, but blinking?

"Then again"—Viola shrugged—"maybe it's just a nervous tick reserved especially for us." She drew a deep breath. "When midnight strikes and the moon is full, we can be quite a handful. Perhaps instead of shocking him out of his shell, we've just fortified the walls. And speaking of walls"—she turned and retrieved a piece of paper from a small marble side table—"give this to your father and tell him to keep his stupid golf game on his side of the hedges."

I stared at the receipt from Connecticut Glass and Mirror.

"He broke my window and shattered my favorite painting with his stupid golf ball. Of course, I expect him to pay for both." She retrieved another sheet of paper. "This is the insurance policy on my Rembrandt. He can either replace the frame and glass or the entire piece. His choice. And"—she turned and grabbed a small brown bag—"tell him here's his precious ball." When I started to open the bag, she held up a hand. "I wouldn't do that if I were you. See, when the ball came flying through and hit the painting, I was a little out of sorts, if you know what I mean."

Full moon. Werewolf. Got it.

I remembered my mother's comment about Viola mistaking the wayward golf ball for a game of fetch.

"Exactly," Viola said as if she read my thoughts. Which, of course, she hadn't. Werewolves didn't have telepathic abilities. Did they?

"It's a small ball," she went on. "So when I opened my mouth to catch it, I swallowed it." She shook her head. "Your father, being the unreasonable man that he is, kept demanding I give it back even though I explained the situation in detail." She let out an exasperated sigh. "The man just wouldn't listen. Kept ranting about my being a thief, which I most certainly am not, and how he's going to file charges and have me arrested. So here." She nodded toward the bag. "There it is."

I let her explanation sink in for a full thirty seconds before my nostrils flared and reality zapped me. I quickly handed the bag off to Max, who held it at arm's length.

"Say, Miss Hamilton, have you met my brother, Max?"

"It's Viola, and no, I don't think I have. But I have seen him before." She swept a gaze from Max's dark head to the tips of his Gucci loafers. "You're even more attractive up close."

"If you like bossy and pretentious," I said.

"I like." She winked at Max before turning her gaze back to me. "Sorry I couldn't be of more help to you. I've met many vampires—and had many of them," she added, her gaze drifting to Max again, "but I've never run into one quite like Francis. Where did you find him?"

"Moe's."

"That explains a lot."

You're telling me.

"Hopefully he'll stop the blinking sometime soon," she added. "If not, I know this really great cosmetic surgeon who could actually sew his eyelids open."

"Thanks, but no thanks. I need him in tip-top shape by this coming Saturday, and I doubt the swelling would be down by then."

"Probably not."

"So, um, how long is that stuff supposed to last?"

"Four weeks. Five if you're not prone to flaky skin."

Four?

"At least you won't notice the blushing until then."

"That's true. Take care, Miss Hamilton. Come on, Frank." I grabbed the exhausted vampire and steered him down the front walk. I smiled as I helped him into the back of Max's Hummer. He collapsed on the seat.

"What about Britney and the twins?" he managed to mumble.

"They're fine."

"Did you feed them while I was gone?"

"Yes."

"Water them?"

"Yes."

"Take them out to tinkle?"

"Yes, and it's pee, not tinkle. Male vamps don't say tinkle."

"They say piss," Max added from the front seat. "At least that's what I say."

"Okay." He sighed and closed his eyes.

I climbed into the front seat beside my brother.

"I'm not an expert, but I know badass vampires aren't orange," Max said as he slid the key into the ignition and steered around the circular drive.

"No," I said. "They're not."

"But you're smiling."

"Because I think the idea has some merit." Let's face it. It was either smile or cry, and I'd never liked to play the helpless, weepy female. Not in front of other people, that is. Besides, I hadn't suggested a tanning appointment because born male vamps didn't have to tan to look mega-hot. But why not? And, if done right, it *would* disguise the blushing.

I glanced at him and noted the strange pallor, and hoped with all my vamp heart that Dirkst could manage to fix him. Otherwise . . .

Not going there, I told myself.

I would not consider failure, or the possibility that I would have to go crawling back to my folks because the entire vamp community blackballed me for handing one of their own over to a spray-happy werewolf who'd painted him Tahitian Sunrise.

So much for not going there.

I swallowed against the tightness in my throat, flipped on the radio, and did my best to focus on the Black-Eyed Peas pouring from the stereo system.

* * *

Max dropped off Francis in Brooklyn and then took me home. I'd just crawled into bed when I heard the alarm clock go off next door. Next came the sound of the early morning news.

I closed my eyes, determined to shut out the announcer's voice and return to my usual state of ignorant bliss.

". . . on the local front, Laura Lindsey, a bank teller from the West Village, is still missing. She's the second woman to disappear in the past two weeks. Police have no clues, but an inside source is saying this could be the work of a serial kidnapper . . ."

Or a serial *killer*.

I remembered everything Ty had said about the number of women and how it would be completely impossible to keep such a huge number alive without stirring any suspicion. I knew he was right—he was hot on the trail of a bona fide murderer. One with a growing list of victims.

The truth made me all the more restless because I knew Laura wasn't just missing. She was dead. Or close to it. And there wasn't anything anyone could do about it.

I spent most of the day tossing and turning and staring at the ceiling. Minus the time spent watching Jerry Springer—today's episode? my ex-lover is a transvestite serial killer—and giving myself a pedicure.

"Maybe he's stashing the bodies in a boat shed," I told Ty when I called him on my way to the office. "Have you checked the boat sheds down near the Hudson?"

"He's not stashing them in a boat shed."

"How do you know?"

"Because I've checked every storage facility in and around Manhattan."

"Oh, well. That's good. At least we can rule that out."

"We?"

"I'm trying to help."

"If you really want to help, don't try to play cowboy next time you suspect something. Call me instead."

And kiss me.

I forced aside the last thought and murmured, "I'm really late."

"Later."

"Yeah, later."

Later ended up being about twenty minutes—the exact time it took me to stop and pick up Evie's latte and settle myself behind my desk.

"What about transvestite hangouts in the area?"

"You think our guy is stashing his victims at a transvestite hangout?"

"That, or just hanging out there."

"Doesn't fit with his profile."

"Maybe the profile's wrong."

"And maybe you should lay off the Springer."

Maybe he was right. The last thing I needed was to waste my energy worrying over Laura. I had much bigger problems. An entire list of them. First up? Francis. I made him an appointment with Dirkst for the next afternoon and then set about returning the stack of phone calls—minus the ones from my mother, of course. I wasn't calling her until I'd scheduled an appropriate date for all of my Huntress Club clients.

First on the list was Sally Deville, a widowed seven hundredish vamp who liked to tango. I spent two hours going over client profiles before I picked up the phone and called one of Max's friends whom I'd once seen tango at one of my parents' anniversary parties. While he wasn't ready to settle down, I managed to convince him of the infinite possibilities—all sexual— by going out with an older, more mature female vampire.

Bingo!

I'd just turned my attention to number two when Nina Two buzzed me on my cell phone.

"I'm just calling you back. So you saw Wilson last night?"

"Unfortunately."

"What's that supposed to mean?"

"That he's a low-life dog and so not worth your time."

"You didn't tell him that, did you?"

"Not in those exact words, but I'm sure he got the message. I mailed him a refund check." A painful task, but I'd managed. "He can find someone else to meet his precious criteria."

"But you can't do that! Then he'll know that something's wrong."

"Something is wrong."

"You like him."

"I do not. Not at all. Really."

"Liar."

"Look, it doesn't matter. Because we're not right for each other. I know that. That's why I want you to find me someone who is right for me."

"Do you think that's wise this soon?"

"This soon after what? We didn't have anything. We're acquaintances. End of story. I wouldn't think of getting serious with him any more than he would think of getting serious with me. Really." She laughed, but it was one of those halfhearted sounds.

My chest tightened.

"I want a man with a much higher fertility rating," she went on. "And you're going to find him for me."

"I am?"

"You have to."

"You don't have anything to prove, Nina. Who cares what Wilson thinks?"

"This isn't about Wilson. It's about me. I'm not out to prove anything least of all that I don't like Wilson. Because I don't. I'm just doing what all vamps my age do. I'm expressing interest in finding The One, and I want you to help me. No reason to let the grass grow under my feet. Fix me up."

"I don't know . . ." I started, but then an idea struck. A fantabulous idea. (I told you I'm good under pressure.) "I don't know why you didn't ask me sooner."

"So you'll do it?"

"You just find the sexiest outfit you can, and I'll have Evie call with the details."

"Thanks, Lil. I really need this. You're the best."

"So true." The last part. As for needing this . . . I wasn't so sure Nina needed a date, aka a distraction, so much as she needed an eye-opener.

Ditto for Wilson.

I pulled his file and punched in his phone number. He picked up on the second ring.

"Wilson Harvey."

"This is Lil." When he started to protest, I rushed on, "Look, I know I told you off earlier, but I've got an amazing woman you just have to meet."

He was silent for a long moment. "What's her orgasm quotient?"

"Off the charts. In fact, she's the current record holder for the Vamp Book of World Records. Single and desperate to find an eternity mate. And she likes opera."

"Okay."

Male vampires were such suckers.

Twenty-seven

❤ ❤ ❤

By the time Saturday rolled around, Laura Lindsey was still missing, I was still watching Springer, and Francis was still orange.

Dirkst had done his best in a three-hour session yesterday and, believe me, it had cost dearly to get him worked in on such short notice. Yep, you guessed it—a date with the lesbian receptionist. Not that I was worrying over that now, particularly after seeing Jerry's episode on "My Boyfriend's Really a Chick and I'm Still Turned On." Besides, I had more important things on my plate.

Today was *the* Saturday. The big kahuna.

The Huntress Club's Midnight Soiree.

I had six matches on for the big event, including Miss Wilhelm, whom I'd finally fixed up with Jeff the *au naturel* construction worker from the Laundromat.

I know, I know. He's human. Fine. Get technical on me.

But flaws aside, the guy had *mucho* qualities that made him the perfect date (notice I said date, not mate) for the snotty, pretentious vampire. Lo and behold, Jeff's mother had been a dance instructor, which meant he could do everything from the cha-cha to the bunny hop to the ever-popular cotton-eyed Joe.

Good looks. Dance know-how. Can't get any more perfect than that.

I'd made five other hookups, as well. I'd paired up mostly human dates with my vamp clients. The females wanted a good time only, which meant dinner and dancing and *dinner*. Thanks to the awesome power of vamp mind control, I didn't have to worry about the humans getting overly nosy or making the other guests nervous. Come morning, none of them would remember where they'd been or what they'd seen. They would just know that they'd had oodles of fun courtesy of DED.

With the exception of Dara and Dorien Cranford. They were sisters. Both widows. Both terribly lonely even if they wouldn't admit it. And so I'd hooked them up with a few born male vamps who'd called DED after picking up my card at their local health club. (Did I get around or what?)

The real issue, and the reason I'd spent over an hour angsting in front of the closet was that my parents would be there. And my brothers. And every other vamp who could trace his or her bloodline clear back to the Stone Age.

This was it. My chance to shine. To prove my stuff. Sort of. I'd intended for Francis to be my crowning glory, but that obviously wasn't happening in his present condition.

Thanks to Dirkst, he now leaned toward a golden orange, but he was still more of a Tony the Tiger than a bronzed Adonis. Nix the whole Lil-is-a-genius thing I'd envisioned during all of those sleepless days (when I wasn't envisioning myself and Ty getting busy on the beach).

Obviously, my mother wouldn't be falling all over herself to beg my forgiveness for not believing in me (fantasy number two). But I did expect, at the very least, grudging acceptance.

Which, in my opinion, kicked guilt's ass any old day.

"I can't do this." The deep voice came from behind the closed bedroom door.

I'd stopped to pick Francis up in Brooklyn, and I now sat on the sofa in his living room, Britney on my left and the twins on my right. I waited for him to put on the new shirt I'd picked up for him on the way over.

"Yes, you can," I told him, setting one of the twins aside as I pushed to my feet and walked over to the closed door. "Everything's going to be fine."

"You've seen me. Who would want to go out with me looking like this?"

"Me, that's who," I told him, and the door swung open. Despite his complexion, he looked good. He wore black slacks and his new shirt. His black shoes gleamed. He had his hair slicked back and—

I reached out and ruffled the hair. There.

"*You're* my date?" I nodded as I worked with a wayward strand that had fallen across his forehead. "A mercy date."

"This is *so* not a mercy date." When he gave me a *get-the-fuck-outta-here* look, I shrugged. "Okay, it's a mercy date. But not in the way you think. You're actually the one taking pity on me. If I don't show up with someone, I'll be fair game for my mother." I finished messing with his hair and noted that he hadn't blushed. At least not visibly.

Just call me the Miracle Worker.

"So *you* need *me*?"

I remembered Thirsten and Theodore, and a sudden desperation gripped me. "More than ever." A strange look fired in his eyes and my desperation quickly morphed into *Boyfriend, pu-lease*. I backed up a step. "But don't go getting any funny ideas. I know I'm hot and totally irresistible"—particularly in tonight's delish ensemble that consisted of a fitted gold strapless dress and a pair of gold Michael Kors sandals that had cost me three full client deposits—"but it's not going to happen between us." *And* I'd borrowed the Tiffany bracelet from Nina One. Add a pair of dangle hoops and a touch of my new bronzer and, *voilà*, ultra hotness. "You're not my type."

He shrugged. "Because I look like Garfield."

"Because you're a client." *And you don't wear black jeans and a cowboy hat and you aren't packing a forty-caliber Sig.* There went the bad voice again. "The orange is just the icing on the cake."

"While it *is* a mercy date," I went on, "tonight will afford you the opportunity to mix and mingle and appear taken to a wealth of born female vamps. Which will make you more attractive despite the tan. Which should help me set you up on future dates." I was keeping my fingers crossed on that one. "Just remember, you're playing it cool and smooth and taken tonight. Act disinterested. And mysterious. And whatever you do, don't blink."

"I'm over the blinking thing." He blinked. "Mostly."

It turned out that the blinking had been the result of lack of sleep. I'd discovered the truth on Tuesday (thanks to yet another sleepless day) when I'd been snuggled in bed, watching the sun set in my mirror. My eyelids had gotten so busy that I'd missed the entire thing. So it seemed Francis—now fully recovered from his weekend with the NUNS—had lost the habit for the most part while I . . .

Blink. Blink.

Well, you get the picture.

"So what do you think?" He stepped back and held his arms out.

I studied the overall picture he made and smiled. And blinked. "I like."

He ran a hand over the black silk material of his shirt. "I actually think I like it, too. Most of the clothes we picked out make me feel stiff and uncomfortable, but this is sort of nice."

"It's primo nice. It's Gucci."

He frowned and slipped into tight vampire mode. "How expensive?"

"Don't be such a fuddy duddy. You can't take it with you."

"I'm not going anywhere."

"Oh, yeah." I tucked the price tag into his cuff. "I'll take it back tomorrow. Just make sure you don't spill anything on it."

"I said not to spill anything." I stood in the main ballroom of the New Canaan Country Club and eyed the dark, gunky splotch on the front of Francis's new shirt.

"I didn't. I got spilled on. That's what I get for braving the buffet line." He shook his head, raked a hand through his hair, and further mussed the part I'd carefully mussed back at the apartment. "I should have eaten before I came."

I knew the feeling. My own stomach had staged a rebellion a half hour ago during a conversation with the chairwoman for tonight's event. Needless to say, she'd sent security out to check the gardens for party crashers playing loud music.

"Since we're stuck with the shirt, would you mind getting back in line and getting me something to drink?"

He turned and stared at the line of guests that wound around the edge of the dance floor.

"You're kidding, right?"

"I'm this close to passing out, which means if I bite the dust, you'll actually have to talk to someone besides me."

"Your wish is my command."

I spent the next few minutes drinking in my surroundings as best I could in between blinks.

I have to admit, we vamps knew how to do it up right. While my own musical tastes leaned toward Outkast and Nelly, I had to admit that the lavish orchestra could belt out a mean tango. The dance floor overflowed with designer dresses and pricey suits. White linen-covered tables had been situated throughout the large room. Large gold candelabra surrounded by a ring of fresh red roses adorned the center of each table. Silver fountains flowed with everything from imported champagne to AB negative. The smell of expensive perfume, lots of money, and rich, succulent blood lent a seductive feel to the air.

I scoped out my couples and noted that while only two were dancing, the others looked to be having a decent time. One pair sat at a nearby table, their heads bent toward each other in conversation. Another stood in the buffet line. Yet another stood on the edge of the dance floor and watched Jeff dip Mrs. Wilhelm in a very polished move that had half the room applauding. Bottom line, no one had ripped anyone to shreds.

Even better, I'd yet to run into my mother for longer than thirty seconds. She'd been in charge of checking invitations at the door. She'd given Francis the once-over and me a tight-lipped "Interesting dress, dear." Which, in mother terms, meant *You should have worn something else.*

I hadn't seen or heard from her since.

Yeah, baby.

"Wilson is here." The statement followed a tap on the back. I turned to see Nina Two looking very nervous.

And hot.

She'd taken my advice, ditched the conservative image, and worn a bright red dress cut up to here and down to there. It hugged curves I'd never even realized existed. She'd pulled her hair up with a ruby-encrusted comb. A matching choker hugged her slender neck and caught flickers of candlelight when she moved.

"He's *here*," she said again.

"You told me to fix him up."

"But not *here*. Not on the same night that I'm being fixed up."

"How goes it with your date?" I stared past her to the well-dressed man standing near one of the champagne fountains. He was tall, dark, and totally handsome. I'd met him at one of the health clubs. He was a born vamp who did his best thinking while on the treadmill. He raised his glass to us before taking a sip.

"He's nice. I guess. It's so loud in here that we really haven't had a chance to talk. Not that we would have much to talk about."

"He's a tax lawyer and you're an accountant. What isn't there to talk about?"

"He does corporate tax."

"Your father owns a corporation that you keep the financial records for. Smacks of good conversation to me."

"He doesn't like opera." Before I could say *good for him,* she added, "And he isn't much for personal investing. He thinks the market is too unstable right now."

In other words, he wasn't Wilson aka the vampire whom she insisted she didn't like.

I shifted my attention to Mr. Harvey, who stood several yards away near the bar, his hands shoved into his pants pockets, his gaze hooked on the tax lawyer rather than the attractive redhead at his side.

Ayala Jacqueline Devanti. She was the daughter of one of my mother's friends and the perfect female vampire. Beautiful. Educated. Orgasm quotient that rivaled even mine (not high enough to qualify her as the record holder, but enough to make her one sought-after vamp). And she desperately wanted to settle down and contribute to the vampire race.

Wilson looked more jealous than interested.

I smiled. "Forget opera. And investing. Go back over there and ask him to dance."

"I don't dance."

"Even better. Ask him to teach you." When she looked doubtful, I patted her arm. "You don't need Wilson. What you need is to have a good time and show him you don't need him."

She stared at me a long moment before realization seemed to strike. "You think?"

"I know. Now *go*. And make it good." I watched Nina Two march back to her date; all the while Wilson watched her.

"Hey." Francis came up beside me, his hands overflowing with two crystal glasses filled with rich red liquid. "What's up?"

I glanced at a second gunky splotch on his shirt. "Besides your credit card bill?" He frowned, and my smile widened. "Not much." I turned toward the dance floor and watched the tax lawyer pull Nina close before sparing a glance at Wilson. His mouth pulled into a tight frown, and his gaze narrowed. "Yet."

"Uh-oh," Francis said. "I think we're in trouble."

"I wouldn't go that far. He certainly looks ready to explode, but it's just because he's coming to terms with his feelings. Once he accepts that he wants her and she's his, he'll step in and tell her. The tax lawyer doesn't have enough invested in the relationship to challenge Wilson, so he'll bow out." I eyed Wilson. "A few more minutes and he'll make his move."

"He looks ready to move now."

"That just goes to show why I'm the matchmaker and you're a client. You have to be able to read people. To decipher each expression, each gesture. Everything means something."

"What about a stake? What do you think that means?"

"What are you talking about . . ." The question faded as I turned and followed his gaze to the entrance.

A male werewolf stood framed in the doorway. He was tall, with sandy brown hair and rich brown eyes. He wore a navy Brooks Brothers suit and looked like any other successful, style-conscious wolf carrying a wooden stake—

Uh-oh.

The sentiment echoed throughout the ballroom as everyone seemed to notice him. The band stopped and people turned and silence suddenly hovered in the air.

"Ayala," he cried. "What the hell are you doing with this guy?" Before she could respond, he shook his head. "This can't be happening. You're mine. *Mine*."

"I am not, James. I've already told you that. You and I—it can't work. You *know* that."

"Like hell. We're good together."

"We're good at sex. That's our only connection."

"It's more than that."

She looked at him with the same pity and tolerance that I'd seen vampires bestow on humans time and time again. "No, it isn't."

"Because of him." His frown deepened.

"Because of you. You're a *werewolf*," she told him. "It was fun. But that's all it was. You shouldn't have taken it so personally."

But he had.

I could see it in his eyes. The total disregard for his own safety (he would be torn into tiny little pieces if he even attempted to hurt a born vampire). The pain and anguish. The undying, 'til-death-us-do-part love.

Okay, so maybe I was reading more into it. Maybe it was more like crazed lust seasoned with just an itty-bitty dash of undying love. Regardless, he felt something powerful for the beautiful Ayala, despite the vamp society's rules against it, and I couldn't help but feel for him.

"It's his fault," the angry werewolf repeated, as if he hadn't heard a word she'd said. "*Him*."

As soon as he spoke the word, his eyes fired a bright red. His lips drew back, and he flashed a mouth full of sharp teeth. He lunged forward, the stake aimed straight for Wilson's heart.

"Wait!" I moved before I could do the math (stake plus angry werewolf equals stay the hell out of it). I stepped in front of Wilson just as the stake came straight at him.

Pain slashed into my shoulder and gripped my entire body. My vision blurred. My pulse pounded in my ears and nearly drowned out the shouts that broke out around me.

Everything seemed to go in slow motion for the next few moments as my knees gave and the floor came up to meet me. A loud *rrripppp!* echoed in my head, and I felt a rush of cool air against my bare skin. I had the fleeting thought that my mother had been right. I *should* have worn something different.

And then everything went black.

Twenty-eight
♥ ♥ ♥

"Lilliana?"

The name pushed past the black fog that held me captive.

"Can you hear me? Open your eyes, dear. It's *Maman*."

Maman.

Suddenly I found myself pulled back in time. I was eight years old again. My mother was waking me for my lessons with Jacques. My life was simple. It was all about conjugating verbs and playing dolls with The Ninas. No worry. No hassle. No electricity bill.

"The minute I saw her wearing that shrink-wrap for a dress, I knew something bad was going to happen."

My eyes snapped open. End of illusion.

"There you are," my mother declared.

She hovered over me and three important things registered. One, I was lying flat on my back on one of the ballroom tables, and two, I was wearing the tablecloth. And three, I was wearing the *tablecloth*.

The linen had been draped over me, the edges tucked up under my arms. My feet, still clad in the gold Michael Kors, dangled over the edge. My toenails glittered a hot pink in the candlelight.

"W-what happened?"

My mother frowned the same way she'd done so long ago whenever I spilled something on my new petticoats. "You nearly died, that's what. What is wrong with you? You don't just run into the pointy end of a stake."

The incident rushed at me, and I remembered Wilson. And the werewolf. And the stake . . .

Ohmigod. I got *staked*!

I stared at the folded towel that covered my shoulder. Blood had seeped through, turning the fabric a bright red. My stomach flipped and my hands trembled.

"I . . ." I couldn't seem to catch my breath. Lucky for me, I didn't have to. But I did have to swallow past a lump the size of Texas.

"You're a very lucky young lady," my father told me. He peered down at me, his face a black mask of anger and concern. "A few inches to the right and you would have been a goner."

I fought for my voice, my tongue heavy. I had to know the worst of it. "My dress?" I managed to croak.

"It split clear up the side and ripped right off when you hit the floor."

Okay, now I really couldn't breathe. Forget being naked in front of an entire ballroom full of vamps. We're talking *Christian Dior.*

I struggled to absorb the news for several long seconds as a dozen other questions raced through my mind.

"What about the werewolf?"

"Your brothers escorted him out."

I'll just bet they did.

I had the vague memory of Max jumping in front of me and Jack pulling the stake from my shoulder. Rob was in there somewhere, along with Francis.

"Oh, no. Oh, no. Oh, no. OH, NO!"

His voice replayed in my head and I blinked frantically to clear my watery eyes.

"Francis?"

"Your escort?" My father stared toward the left and I followed his gaze to Francis, who sat in the corner surrounded by a half-dozen female vampires. "Your mother and I weren't so pleased when we first met him—his coloring is a bit off—but he turned out to be one fine strapping young man." One sleeve of his new Gucci shirt had been ripped clear off, and the rest of the material was in shreds. His arm was scratched and his hair mussed, and he looked about as sexy as I'd ever seen him. Apparently I wasn't the only one who thought so.

"What did you say he did for a living?"

"He's in real estate."

"As in broker?"

"As in France. He owns most of it. He's Francoise Deville. Of *the* Devilles."

Both my mother and father smiled.

I struggled to sit up. Pain stabbed at me, and I fought down a wave of nausea.

"Take it easy." My father reached out and helped me into an upright position while I held the damp towel in place.

I glanced around. The ballroom was a pitiful sight. The band had stopped playing, the instruments abandoned in the face of danger. Tables were overturned. Chairs lay in bits and pieces here and there. The remaining guests clustered in groups and whispered to themselves. The fountains had been overturned. Waiters rushed here and there, picking up debris and cleaning what was left of the lavish room.

My gaze caught and snagged on Wilson and Nina Two. There wasn't a sign of Ayala or the tax lawyer. It was just the two of them amid the chaos that remained of the room. He lay on the floor, and she knelt beside him. She cradled his head on her lap and smoothed a hand over his forehead.

"Fifty years and the annual soiree has always gone off just beautifully. Until tonight." My mother shook her head. "I told you this dating business was a huge mistake. I told her," my mother told my father before turning back to me. "I hope you know that you're responsible for this, Lilliana. You and that ridiculous business of yours."

Wilson caught and held Nina Two's hand, and I smiled. "You're right. I am responsible."

Damned straight I was, and I couldn't have been more proud.

I needed to sleep in the worst way.

Exhaustion tugged at my pain-rattled senses as I headed back to the city, tablecloth wrapped around me like a sarong. The towel on my shoulder had been replaced with a large bandage courtesy of Dr. Sheridan, my mother's personal physician, who'd made a house call—or, in this case, a ballroom visit—the minute my mother had called.

I'd left Francis with Geneva Gray, a successful, single female vampire and the leader of his new fan club. While she'd looked ready to devour him in one bite, he'd looked more than capable of handling her. The fight had stirred his baser side and cracked open his shell in a major way.

Finally.

My mother and father had been stuck helping with the cleanup—in other words, they'd been dictating orders to the crew in charge. Jack and Rob hadn't been seen since escorting the werewolf outside, and I knew they'd had their wilder side stirred up so much that they'd needed to work off some of the energy. The cure? Some heavy-duty sex.

Max looked ready to bust himself, his expression fierce as he drove me home. But he was the oldest, and more controlled, and so he managed the forty-five-minute trip without spontaneously combusting. I knew once I was out of the car, however, he would go on the prowl and find a woman to help him use all that vamp energy. Lucky girl. There was sex. And then there was *vampire sex*. She was definitely in for the most memorable night of her life.

I felt a pang of envy because, it seemed, everyone would likely be having sex tonight except for me. But then we hit a bump. Pain exploded and coursed through my body. I clamped my teeth together and went back to thinking about my soft, warm bed and blessed sleep.

"Are you going to be all right?" Max stood just inside the doorway to my bedroom. "I could stay if you need me."

"Go." I waved him off from where I'd collapsed on the bed. "I'll talk to you tomorrow."

"Try to sleep. That'll make everything better."

"I'm way ahead of you on that one," I told him, my eyes already closed. I buried my head beneath the pillow even before he killed the lights.

I didn't even hear footsteps. Just the sound of the door opening and closing, and then he was gone.

My shoulder throbbed as I unwrapped the tablecloth I was wearing, tossed it aside, and climbed beneath the sheets. I closed my eyes and, for the first time all week, welcomed sleep. I was too tired to think, much less worry over missing girls and credit card bills and ruined dresses. Sleep, I told myself. Just sleep.

I was almost dead to the world when I heard the front door.

Since the sun had yet to come up, my senses should have been more alert. They would have been if I hadn't come *this* close to being a vamp shish kebab. It wasn't until I felt the cool hand on my forehead that I managed to open my eyes.

I saw the large shadow looming over me and I jumped. Pain zigzagged through me and I yelped.

"What the hell happened, sugar?" The deep, familiar voice slid into my ears.

"What . . . ?" I blinked. I had to be seeing things. No way was *he* here. In my bedroom. Now.

Sure, he'd paid me just such a visit many times, but that had been in my fantasies.

Then again, my shoulder hurt like a sonofabitch, which definitely screamed reality.

I cleared my suddenly dry throat. "What are you doing here?"

"What happened?" Ty stared at my shoulder, his gaze dark and hooded, as if a dozen thoughts raced through his head. None of them pleasant.

"I got staked." I explained about the jealous werewolf.

"That was a stupid thing to do."

"I don't know. I thought it was quite brave. Noble, even. And, of course, very professional. Wilson is my client, and I did get him into the predicament in the first place. I couldn't very well leave him to fend for himself. Sure, he's an ignorant jerk, but he came to his senses." I told him about how he'd left with Nina Two and how they'd looked so happy.

"I should have known."

"What's that supposed to mean?"

"That you're a sucker, and I'm not referring to blood." His gaze narrowed, and he gave me the once-over, which made me suddenly very aware of the fact that I was completely naked beneath the top sheet. "Are you sure you're a vampire?"

Unfortunately.

Now where had that come from? I liked being a vampire and doing vampy things and living forever.

I struggled to a sitting position, the sheet tight under my arms, and my shoulder screamed with a pain unlike anything I'd ever felt. I had the sudden urge to crawl into a fetal position and disappear. My eyes blurred with tears.

Okay, so I liked the whole vamp thing most of the time. Now *not* being one of them.

"It's okay." But he didn't sound as if anything was okay. He sounded awkward.

"What's the matter?" I sniffled. "Never see a vampire cry before?"

"Well, actually, no."

"If you say vampires don't cry, I'm going to hit you with my good arm."

He grinned and reached out. He caught a fresh tear with one rough fingertip, and I shivered from the feel of it.

"Lie back down," he murmured.

Mmm . . . I thought he'd never ask.

He settled me back onto the bed and just when I closed my eyes, ready to feel his kiss, I felt a rush of air as he moved away. I heard the refrigerator door open and close. Glasses clinked. And then he was back.

The bed dipped and his hard thigh pressed against my side.

"Drink this." His hand slid under my neck as he helped me lift my head. "It'll help you regain your strength." He held the glass to my lips, and my gaze hooked on his wrist. Blue veins bulged, pulsing with a life force that would help me much more quickly than the bottled stuff I'd become accustomed to. His pulse echoed in my head, and hunger grumbled deep inside me.

"Go on," he said.

I met his gaze and saw the meaning deep in his eyes. He knew what I was thinking, and he was thinking the same thing.

I licked my lips and felt my fangs graze the fullness of my tongue. His pulse thrummed louder in my ears, and my insides tightened.

I wasn't going to do it, I told myself. I couldn't. I was made of stronger stuff.

But then my shoulder screamed and the pain was too much and he was right there and—

My lips closed over his wrist, and I took what he offered.

The delicious wet heat filled my mouth and slid down my throat. I could feel his life force pulse through me. It traveled at the speed of light. Spread to my fingers and my toes. Raced to the wound on my shoulder. The pain eased and a different sort of ache took its place. One just as fierce, and much, much lower.

He tasted even better than I'd anticipated. Sweet. Bold. Decadent. Addictive. *Yum.*

"Ahhh . . ." His deep groan echoed in my ears and jerked me back to reality.

I glanced up to see him sitting at my side, his head thrown back, his eyes closed as I fed from him. His fingers still held the glass. I sucked harder. He groaned again, and his knuckles went white. The glass shattered. Red splattered my crisp white sheet.

Oops.

Not *oops,* I'd ruined my favorite bedding. But *oops,* I'd broken a major vow to myself and chucked my entire belief system for a few seconds of instant— albeit really terrific—gratification.

Major oops.

I pulled away and licked my lips. "I . . . I'm really sorry. I shouldn't have . . . I mean, I never . . ." I wiped at the corner of my mouth. "I mean . . . Oh, hell, I don't know what I mean." I shook my head and reached for the tablecloth I'd worn prior to crawling under the sheets. I pulled it up to my neck, all the while pushing the soiled sheet toward my feet.

Ty's strong hands grazed the inside of one knee as he bent to help me. He wadded the top sheet into a ball and disappeared into the kitchen.

By the time he returned, I'd managed to write off the whole wrist-sucking incident to delirium brought on by an indescribable amount of pain, i.e., temporary vamp insanity.

"So what exactly are you doing here?"

"The police found a body."

"Laura?"

"They think so. They can't be sure until they match up the dental records—it looks like whoever dumped the body tried to barbecue it first."

"That's pretty gross."

"Yeah." He ran a hand through his hair. "While no one wants to upgrade the kidnapping to a murder, the police are actually hoping it turns out to be Laura. A body means clues. If it's the right body."

"And you don't think it is?"

"It just doesn't fit. This guy's taken a lot of women, and not one body has been recovered. Why now?"

"Maybe he's getting sloppy."

"The body was found in a Dumpster near the Hudson River." He must have read the I-told-you-so-look, because his gaze narrowed. "A Dumpster, not a boat shed."

"Storage is storage."

"It's trash. Not storage."

"Storage for trash," I pointed out. "And close enough to send Jerry a thank-you letter."

He flashed a quick smile before the expression faded into business as usual. "The body wasn't even stuffed deep inside. It was just sort of lying there, near the top. As if someone had been in a hurry and had just chucked it." He shook his head. "This guy doesn't hurry. He's methodical. Careful."

"I would think the police would know that."

"They do. But with no leads, the locals are under pressure to find the missing girls, dead or alive. Otherwise, the feds will step in."

"Maybe that's a good thing."

"Maybe. And maybe it'll just send the killer running to another city." He ran a hand over his face and for the first time I saw past the dark good looks and noted the exhaustion rimming his eyes. "I've already chased him clear across the country. I want it to stop. Here."

He looked tired.

As tired as I felt.

Crawl right on in, I wanted to say. *The bed's big enough for two.* But I knew that if Ty were to climb between my sheets, the last thing we were going to do was sleep.

"Thanks for stopping by."

As if he read my thoughts, he nodded. "You really should keep your doors locked."

"I don't need a deadbolt. I'm a vampire."

"You keep saying that, sugar, but I'm not so sure I buy it." He grinned, his lips parting to reveal a row of straight white teeth. "A real vampire would have jumped my bones the moment I walked into Dead End Dating."

"A real smart vampire would have kicked your ass out quicker than you could say Bela Lugosi." I eyed him.

"Better late than never? Is that what you're saying?"

"Exactly. Out."

"One day," he vowed as he pushed to his feet, "you'll be begging me for sex."

"Sex isn't the issue here."

"Sex," he murmured just before he closed my front door, "is inevitable."

That's exactly what I was afraid of.

TWenty-nine
❤ ❤ ❤

Any satisfaction I'd felt at getting Wilson and Nina together drained away the moment I dragged myself into work on Monday and picked up line four because Evie had her hands full with lines one, two, and three.

Once I'd finally managed to fall asleep after Ty left—we're talking *hours* and a spectacular sunrise— I'd slept the entire day and night away (thanks to Ty's blood, a little detail I'd decided *not* to think about). I'd opened my eyes just as the sun had started to sink to find my shoulder healed and the pain completely gone.

A good beginning for any Monday, I had to admit, but it didn't last. I forgot my wallet at home and half-way in to work had to turn around. Then the latte machine broke just as I was getting a cup filled for

Evie. *Then* I stepped in dog poop and stained my new champagne-colored leather Miu Miu boots.

And now this.

". . . responsible for the charges incurred on your account. While we here at Ford Bank understand that everyone goes through difficult times, we still have rules and regulations that we must abide by. In particular, the minimum amount due."

"But I sent a payment in just last week." For the now ruined Christian Dior dress and my Miu Mius.

"You sent the scheduled payment for charges."

"Exactly."

"But not the additional late fees from the two previous months, which, under our contract, you are required to pay in full as part of the minimum monthly payment. In order to bring your account current, we need a total of . . ."

My eyes widened as he recited the amount. While business was going better than expected at this point, it wasn't going *that* well.

"I'm afraid you now owe another late charge for this month. That is, unless you would like to set up a payment over the phone, in which case we can avoid any further late fees and bring your account current."

"I guess so . . ." Short for *What choice do I have since you've cornered me and I can't pretend to be the answering machine?* I gave him the required bank information, did a quick mental evaluation of what was left, and moped for the next fifteen minutes while lusting after practically everything in the new Ann Tayler online catalogue.

I was busy envisioning myself in a red Grace Kelly-ish top when Evie walked in. She wore a Rozae Nichols net cardigan with metallic beads and a silk jersey skirt—both last season but oh so cute anyway. Suede wedges and a leather cuff bracelet completed the ensemble.

Maybe things weren't all that bad.

If Evie could look great in last season, so could I. There was more to life than money and a decent line of credit. Or so I desperately wanted to believe.

"I've got good news, bad news, and really bad news. Which do you want first?"

"Give me the good news." What can I say? I'm the eternal optimist.

"Melissa called this morning and said she didn't have much luck with either of the last two guys you set her up with, but that she's willing to try again. So I did a little checking and came up with what I think will be the perfect match. They're meeting"—she glanced at her watch—"right about now."

Which meant she'd given up the infatuation with Francis. Definitely good.

"And the bad news?"

"Francis called and said Britney is sick and that he has to cancel tonight's date."

"He has a date tonight?"

"That's the really bad news. She isn't one of our clients. In fact, he met her Saturday night and she asked him out, along with a half-dozen other women."

"Because they met him at the soiree, which he attended with me."

She thought about the information and smiled. "That does make us responsible, doesn't it? Then I guess today isn't so bad, after all." She disappeared out front and I reached for the two files she'd placed on my desk.

The first belonged to Melissa and the second to Jerry Dormfeld, also known as the Chili Dog Guy. I opened both files and placed them side by side. I read Chili Dog's likes and dislikes when it came to the perfect woman before shifting my attention to Melissa's profile.

Single. Never been married. No children. Family out of state. Waitress at a local restaurant.

Evie was definitely on to something. Melissa answered the guy's wish list to a T. On paper, she was the perfect woman for him.

Or the perfect victim.

As soon as the thought struck, I pushed it back out. Or I tried to. But then my attention shifted back to the first file, and I could practically hear Ty's voice reciting the kidnapper's modus operandi (I'd finally tuned out Jerry and tuned in *CSI*).

His victims are all single. Never been married. No children. No immediate family. No real career.

On top of that, she was new to the city. She hadn't had time to make many friends. She was new on the job. There would be no one to really miss her right away.

Until it was too late.

I should call Ty.

At the same time, what did I really have to tell him?

Just a hunch. A big one. But a hunch, nonetheless.

Chili's profile read like a half-dozen others in my file. Even more, I hadn't picked up one questionable thought racing through his mind when I'd met with him face-to-face. He was a guy. With a one-track brain. One that featured a chili dog. End of story.

Chances were he wasn't the kidnapper at all and I was simply having a breakdown. I had been staked and had drunk Ty's blood—all in less than a few hours. It only stood to reason that so much sensory overload in so short a time would send me over the deep end. Cripes, I was just a vampire. Not Wonder Woman.

I studied his folder again, and my gaze hooked on his previous address. A Chicago address.

My stomach hollowed out.

Hel-lo? Lots of New Yorkers are from Chicago.

I pressed the intercom and buzzed Evie anyway. "Where did you say Melissa was meeting her date tonight?"

"I didn't, but I can take a look-see." She paused and I heard her fingers tapping her keyboard. "Carmine's. It's that Italian place over on the Upper West Side. Great chicken parmesan and an impressive wine selection."

"Give me the address." I jotted down the information on a sticky pad. Grabbing both files and my purse, I pushed to my feet.

"By the way," Evie started when I walked into the outer office, "Francis wanted you to call him when you get a free moment . . ." Her sentence trailed off as she noted my purse. "Is something wrong?"

"Nothing," I said as I headed for the door, my heart beating so fast I thought it would pop out of my chest.

At least nothing I could prove.

Yet.

I'd been dead wrong. Chili Dog wasn't the kidnapper.

Nope. The ferocious-looking vampire standing next to him was the kidnapper.

I stood in the shadows of Melissa's apartment building and watched as the feral-looking vamp stared deep into her eyes and willed her into a limp noodle. The smell of German chocolate cake floated across the distance and filled my nostrils.

Make that a feral-looking *born* vampire.

It had been an hour since I'd left the office and headed for Carmine's, only to find that Melissa and her date had already left the restaurant. I'd tried her apartment first—the hunch thing again—only to find the place still locked up tight. The only sound that had come from inside had been the faint yapping of her dog, Daisy.

I'd taken that as a good sign.

If I were a mass murderer, I would definitely have silenced all that yipping first thing. Which meant they probably hadn't gone back to her apartment. They'd gone somewhere else.

I'd been about to head for the address Chili Dog had listed when my super vamp senses had picked up a faint noise coming from the alley behind the building. I'd tiptoed into the shadows and felt my way along the cold brick until I'd reached the corner that led to the rear. I'd peeked around and hit pay dirt.

"I . . ." Melissa's words faded into a choked gurgle as a glazed look came over her eyes.

She stared up at the six-foot-plus stranger who towered over her. He wore classic vamp: black slacks, black silk shirt, and Gucci loafers. He had dark hair that curled down around his shirt collar and smoky gray eyes. Overall, he was good-looking.

Or he would have been if I hadn't sensed the violence that lurked just beneath the surface.

He didn't just want her blood.

He wanted to drink from her, and then he wanted to watch her die.

Dread played up and down my spine as I watched Melissa melt in front of him. He caught her effortlessly, tossing her over his shoulder like a laundry bag. He was little more than a blur as he moved toward a black Rolls-Royce fully decked out with leather seats, expensive rims, and a DVD player. (What can I say? I notice these things.) He dumped her into the backseat of the idling car before turning back to Chili Dog.

Suddenly, it all made sense. Jerry Dormfeld—if that was even his name, and I wasn't placing any bets— was this guy's minion. His servant. His lap dog.

That's why I hadn't been able to read anything in Jerry's thoughts. Because he didn't have any thoughts of his own. He existed solely for the purpose of doing his master's bidding. He thought of only one thing: whatever it was his master planted in his mind. In this case, a great big hot dog with extra chili and double onions.

The minion went out and did his master's bidding, answering ads and visiting dating services in search of women who fitted the profile, and then Super Vamp stepped in and abducted them.

And sucked them dry.

Super Vamp then watched his victims turn into vampires (a painful, agonizing process, from what I've been told) and left them to the daylight. The sun fried them to a crisp and turned them to dust.

Bye, bye, evidence.

No way, a voice whispered. *You definitely shouldn't have started watching* CSI.

At the same time, it added up. Born vampire. Missing women. No bodies.

And Melissa was about to be next.

I pulled out my cell phone and punched in Ty's number.

"Hey," his deep voice rumbled over the line. "I can't pick up right now, so leave a message." *Beeep.*

"It's me," I whispered. "Help!" I told him as quickly and as quietly as I could what was happening and then I phoned Evie.

"Something's wrong with Melissa's date," I said in a frantic whisper.

"Is he a loser?"

"Actually, he's a murderer." *The* murderer. "I need

you to call this number and keep calling it until Ty Bonner answers."

"The hottie bounty hunter?"

"Yes. Give him this license plate number and tell him I don't know where they're headed, but I'll call as soon as I can with a location."

"And if you don't?"

"Call the police."

"Shouldn't I call them anyway?"

And have the whole lot of them get slaughtered *if* they managed to find Super Vamp? I wasn't going to have *that* on my conscience.

Then again, if I didn't call with a location, it would mean that I'd gotten slaughtered, too. Which would mean there was little chance I'd be sitting around in the future feeling guilty.

I shook away the thought. "There's nothing to tell them right now. Just get in touch with Ty. I have to hang up."

I ducked down behind a garbage can just as Super Vamp turned toward the cluster of shadows where I was hiding. He'd heard me. I knew it even before I sensed his presence moving closer.

The hair on the back of my neck prickled, and I closed my eyes.

I focused my own thoughts on the first thing that came to mind—Britney. In a matter of seconds, I'd morphed into a clone of the obnoxious little cockerdoodle.

The garbage can flew out from in front of me and

slammed into a nearby wall as Super Vamp tossed it aside. Piercing gray eyes stared down at me.

I wagged my tail and let loose a string of high-pitched barks.

"Annoying little shit," he growled.

Okay, so I wasn't Britney's biggest fan, but I wouldn't go that far.

I barked some more and even nipped at his ankles until he turned and strode back to the car. He disappeared into the front seat. The doors slammed shut, the motor revved, and the car rolled out of the alley, leaving me and Chili Dog staring after him.

Once the car disappeared, the minion turned and left the alley. His work was done for the night.

And mine had just begun.

I focused again and a heartbeat later I was standing there just as I'd been before, minus my Miu Miu boots. That was the thing about morphing, especially if you didn't do it that often. There was a tendency to get rusty, which meant sometimes you got it right, and sometimes things got scattered in the crossover. A pair of shoes. A handbag. A cell phone.

I adjusted the notebook clutch under my arm, cell phone still tucked safely inside along with both folders, and tried to ignore the damp wetness beneath my bare feet. I knew my boots were probably somewhere nearby, maybe in the trash can that lay on its side on the ground, or a nearby pile of cardboard boxes, and I would have made a mad search for them if I'd had time.

But the clock was ticking for Melissa and so I fought down the urge and closed my eyes.

A little more concentration and the sound of beating wings filled my suddenly tiny ears. My vision grew even sharper, and I suddenly felt as light as a feather. My teeth grew smaller and pointier and very batlike. I could only hope as I took flight that I'd gotten the color right. Black in this instance. The pink definitely did not fit with low profile. I left the alley behind, spotted the car just as it pulled onto one of the main streets, and then I followed.

Thirty

It wasn't a boat shed.

It was a lavish two-story house in an upscale Jersey neighborhood lined with large brick homes and carefully manicured lawns. The car pulled into the driveway, and the garage door rumbled open. The Rolls disappeared inside, and the door closed again just as I landed behind a row of hedges and changed from sleek bat back into my usual self.

Minus my favorite Gucci bangle bracelet and the mini suede jacket I'd been wearing.

I fought back a wave of dread. What had I expected? Use it or lose it. That's what Max always said. I hated when Max was right.

I forced myself to look on the bright side. I still had my purse and my cell phone and my health. What more could a single female vamp ask for?

I checked the number on the mailbox, punched it

into my phone, and text-messaged it to Evie at the office. And Ty. I didn't want to chance a phone call. Super Vamp had heard me once before, and I wasn't about to take that chance again. The goal was to lay low, and, with any luck, the cavalry would arrive soon.

Not soon enough, I realized when I circled the house and found Melissa in one of the back bedrooms. She lay on a red satin coverlet, her body completely nude, her hands and feet handcuffed to the bedposts thanks to the vampire who leaned over her. The sharp scent of oil made my nostrils flare. I watched through the window as Super Vamp finished adjusting the last of her restraints and leaned back to survey his work. He checked one wrist and then the other before his gaze swiveled toward the windows that ran the entire length of the bedroom wall.

A wall that faced the east.

Good morning, sunshine!

What could I say? I was the complete package. Looks and brains. Satisfaction washed through me, followed by a rush of panic as I ducked to the side to avoid being spotted. Seconds ticked by until I felt the vamp's attention shift back to the woman handcuffed to the bed.

I peaked around the edge in time to see him trail his hands over Melissa's body. She arched into his touch, tugging at her restraints, her eyes glazed, her face a mask of hunger. She liked what he was doing, and she wanted more.

His hands.

His mouth.

His fangs.

Duh. She'd been vamped. Reduced to a quivering mass of need and only Super Vamp could give her what she so desperately thought she wanted. But it wasn't real. It was a vampire-induced illusion, and by the time she came to her senses, it would be too late.

She would be a vampire herself. And doomed to the sun's painful light.

All right, already. Enough with the doom and gloom. Do something.

I moved then, as fast as my preternatural bare feet could carry me, and rushed back around to the front of the house. I said a prayer—and hoped the Big Vamp Upstairs had a free moment—and rang the doorbell.

"Hi." I smiled brightly when the door swung open and Super Vamp stared back at me. His gaze was dark and hungry and very unhappy. Whew. He hadn't bitten her yet. "I'm Lil." My smile widened. "Your neighbor. I've been meaning to stop by and welcome you to the neighborhood. You just moved in, right?"

"A few weeks ago. But I won't be here long. I'm just renting. I travel. On business."

"That's no reason to be a stranger." I smiled again and decided to go for broke. It wasn't like he wouldn't know I was a vampire. A born one, for that matter. "It's so nice to have one of my own kind nearby. I can't tell you how lonely I've been living around here with all these humans." My voice lowered a notch. "And werewolves." I shook my head. "And I won't even mention Mrs. Abercrombie on the corner. You don't even want to know what she does once the sun goes down. It's really tough being a vampire these days."

He stared suspiciously at me before he finally shrugged. "It's certainly not like the older days."

"And how long ago would that be?"

"Eight hundred years."

I whistled, and my mind started to race. If things didn't work out with Francis, maybe I could turn this guy into viable eternity mate material . . . Nah. Geeks were one thing. Vicious, murdering vamps . . . well, who could trust them?

"I'd love to dish. Why don't I come in and we can have a nice long talk about old times—"

"No. I'm busy. I don't have time."

"Not even for a little visit?"

"No."

"Just settling down to dinner?"

"Something like that."

"I'll join you. I hate to eat alone."

"I like it."

"Come on." I made a face. "It's no fun to eat all by your lonesome." What was I saying? Vamps always ate alone. Unless you counted the entrée, that is. "Be sociable."

He stiffened, and his frown deepened. "I don't want to be sociable."

"Lighten up."

"I don't want to lighten up." He shook his head. "Listen, get out of here. I like my privacy." Before I could say another word, he slammed the door shut in my face.

I rang the bell again and it lurched open before the *ding-ding* managed to fade.

"What?" he growled.

"I was wondering if you'd like to buy some Girl Scout cookies."

"*What?*"

Yeah, *what?*

"I, um, that is, I thought you might want to take them to the office for your, um, colleagues. Or maybe you've got a maid or a gardener. Why, I'd bet they would love a box of Thin Mints. Talk about terrific." When he stared at me as if I'd grown a halo, I rushed on, "Not that I know firsthand. I certainly can't eat cookies, as you well know. But I do have human acquaintances who say they're majorly delicious." Okay, so it sounded lame, but he looked really pissed and I was really nervous and I had to say *something*.

"You don't have any cookies with you." His gaze swept me from my head to my bare toes.

"Well, no. But I could go and get them. In fact, you could go with me. You can pick out your own."

"Get lost." He slammed the door.

I pressed the button again. "I'm taking that as a no," I told him when he hauled open the door again.

"*Hell,* no." He slammed the door again.

I was about to lay on the bell again when I heard Ty's deep voice behind me.

"Where is she?"

I whirled to find him standing so close that my chin

bumped his chest. I jumped. "Geez, it's about time." I pointed around the house. "She's back there."

We reached the wall of windows just in time to see the vampire walk back into the bedroom. He muttered something about "nosy fuckin' neighbors and Girl Scout cookies" and Ty shot me a *what-the-hell?* glance.

I shrugged. "What can I say? I'm not used to thinking on my feet."

The vamp moved closer, and Ty drew a very deadly looking forty-caliber Sig from his pocket.

"That's not going to do anything," I told him.

"It's going to slow him down enough for me to subdue him and get some answers."

"Oh."

"Step back." He aimed. The red beam caught the Super Vamp square in the shoulder.

Ty was about to pull the trigger when the doorbell rang.

Everything happened really fast after that.

The vampire flew into a major rage. He whirled. Ty pulled the trigger. Glass shattered. Someone screamed.

And kept screaming.

My mouth opened even wider when I saw Francis framed in the bedroom doorway—wait a second. *Francis?* Evie followed on his heels, and the now-wounded vampire turned on them.

Ty lunged through the broken window, but he was too far away. The wounded vampire grabbed Francis and threw him against the far wall. He grabbed Evie next. She flew through the air and landed in a heap in the corner.

Frank got back up. Evie didn't.

I reached her limp body just as Francis launched a counterattack (go Francis). He took Murder Vamp down with a running tackle and a head butt to the middle, and Ty joined him.

Ty got the murdering vamp into a choke hold while Francis landed some pretty ballsy punches to the guy's jaw. Murder Vamp managed to pull his legs up and send Francis flying, then he chomped down on Ty's arm, which hugged his throat.

I wasn't exactly sure what happened next. I just knew that one minute Murder Vamp was fighting Ty off him and the next the murdering vamp was flying across the room. (Ty packed quite a punch.) He landed in a tangle of arms and legs at my feet.

That should have been the end of it. It would have been if he'd been human. But no. This guy was a vamp. As in pigheaded. As in he just had to get back up.

He staggered to his feet, and I felt my hand close around a large shard of glass from the shattered window.

"Hey." I tapped him on the shoulder and he turned on me.

I thrust my hand forward and the glass sank into his chest. He went stiff; his mouth opened and white foam dribbled out (ewww) and then he turned to dust. Flesh. Bones. And poof, he was gone.

I angsted all of five seconds—hey, this guy was E-V-I-L—and then whirled toward my fallen assistant.

"Evie?" I felt for a pulse. It thrummed against my fingertips, and my panic eased.

"What happened?" she asked a few seconds later when her eyelids fluttered open. "Did he hit me?" She glanced around, but there was no *he* to be seen. "Where did he go?"

"It's a long story." One I wasn't about to tell her. "What are you doing here?"

"I couldn't sit at the office and do nothing while you went after a dangerous murderer. I had to help you."

"What about Francis?" I motioned toward the vampire who was struggling to free a now squirming Melissa. When Super Vamp had vanished, so had his hold on Melissa. She was now shrieking. Her high-pitched voice nearly drowned out the sounds of approaching sirens.

"He called right after you text-messaged me. I was upset, and I sort of blurted out what was going on. When he found out Melissa had been snatched, he got a little crazy. Did you know he liked her?"

"He mentioned something a while back." And I'd tried to dissuade him. Human. Vamp. It wasn't supposed to happen.

"He picked me up," Evie went on, "and we came to help."

Melissa's shrieking faded into a sob as she stared at the vampire uncuffing her left wrist. "You really got crazy"—Melissa stared at Francis—"when you heard I'd been abducted?"

"Well, yeah. You're nice. I didn't want anything to happen to you."

"I didn't think you liked me. You never called."

"I didn't think you wanted me to call."

"Didn't Lil tell you . . ." Her voice trailed off as both pairs of eyes fixed on me.

I shrugged. "People make mistakes, you know. Nobody's perfect." I busied myself helping Evie to her feet while Ty went to the front of the house to greet the police.

Humans and vamps. Go figure.

A half hour later, I stood out front in my bare feet at the edge of the driveway with about a dozen neighbors. The house crawled with police and FBI. Yellow crime scene tape surrounded the perimeter. An ambulance sat near the curb. Melissa lay on a nearby stretcher. Two paramedics tended to several small cuts on her arms and torso—courtesy of the shattered window—while Francis held her hand.

Another ambulance was just disappearing around the corner, Evie tucked safely inside. She had a minor concussion, which required twenty-four hours of observation at a nearby hospital.

I'd wanted to go with her, but I'd had to hang around to give a statement. Which, hopefully, I would be able to give sometime this century.

I eyed the cluster of officers near the front door and gave a little wave. "Hey, remember me?"

"How could I forget?" Ty's deep voice slid into my

ears, and I turned to find him standing beside me. "You were really something in there."

"I didn't really do anything. I mean, I *did* stake him, but I had no choice. Otherwise, I didn't do all that much."

"You screamed. Loud. I don't think I've ever heard a vampire scream before."

I shrugged. "Just one of my many talents."

"Seriously, you did good tonight."

I'd managed to stake another vamp and end his existence without losing my lunch or collapsing into a crying heap. I guess that was sort of good.

Even if it didn't feel so good.

"Personally," Ty went on, "I would have stalled with something besides Girl Scout cookies, but hey, that's just me."

I smiled despite the strange sadness weighing on my chest. "It worked, didn't it?"

"Yeah." He shook his head as if surprised. A grin lifted the corner of his mouth. "It did. It sure as hell did."

Silence settled between us for a few moments, and I shifted my gaze back to the house. But not my attention. That was centered fully, completely, on the man next to me. And the fact that he stood close, just an inch shy of actually touching me. Awareness zipped up my spine.

"You look cold." Soft leather slithered over my bare arms as he settled his jacket over my shoulders. His intoxicating aroma surrounded me. "I'd give you my boots," he went on, "but I don't think they'd fit.

Then again, the cold probably doesn't really bother you."

I realized then that Ty didn't know any more about born vamps than I did about made ones. Which, in this particular case, was a good thing.

"Actually, I am a *little* cold, but I'll make do." I snuggled deeper inside the jacket and faked a little teeth chattering. "Thanks."

"No problem." He looked as if he wanted to say something else. Or touch me. Or both.

Please!

So maybe the cold *was* getting to me. I was delusional. Out there. I wasn't supposed to want Ty and he wasn't supposed to want me and the world just wasn't supposed to work that way—

"I'll be back." Ty's deep voice cut into my mental rambling and jerked me back to the present.

"Will you?" The case was now solved. Closed. History.

"Sure. I have to give the police a statement and then I need to talk to forensics about the suspect's body."

"There is no body."

"Exactly." Before I knew what was happening, I felt his lips on my forehead as he gave me a quick kiss. "I'll be back."

A girl could only hope.

"So you're a matchmaker?" one of the neighbors asked after Ty had walked away.

I turned toward her, and she flashed a card that Evie—flat on her back on a gurney—had handed out.

I nodded and she added, "My husband passed away last year and I've been meaning to get back into the swing of things. But it's hard, you know? I mean, dating can be murder."

My mind raced back through tonight's events, and I stared down at my blood-spattered tank visible between the edges of Ty's leather jacket. "You don't know the half of it."

Epilogue

♥ ♥ ♥

The pleasure of your company is requested at the commitment ceremony of Mr. Wilson Harvey to Miss Nina Wellburton . . .

I sat in my office on a clear, star-studded, moonlit night and held the thick, glossy vellum embossed with gold lettering. My heart gave an excited thump.

"I've never seen a marriage invitation phrased quite that way before," Evie said as she stared over my shoulder. "That is what this is, isn't it?"

"Yes." Or rather the vamp equivalent. Complete with a lavish reception and the most hideous bridesmaid's dresses I'd seen since my aunt Clarabella from Louisiana had exchanged commitment vials down in Shreveport just before the start of the Civil War. Picture *Gone with the Wind* meets *Prom Massacre Part IX.*

Uh, yeah.

Not that I was complaining. I'd wear hoop skirts

and double as a giant pitcher of Tang if it meant seeing Nina Two happily hooked up to the vamp of her
dreams for all eternity.

Hey, what are friends for?

"I guess they're going the cheap route. It says
BYOB."

I wasn't explaining *that* one.

Evie still hadn't figured out my little secret. As far as
she knew, I was the eccentric—and obviously tasteful—
boss with an impressive collection of bangle bracelets
and designer belts.

And how goes it with everyone else?

Well, Nina One still had her shopping addiction,
although Nina Two and I had persuaded her to tone
it down a bit. Then again, maybe it was her father
tightening the purse strings that did that. My brother
Max was still a playa-playa. Jack and Rob were still
trying to follow in his footsteps. Esther Crutch was
still waiting for me to hook her up—in between Botox
injections and cellulite massages. My father was still
fighting over territorial rights to the hedges on the
east side of his property. My mother was still trying to
fix me up. And Ty was still haunting my fantasies.

And most of my reality, as well.

He'd helped out the locals with several unsolved
cases, and they'd been so happy with his work that
they'd asked him to stick around Manhattan for a little while.

I *know*. Am I in trouble, or what?

To my credit, I hadn't sucked his blood—or any

other part of his person—since that night at my apartment. And I sure as hell hadn't kissed him.

Yet.

"This is so exciting," Evie went on, effectively distracting me from the whole Ty issue, bless her human soul. "Our first official marriage. We'll have to frame the invite and hang it on our Happily Hitched wall."

"Since when do we have a Happily Hitched wall?"

She waved the invite. "Since right now."

I smiled, despite the fact that things hadn't turned out exactly as planned. Namely, Francis had chucked his newfound hotness, turned down the half-dozen born female vamps who'd fallen for him at the soiree three months ago, and was now living with Melissa.

Sure. They were happy. And sort of hitched. If you considered total monogamy and matching sweaters expressions of their undying devotion. But they weren't planning a nursery or wearing each other's blood around their necks. Which meant they were far from the perfect example of a vampiric happily ever after.

But while I hadn't managed to find an eternity mate for the oldest, geekiest vampire in existence, I *had* managed to find one for the pickiest vamp. Aka Wilson Harvey.

I'm definitely da bomb.

The extra word-of-mouth I'd received because of the kidnappings/murders hadn't hurt, either. While Ty had managed to put the Jersey incident to bed very quietly thanks to a few of his buddies in very high places—who woulda known the FBI had a real paranormal investigations unit headed by, *ta-da*, a vampire?—there had been quite a bit of speculation among the local authorities. My name had been tossed around by New York's finest more than once. Needless to say, I'd gained somewhat of a reputation over the past few months and had taken on a rather impressive client load of born vamps *and* lonely cops.

Among other creatures.

I told Evie good-bye and waited for her to leave before I picked up the message she'd left on my desk.

Please call Viola Hamilton. It's urgent . . .

Urgent? What could the queen of the werewolves want with me that was *that* urgent?

I ignored the sudden butterflies in my stomach, picked up the phone, and punched in the number. I'd faced off with a murderer, hooked up my best (and most boring) friend in the entire world, and managed to have a pair of Miu Miu boots cleaned *without* any spotting. There wasn't anything I couldn't handle.

At least that's what I told myself.

And there was only one way to find out.

If you fell in love at first bite with
Dead End Dating,
read on for a sneak peek at

Dead and Dateless
by
KIMBERLY RAYE

the next delectable novel
in the Dead End Dating series!

"I need a man." The attractive woman sitting
across the desk from me leaned forward.

Her name was Viola Hamilton, and she was the latest
client to come walking into the small but well-furnished
office that housed my latest business venture—Dead
End Dating. Manhattan's first and only hook-up service for vampires. And humans. And any other creature who could fork over my pricey (but well worth
every red cent) fee.

I'm the Countess Lilliana Arabella Guinevere du
Marchette. Lil for short. The latest and greatest when
it comes to matchmakers, and a five-hundred-year-
old born vampire with an ever-expanding wardrobe
and a serious cosmetics addiction.

Okay, *okay.* I'm a five-hundred-year-old born vampire with an ever-expanding wardrobe, a serious cosmetics addiction, *and* enough outstanding Visa charges to fund a small third-world country.

But enough about the ever-fantabulous me.

"Actually," Viola went on, "I need twenty-seven men to be exact. Tall, dark, handsome, smart. Preferably human. But with only two weeks until the full moon, I'm willing to negotiate on that last point."

Viola had long, dark hair, jet black eyes, and lips slicked with Chanel's Crimson Dream. She wore a black Gucci jacket and matching slacks. A Cartier watch with a diamond band glittered from her slender wrist. She was president of the Connecticut chapter of the Naked and Unashamed Nudist Sisterhood aka the NUNS aka a group of female werewolves who met weekly at her Fairfield estate.

She was also the reason my father had nearly decapitated himself with a pair of hedge clippers last weekend. My old man detested thick, overgrown bushes almost as much as female werewolves, and so he religiously trimmed the azaleas that separated the two estates. Viola, on the other hand, detested short, puny vegetation and snobby, pretentious born vampires, and so she religiously put up a fight.

I, on the other hand, welcomed any- and everyone with my arms wide, my mind open, and my deposit slip ready.

A smile spread across my face as I mentally calculated what twenty-seven men (preferably human) meant in terms of outstanding credit card payments.

"So can you help me?"

"That depends," I heard myself say. Wait a second. I knew Viola could fork over the cash. I should be shouting *Yes!* After all, I'm a born vampire. The PC term for unconscionable, pompous, money-hungry, bloodsucking aristocrat.

"On what?"

"On what you're going to do with twenty-seven men." Okay, so I'm not exactly PC. Sure, I could be as pompous as any ancient-born *vampere*. I was most certainly money-hungry. I'd also recently fallen off the wagon on the bloodsucking part (I'd been going for the bottled stuff up until a few weeks ago when I'd been staked in the shoulder and nursed back to health by a megalicious made vampire named Ty Bonner). *And* I was also an aristocrat (French royalty and all that). It was the unconscionable part that I had trouble with. "I'm a matchmaker, not a personal chef."

Viola smiled, revealing a row of straight, white teeth. "We're not going to eat them, dear. We're going to have sex with them." She stubbed out her cigarette in the small crystal ashtray on the corner of my desk. "And procreate. Female werewolves only ovulate during a lunar eclipse, which means we get one, maybe two shots a year to actually conceive, if any at all. Last year, we got nada. Since we females carry the actual were gene, we can mate with any creature and still produce a were baby. We NUNS feel a social responsibility to keep our race as pure as possible, and so we prefer humans. That way we don't have to worry about any otherworldly genes mixing in with our own."

Okay, so I already knew this. Not firsthand, mind you. While I am now a hot, hip, happening vampire, I was raised in a very sheltered environment. Most of my friends were born vamps, and so I'd never actually talked to a real werewolf. Of course, I was as educated as the next born vamp, and so I'd learned all about sexuality and the various species early on. But hearing it told by a holier-than-thou *vampere* tutor whose lesson had been extremely brief (other creatures weren't deemed worthy of our precious time) and hearing it straight from Viola (complete with details) were two very different things. She spoke from actual experience.

"Why not a male werewolf? Wouldn't that be the ideal?"

"Do you know twenty-seven available male werewolves?"

"Not at the moment."

"Neither do we. There are a total of fifty-two members of our organization, nearly half of whom have mates and don't need your services. I'm here on behalf of the single, uncommitted, aging NUNS. Unlike you vamps, we only have a small window for procreation. Fifty years to be exact. Desperation always makes one less choosy. Besides, male werewolves are bossy and overbearing and extremely territorial. You have their child, and bam, they're ready to pee on every tree in your front yard. While I wouldn't mind it if I found the right male werewolf, I haven't, and I seriously doubt I'm going to in the next two weeks."

"Why not just go to a sperm bank?"

"We only ovulate during an actual sexual encounter. Our reproductive system requires a barrage of stimuli. In other words, there's no kissing or touching or nibbling a turkey baster, dear."

"I see your point."

"Wonderful." Viola smiled and opened her Christian Dior clutch. "I'll write you a check."

I was just about to reach across the desk and kiss this month's bills good-bye when the intercom buzzed.

"Lil?" Evie Dalton's voice floated over the line. Evie is my devoted assistant. She had great taste in belts, lived for the lastest MAC lip gloss, and could spot a fake Fendi at twenty paces. Had I been a lesbian human instead of a heterosexual born vampire with a screaming biological clock, I would have married her on the spot. "I know you're with a client, but could you come out here?"

"Give me just a second." My fingers closed around the check.

"It's really important."

"So is this." I stared at the five-figure sum. While it wasn't my ultimate fantasy (me plus the megalicious Ty Bonner plus this cute little number I'd spotted over at La Perla), it was certainly a dream come true to a struggling entrepreneur.

"There are some men here to see you."

"If Brad Pitt isn't one of them, they can wait." I smiled at Viola, slid her payment into my top drawer, and turned toward my laptop. "Let me get you a receipt and—"

"They're not really into waiting."

"They'll have to make an exception." I punched the off button. The light blinked and the intercom buzzed again, but I ignored it.

"That's twenty-seven matches," I said as my fingers flew across the keyboard. "At the usual amount per match, plus a bonus for our deluxe, ultra-speedy service—"

"You can't go in," Evie's voice rose to a shriek a split second before the door crashed open and a half-dozen men clad in cheap suits burst into my office, none of whom looked even close to Brad Pitt.

"Lil Marchette?" The question came from the first man to reach my desk. He wore a navy blue suit, a haggard expression, and the worst tie I'd ever seen.

"She's not here," Evie shouted from the doorway. "She left early. This woman is her assistant. Because if she wasn't her assistant, she would be in big trouble."

"How big?" I asked, my gaze darting from one man to the next.

"Plead the fifth," Evie blurted before two of the men managed to push her back into the outer office.

"What's going on here?"

"We need you to come with us," the man said as he flashed a silver badge and motioned to two of his underlings. They quickly pushed Viola out of the way and rounded the desk for me.

Detectives. Badges. Handcuffs.

The pieces started to fall into place, and panic bolted through me.

"But you can't!" I wiggled away as he reached out. "I didn't mean to put a dent in that soda machine. I was just trying to get my money back and—"

"I don't know anything about a dented soda machine."

"I meant to call about that jury summons," I blurted, rushing down my mental list of offenses, "but my cell phone's been out and I don't like to use my business phone for anything but—"

"It's not the jury summons."

"I didn't mean to take that towel from the gym. It just got mixed in with my change of clothes."

"Nope."

"That cabdriver said he didn't mind if I didn't have enough cash for the entire fare—"

"Guess again." He pulled out a pair of handcuffs as two of his men fought to get a grip on my arms. Not easy considering I have preternatural strength and a severe allergy to polyester.

"Then what did I do?" The cuffs slid on, and I found myself pulled around the desk. "Because whatever it is, I won't do again. Cross my heart and hope to—"

"—die?" the detective finished for me. "You just might."

"What's that supposed to mean?"

"You're being arrested for murder."